THE CALLING
OF THE CLAN

parris afton bonds

NEW YORK TIMES BESTSELLING AUTHOR

Blue Bayou	*Made for Each Other*
Blue Moon	*Midsummer Midnight*
The Calling of the Clan	*Mood Indigo*
The Captive	*No Telling*
Dancing with Crazy Woman	*Renegade Man*
Dancing with Wild Woman	*Run To Me*
Deep Purple	*Savage Enchantment*
Dream Keeper	*The Savage*
Dream Time	*Snow And Ice*
Dust Devil	*Spinster's Song*
The Flash Of The Firefly	*Stardust*
For All Time	*Sweet Enchantress*
Kingdom Come: Temptation	*Sweet Golden Sun*
Kingdom Come: Trespass	*The Wildest Heart*
Lavender Blue	*Wanted Woman*
Love Tide	*Widow Woman*
Wind Song	*When the Heart is Right*
The Barons	*The Brigands*
The Bravados	*Doorway To The Moon*

THE CALLING OF THE CLAN

PARRIS AFTON BONDS

The Calling of the Clan

Published by Motina Books Publishing
Copyright 2020 by Parris Afton Bonds
All Rights Reserved

This is a work of fiction based on history and a product of the author's imagination. No part of the publication may be reproduced, distributed, or transmitted in any form or by any means, or stored in a database or retrieval system, without the prior written permission of the publisher.

Published by Motina Books, LLC, Van Alstyne, Texas
www.MotinaBooks.com

Library of Congress Control Number: 2020946934
 Bonds, Parris Afton
 The Calling of the Clan

ISBN-13: 978-1-945060-23-6

In honor of the beautiful Scottish river, I was given the middle name of Afton, as were my mother and grandmother, as well as my niece and granddaughter (and, also, the youngest of my five sons, after I surrendered any further attempts at producing a female bairn). THE CALLING OF THE CLAN, like its prequel, THE CAPTIVE, bears witness to my author's rather vivid imagination of my Scottish heritage ~ and, aye, the film THE LAST OF THE MOHICANS with its majestic music score and complex hero Hawkeye inspired me.

FOR MY SAUCY, SASSY, AND REDHEADED BFF,
ANNE BEHL

Wanting a bride, the proper bride, twenty-five-year-old Jacob Dare reckoned Campbelton's annual Gathering of the Clans festival would be the most likely place to seek one. At least, the one he wanted.

A port on the Cape Fear River, Campbelton was in 1776 the mercantile and political life of the royal province of North Carolina. Rich merchants, high ranking officials, and wealthy landowners – almost all exiled Highlanders – mixed with crofters, cotters, and poor immigrants from Cross Creek, one mile away, on the opposite side of the Cape Fear.

From somewhere among Campbelton's Gaelic gentry, he was determined to find a young woman to recreate the home that his father's Dare Castle in Paddington, England must have been. She would have to be well-bred, well-read, and gifted with the ability to turn the primitive into the palatial. If she was favorable to look upon and sweetly dispositioned, that would be even better.

That unusually warm April afternoon he and the much shorter forty-year-old Fergus Munroe observed the festival from a sycamore stand, where the shade was dense and impervious to the sun. "Yewr forking in the wrong direction, lad," Fergus said, shaking his bush of salt-and-pepper hair that nigh matched the shade of his bedraggled coonskin cap.

"No. I want one from here."

"Why would a high-born lady live in an injun-'fested settlement sech as Kinsfolk Landing?" The Ulster Scots fur trapper had built a trading post at Jacob's settlement in exchange for the five acres Jacob had given him and ten percent of the profits.

Jacob's dark face flashed a startling white grin. The dark eyes did not. His voice had a quiet, measured, and determined sincerity. "Because I do not take no for an answer."

The tobacco plug Fergus spat dinged the dirt. "Campbelton's Highland lasses are accustomed to foot servants and ladies' maids. Ye know – high-stepping horses drawing fine carriages and a slew of overhead candles dripping hot wax at fashionable balls. The lass ye selected would have to be *glaikit* to agree to settle on a wild creature fer a mate."

He was already surveying the crowd gathered on the parade grounds. "You settled for Coowee."

"She's hung on like a tick," he said grumpily. "Besides, no blue-blooded father worth his salt would give over his daughter's dowry to the likes of yewrself."

He was not listening. His vision, keen from constantly switching between a killdeer's tiny tracks in the mud before him and a bald eagle perched on an outcropping of the distant Blue Ridge Mountains, searched now for a hike of ruffled skirt or toss of a beribboned and lacy white cap.

The afternoon's festivities, a holdover from a feudal era, were a pageantry of military processions and games of brute strength and skill, demonstrated by clansmen brandishing their claymores. The games were invariably accompanied by revelry and heavy drinking – and especially dancing.

Despite the royal ban in England on tartan kilts, the Highlander men of the North Carolina colony flaunted their kilts during the Sword Dance as saucily as would a maid her petticoat. His mouth twitched. That feminine-like clothing would not serve well here, what with the snakes, briars, nettles, and poison ivy. Even when in breechcloth, he was not foolish enough to venture into the woods without his wrappers.

All was not gaiety that afternoon. Five weeks prior, back in February, these Highlanders, loyalists to King George, had clashed with a combined force of North Carolina Continental and militia at the bridge over Widow Moore's Creek and had suffered a resounding defeat. More than 850 survivors had been taken prisoner. The

Royalists' first armed conflict with the rebels on American soil signaled a mighty discontent stirring throughout all the colonies.

Feared even more at the present were the intensifying conflicts with Indian nations, chiefly the Cherokees – and chiefly the reason Jacob found himself traveling in the river port area. Since he had to be at Fort Charlotte on April 15th, that left him only four days at Campbelton to court a potential bride.

His eyes swept a semicircle, past sweating foot racers churning up the dirt along one side of the parade ground. On the other side a kilted pipe band in spats, jacket, and sporran massed for a last practice competition. Their bleating and thudding was a painful screech to his ears, accustomed to more subdued chattering of forest critters. Farther along, a horse procession with standard bearers carried flags representing their Highlander towns.

His reconnoitering gaze reigned in abruptly at a large stage erected amidst a clump of great oaks and decorated with evergreens, floral wreaths, and garlands.

On the platform, near the royal standard, two women stood. One, a middle-aged woman in tartan and feathered bonnet, was addressing the fashionably dressed gathering. She spoke in that strange tongue native to the Gaelic aggregation and to the Royal Highland 84th Regiment of Foot. As she paused, enthusiastic applauding erupted.

"Who is she?" he asked of Fergus, while his own fascinated stare remained riveted to the stage.

Squint-eyed, Fergus had a wide tongue that rolled his every word. "She be the famous Flora MacDonald. The wee lass helped Bonnie Prince Charles escape Scotland. She and her family took refuge here a couple of years back. Her menfolk were captured at the battle at Moore's Creek."

"No, not her. The tall one."

"Och, that be the Lady Catriona Kincairn. But don't be getting any ideas about her, lad. Her mother was the chieftess of the Afton clan before emigrating here. The Kincairns be the most prominent family in the area after Flora Macdonald's, and ye could not have chosen a lass less likely to accept yer courtship."

"Wait for me."

Long rifle in hand, Jacob strode across the trod-down grass, his focus never taken from the winsome Catriona Kincairn. Extravagantly tall, she had soft curves that enticed and, beneath a beflowered, straw wide-brimmed hat, hair flame-red enough to heat the most bereft heart. He knew he was bent on undertaking a seemingly impossible mission. But that had never stopped him. Not in the time spent with his mother's Wolf Clan nor that with his father's military peers.

Flora had finished exhorting the Loyalists to a skirl of bagpipes. A blast of bugles brought the younger woman forward. As she began to speak in that strange Gaelic tongue, he reached the edge of the red-haired-and-ruddy crowd. Taller than most, he could easily espy his quarry over their heads.

Her wide-set, lively gray eyes roamed with affection among the faces of the listening Highland Gaels. Her modulated voice, warm and lyrical, spoke in appealing tones. Then she switched from Gaelic to the King's English.

Throughout all of this, a slow tremor started in him, like a small earthquake. He was thunderstruck. He could not believe what he was experiencing. But he could not deny the feeling either. Simply, he was overwhelmed by the wonder of it – a joy too great to hope for.

Yes, this was the one he knew he would take to wife. Something in the way she held herself, in her calm and poise, bespoke a strength. A strength she would need if she were to stand by his side in the primeval forests beyond civilized society – upriver, past where Hollering Squaw Creek mated with the wide Cape Fear and where he had claimed his father's six-hundred acres and lumber mill.

Now all he had to do was make the impossible happen and claim the maiden, as well. That she could ever come to love him was irrelevant.

"I speak in behalf of me mam today," she was telling the crowd. Her plaid, secured at her shoulder by a silver brooch, was slung back, as if rebelling against constraint. Amazingly, the maiden's eyes altered shades. Earlier the lively gray of quicksilver, now the gray nothingness of dead peat moss. "Me mam attends me da, who is having a bad day. He was gravely wounded at the Battle of Widow Moore's Creek."

Sorrow muted her voice to an almost intimate whisper, and the listeners inclined their heads or leaned forward, as if fearful of missing a single word that lilted from her lips. "Aye, and three of me brethren were taken prisoners there, as well."

She paused, then her tone echoed the funeral dirges of old.

"We Highlanders ken the painful aftermath of unsuccessful revolutions . . . our lives and property forfeited at both the battles of Fifteen and Forty-five. Perforce, after the Battle of Culloden we were obliged to sign the Oath of Allegiance to George III. We canna go against our word. Still, if we canna be of service to the American cause, me mam pleads let us not be of injury to it."

Her impassioned gaze alighted on first one face, then another, and her voice assumed the staccato notes of a fiddle, catching the listeners by surprise. "Although we have suffered defeats before and suffered a bloody defeat at Widow Moore's Creek only weeks ago, we Scots, the backbone of North Carolina loyalism, will never surrender our right to freedom."

From among the throng, a cheer went up and steel blades with iron basket hilts and shagreen grips swished the air. "King George and broadswords!"

He circumvented the crowd and met her as she descended the plank steps with untutored grace, her forest-green skirts carefully raised, revealing a glimpse of green mules and sheer white stockings. As inordinately tall as he was, the top of her fiery tresses nevertheless cleared his shoulder. "You will surrender."

Her head jerked upward. Brilliant eyes met his with a puzzled stare. "What?"

"You are not like them. Not the kind to ride the fence. Your mother may believe temperance is wise. But you do not. Temperance is not your nature. Yet, you will surrender."

Her head tilted, so that she could peer up at him from the brim of her engagingly angled hat. Her thickly lashed lids narrowed. "Who are ye?"

"Jacob Dare. Of the Dare Plantation in Kinsfolk Landing."

Her dismissive gaze absorbed his long, lank raven locks, unpowdered and unclubbed. Then her eyes drifted lower, to his thigh-length, coarse muslin shirt, tightly belted. Next, they inventoried his pipe tomahawk, knife sheathed in deerskin holster, and Doune pistol, all secured at his waist. Lastly her gaze leisurely inventoried his skintight, travel-stained buckskin breeches and worn wrappers secured by deer sinew, both below the knees and at the ankles, above his moccasins.

Obviously, his attire did not elevate him in her opinion, because the maddening twitch of her lips told him she did not find him or his statement of any worth. Her steady eyes met his once more with a calculated indifference. "I dunna know ye."

His amusement palled. For an awful fleeting moment, he was once more at Fort Dobbs. He was once more Colonel Martin Dare's skinny and half-naked, half-breed bastard. Then, he shifted his long rifle and his stance and gave her an easy smile. "'Tis no matter. Marry me, you will."

At that, she shook her head of glorious red hair and chuckled. A soft trill that came from deep inside and was as lovely, he thought, as the cardinal's in spring. Then, purposefully her trivializing stare once again appraised his wiry, sparingly built physique. "Ye have as much chance of winning me for a wife as ye would at winning the toss of the caber."

"Then I challenge you for the right to court you should I win the caber toss."

She grinned out right, and dimples appeared miraculously beneath her full cheekbones. "Ye are no match for our brawny Scots lads. A mon such as ye with nothing but hank and bone to him might as well petition the wee people for a pot of gold."

"Do you accept or not?"

With a toss of her strong chin, she said, "So done."

He pivoted away, but she called out after him, "Mind ye now, should ye come a courtin', I would laugh ye out – "

He continued on, crossing back to Fergus, waiting patiently beneath the sycamore shade. "What do you know about caber tossing?"

The Scotsman's hooded lids managed to widen. "Yewr jestin', tell me true?"

~ ~ ~ ~ ~ ~ ~

Almost two hours later, he and Fergus made their way to a meadow adjacent to the Bluff Presbyterian Church, where a dozen or so men were already lined up at one end. On either side, a crowd had gathered to cheer, jeer, and place bets.

At once, Jacob's gaze arrowed straight to the statuesque young woman. Where she stood seemed washed by sunlight. She had removed her hat, and the sunlight burnished her hair with the colors of metals forged by heat. Copper, gold, bronze, cinnabar – and even the rust that could dominate those other metals.

She was talking to a man of equal height, despite her high curved heels. His fair-colored natural hair was clubbed. Her smile, the tilt of her head, her body inclined slightly toward his broad one, all these told Jacob she was favorably disposed to the handsomely attired gentleman.

Removing his mustard-colored linen coat, the man passed it along with his tricorn to her. Like most upper-class Tidewater planters, his suits had obviously been ordered custom-made to his measurements in London. Suits such as he wore had to have been specified cut from expensive fabrics, embellished with imported buttons, and made without lining to stave off inordinate perspiration caused by the colony's humidity.

He said something that brought a transforming smile to her face. With that, he blew her a playful kiss and then set off in the direction of the caber-tossing arena. The way he sauntered, never glancing down, told Jacob this solidly built man was supremely confident that the ground, and the world, would always rise up to meet him.

"Get yon Barrett Fairfax to fetch ye yewr cable," Fergus grumbled. "Mayhap, he will throw his back out."

"What do you know of him?"

"Dunna underestimate this competitor, lad. Whether for the tossing of the caber or wooing of yon bonny lass. The Sassenach sold his Lieutenant Colonel's commission to become a tobacco factor. Educated at Oxford, he was."

And that, that one advantage, therein set Barrett Fairfax far above mere mortals who comprised most of the colonists – but not, in Jacob's studied estimation, above himself.

"Now, listen to me, lad, ye may be lang and skinny as a string bean, but the mighty width of yewr shoulders will be an asset. Tis the running that twenty or so feet, the momentum afore ye toss the caber, that will matter more than strength."

Jacob's eye was on Fairfax who was approaching. The man possessed the stiff carriage, as straight as a saber, reflective of a born soldier. Jacob passed Fergus his twelve-pound flintlock rifle, which normally he kept with him at all times and could fire and reload on the run, which no British soldier could do – not even Fairfax.

Totally ignoring Fergus, the energetic Fairfax nodded at Jacob and allowed a smile, however briefly. "I understand you scout for Caswell's colonial militia?"

Jacob said nothing, only waited, and returned Fairfax's condescending stare with his own blank one.

Nonplussed, Fairfax was forced to fill the silence. "That makes us vying not only to determine the best man at the caber toss today, but also vying to determine which side shall dominate here – Crown or Colonial."

Then Lady Catriona had refrained from sharing with Fairfax that she now had an additional suitor vying for her hand. Interesting. "I have no loyalty to governments."

Fairfax's muscled frame stiffened. "There is such a thing as duty and honor to our country above all else."

He met Fairfax's perturbed glare with an expressionless look that might, or might not, have been challenging. "There is such a thing as a man's right to decide for himself. Beholden to none."

"That consideration is subordinate to the interests of the Crown." The man, who was maybe thirty, emitted a grunt of disgust and shouldered past him.

For all Fergus's advice about the best form to use in the caber toss, the mere cupping upright in one palm at elbow height the seventeen feet of tapered tree trunk, weighing more than 175 pounds, was a feat in itself.

Jacob watched one after another competitor hurl the caber end-over-end so that it fell, if lucky, with the larger end hitting the ground first and then the tapered end falling perpendicular to the tosser at the twelve o'clock mark.

After each toss, applauding ensued. When Fairfax took his turn, it seemed the spectators' breath suddenly ceased, as if they had attended the week-long games solely to be a part of this ten-second demonstration of mythological performance. Fairfax took his running steps. His shoes, of the best London-made cordovan, anchored in the turf. With a mighty surge of his last step, he hefted and tossed the caber.

After those ten seconds, Fairfax clearly bested all previous competitors. Cheers erupted. Fairfax waved at the crowd and executed a brief bow in the Lady Catriona Kincairn's direction.

Knowing that the winning toss had been witnessed, spectators were already drifting away, toward the *Maide Leisg* – the Lazy Stick competition. Jacob would not glance at Lady Catriona, to see if she had stayed or was departing on Fairfax's arm.

His turn was next. He had studied Fairfax's effort, noting even the man's approach to the perilous toss-line. Its divots dug up by the boots and brogans of all the previous competitors could easily trip up the unwary.

And yet . . . could he not make those divots work for him rather than against him?

Sweat plastered his muslin shirt to his back. It took all his strength and coordination just to keep the caber upright as he hoisted the nearly two-hundred pounds in his palm. With the weight balanced against his shoulder, his moccasins churned out the twenty yards' approach.

Planting his feet solidly in the divots for purchase, he flipped the caber up and out – and watched with lung action suspended as the caber spun like a mere throw of his tomahawk through the air. After what seemed interminable time, the caber landed. It tipped over exactly at the twelve o'clock mark and more than an ell's length past that of Fairfax's.

Silence stunned the afternoon. Next, exuberant whoops rang out. Only then did Jacob allow his gaze to seek the striking young woman. Her dismayed glance clashed with his. Abruptly, she pivoted toward an equally dismayed Barrett Fairfax and accepted the arm he was slow to proffer.

If Jacob thought the caber toss required all the physical skills he possessed, wooing the young woman next would require all the social skills he did not possess.

Dancing to the fiddle, tin whistle, or drums and pipes was held nightly during the games on the Commons, encircled by a tree-lined cobblestoned walkway that took in the public stocks, gaols, and parade grounds. The flames of candles also danced within the four-paned streetlights placed around the village green.

The Highland sword dance competition was performed, as well, to the accompaniment of bagpipe music. But Catriona looked forward to the lively country reels that sang to her spirit and beckoned her feet, shod in the flat-soled ghillies, to participate.

As she dipped a curtsey before Barrett Fairfax, a grin hovered at the corners of her lips. "Aye, I would be delighted to partner with ye."

Of course, they both knew the wording of his request for a dance and her response expressed far more. He had been openly courting her for a little over three months now, since he returned from England to the royal province last Christmastide. Before that, they had been childhood friends. Like child pranksters everywhere, she had locked him in the outhouse, and he had dipped her pigtails in the inkwell.

The enterprising businessman planned to ask her father for her hand in marriage as soon as her father recovered from the wounds made by ball and saber at the battle of Widow Moore's Creek. Come Christmastide next she would be, at last, a married woman at three and twenty, far past her prime. She had no one to blame but herself. Giving up her inclination for independence and the right to resort to her own judgement did not come easily for the daughter of a Highland clan chieftess.

She and Barrett took their positions in one of the squares formed by three other couples. The fiddler flung his skill into the energetic *Glenzier*, and she turned to face the handsome Barrett. He wore a fashionable wig tonight – and a devastating smile. His phenomenal success in expanding his holdings by acquiring plantations whose owners had gone over their head in debt, as well as, the high esteem in which he was held in the royal colony, was not to be overlooked when considering a husband.

The fiddler attacked the hearty jig with a perfect coordination between fingers and his sawing bow. She and Barrett dipped a curtsey and bow, then began the rapid foot movement around the square in a figure-eight style and an entwining of arms to the song's energetic pitch. Her underskirt, richly ornamented with lace and ribbons, flashed. His yellow jacket panels flapped like the wings of a powerful falcon.

Her laughter joined his. It had been weeks since she had laughed, since the awful battle that had cost so many lives of her clan. At night, she would jerk upright from sleep, worried by vague dreams of her three older brothers taken prisoners at the battle. Andrew, the middle brother, had never been in the best of health since he had come down with pleurisy at twelve.

And, as far as health concerns, her father was not recovering from his wounds as quickly as she would have expected, despite her mother's ceaseless tending. At one point, amputation of his badly infected leg had been feared necessary. It was still a touch-and-go battle with the infection.

After she and Barrett exchanged partners three times in the reel, they, at last, reunited, his warm hands clasping hers. Adoration shone clearly in his strong features. On the sidelines, people clapped enthusiastically. Breathless with the frolicking exertion, she should have been fully caught up in the moment.

Nonetheless, she stilled for yet another moment, acutely aware of another's heavy stare. Perhaps, instead of the dance's demanding footwork, that sense of being watch accounted for her breathlessness. As a child, she had experienced that same acute sense of surveillance; but then, the imaginative minds of children, and especially hers, were prone to flights of fancy.

Although she could not see the man, she sensed he watched from the trees, beyond the crowd, beyond the Commons. This tall heathen, who had boldly announced he would court her. And even more boldly assessed her, his narrowed eyes measuring her from pumps to hat.

She could not remember his name. But, aye, the dark eyes in the dark face, those she did remember vividly. Yet, after winning the caber toss, he had yet to make a move to indicate his continued interest.

She swept up her skirt and petticoat once more in a curtsy to Barrett and then allowed him to lead her back to Flora and her married daughter, Anne Macleod — but not before glancing over her shoulder into the shadowed forest.

"What is it, Catriona?" Barrett asked, watching her quizzically.

She shook her head. "Nothing . . . merely the spell of the music that calls me."

Indeed, the fiddler was now wielding his bow more slowly, like a magic wand, coaxing a hypnotic melody that was rhythmic, repetitious and relentless . . . and so subtle it was difficult to pick out its variations, even for a practiced dulcimer player such as herself. "What was his name, the mon who won the caber toss today?"

Barrett's hazel eyes, blessed with long, golden-brown lashes, flicked over her flushed features. Then he gave her his tongue-in-cheek smile. "Why? Do I have a rival?"

She smiled. "Hardly. I dunna recall seeing his face before." The way the man had selected his words, as if tending as much care to their sound as their meaning — could he be that determined to be a gentleman?

Barrett straightened the frothy lace of first one of his cuffs and then the other. "Most likely a backwoods lout who meandered into Campbelton at the right moment and got lucky at the toss."

Rejoining Flora and her daughter, she told the two, "Ye should be dancing,"

Flora smiled despairingly and lifted her skirts to display silver shoe buckles popular among women of wealth and style in Britain and its American colonies. "Tis been a long time since these old feet danced."

Her daughter Anne slid Catriona an arch smile. "'Tis a splendid couple you make dancing."

The entire community of Campbelton, comprising perhaps a hundred and fifty residences or so, as contrasted with Cross Creek's nearly 1500 homes, viewed the two blue-blooded citizens as a duly expected union.

Many of the community were clansmen. In voluntarily sharing the exile of their countrymen in 1746, her parents had been issued by the Crown the rich river bottom land grant along the Cape Fear, on two conditions – their sworn fealty to the Crown and the payment of a small fee for surveying and registration costs. The land grant, graced now with Afton Manor, was worth a king's ransom these days.

Barrett executed a flourished bow. "My privilege to be in the presence of the lovely and primordial Three Muses."

"Barrett is only flaunting his Oxford education," Catriona teased.

Anne, only a little older than Catriona but already married with children of her own, rapped him on his coat sleeve with her ivory-handled fan. "Ye are such a blathering charmer. Were your sights not already set on Catriona, I would be tempted to leave me husband for ye."

This time, he made only a slight bow. "Tis sorry I am about his capture and imprisonment. Both your husband and yours, Mrs. MacDonald. The gaol at Halifax is it not?"

Flora's sigh echoed the depression that had overtaken her. "Nae, me menfolk have been transferred to a prison in Philadelphia. He writes me that I should leave our home at once. Return to Scotland afore the rebels seize control over the entire continent."

"Ahh but the gate swings both ways, does it not? So many faithful fleeing, yet so many arriving." He turned to bestow a light kiss on the knuckles of Catriona's fingerless glove. "Until your *ceilidh* tomorrow night."

After he departed, she glanced over her shoulder to the dark forest beyond. At that same moment, the fiddler's music crescendoed to an unbearable pitch that was released by a thrilling and exuberant pyrotechnical display overhead. Face tilted up to watch with childlike awe, she thought the splendor in the sky too much beauty for one soul to bear alone.

~ ~ ~ ~ ~ ~ ~

The twitters of barnyard swallows and the raucous crow of the neighbor's strutting cock awoke Catriona. The first thought to breach her sleepy mind was, as usual, a melody. Music, by nature, ran in both her mind and veins. But this melody, the insistent one from last night, it verily plagued her. As did the daunting image of a lean, dark jaw and dark eyes above cliff-like cheekbones.

She would not let yesterday's absurd encounter ruin her day to be capped by the *ceilidh* that evening. Lids closed, she stretched her long frame on the imposing four-poster's goose-down mattress with its welter of pillows. From the open mullion windows, she inhaled the familiar scents that came off the river – the sweet-smelling magnolia trees and jasmine vines and the pungent pines.

At last, she stirred, sat up, and ran her long fingers through her mass of sleep-matted curls of which, aye, she was horridly proud. A variegated red, her hair stood out in a town filled with ordinary redheads. Surely, given her flaws and shortcomings, she was entitled to a smidgen of pride.

She reached for Tom Paine's *Common Sense*, published only three months before, to leisurely resume her reading. Only peripherally did she take note that sunlight was streaming far across the fine grain mahogany floor to spangle the armoire.

She had overslept!

Foregoing ringing for her lady's maid, she quickly performed her ablutions, brushed her hair into a semblance of order, and donned a lavender sprig muslin daydress and lace-frilled cap. In her hurry, she nearly tripped down the beeswax-polished staircase. Ungainly, she never had considered herself. She could hold her own with her brothers in any skill of agility. What had changed overnight?

Her father had backed his throne-like chair at the breakfast table against the wainscoting to make room for his arm sling and heftily bandaged thigh, its leg propped on another chair. Descended from an illustrious line of lairds, Ranald Kincairn looked, indeed, like some Scottish king of mythical mists. Women of all ages throughout Campbelton still swooned when in his company.

Despite his pallor from infection, he was still of daunting prowess. His body had been riddled with four bullets and two swan shots when he had led a picked company of swordsmen in a fruitless charge to reach his three sons at the front.

She kissed his weather-polished cheek and slid into her chair.

The damask tablecloth was set with Limoges porcelain, Waterford crystal, and solid sterling. "Ye are out of bed today, Da. Are ye feeling better?"

"Aye, your mother makes too much of me wounds."

"Where is she?"

"At Anne's. Flory is wanting to draft a petition to that damned upstart Provincial Congress for the release of our sons."

"That could take years." She wrinkled her nose and cut a grin at Phoebe, who had bumped open the dining room door with her bony hip.

"And at this rate, Missy," the woman groused, "it will also take years for ye to settle on a husband." In her mid-forties, Phoebe had buried three. Her askew white cap covered hair already iron gray. She carried a tray laden with a bowl of porridge, a ceramic jug of molasses, and a pewter cup of steaming coffee. She placed them in front of Catriona. "Tis yewr bairns I want to see before I meet me Maker."

Catriona reached for her cup. "Perhaps this year I shall yet surprise ye and marry."

"That would surprise me, too," her father said, shifting his weight to better accommodate his propped leg. He was chafing to get back to his command of the Royal Highland Emigrants.

"Why? Barrett has much to commend him. Despite being a Sassenach, Da," she added, jesting. Barrett and his parents had emigrated from England when he had been but five.

A prosperous land speculator, his gregarious personality made him popular among the colonial aristocracy. Furthermore, he was a brilliant speaker at the General Assembly – well, he was until days ago, when the rebels scheduled a provincial assembly in New Bern, preempting the royal one. Chaos seemed to rule the land, and she worried that conditions were dangerously ripe for anarchy.

Her father lifted a dark brow. "Ye do have more than one suitor to choose from, *mo ulaidh*."

Phoebe cackled. "Ye mean Widower Bridewell – who pinches his pennies until they yelp?"

"No. I mean Jacob Dare."

The coffee sloshed in Catriona's cup. "Who?"

"He appeared at the door this morning. Asked for ye, he did."

Her fingers flew to her throat, as if she could prevent the betraying pulse from pumping there. "Did he, now? What did ye tell him?"

Watching her expression closely, her father said, "*He* told *me*. Said he wanted to make known his aim – that he planned to begin courting me daughter this evening at our *ceilidh*."

She found her breath and demanded, "And what did ye say, Da?"

He fixed her with that unrelenting stare that had quelled her and her brothers as children. And still did. "How do ye know him?"

Her dark brows lowered. "I dunna know him. The scurvy knave introduced himself at the Games yesterday and announced he would be marrying me. Marrying me! Can ye believe it? He must be daft."

He grunted. "I understand ye are affronted. Ye deserve to be cherished, to have the best laid at your feet." He delayed whatever he had been about to say by pausing to dollop his scone with thick clotted cream.

Then he cleared his throat. Still, his voice rasped like a file. "Nearly thirty years ago, *mo ulaidh,* I abducted your mother against her parents' will – and hers."

Only a few times did her parents obliquely discuss this, and the knowing look and secret smile they exchanged told Catriona this was a private memory for them alone.

A faraway look hounded his deep-set eyes. "Can I gainsay a mon who has, at least, informed me of his intentions?" He smiled faintly. "I am bored by my convalescence. Confined like a rabbit to a cage. Tonight should prove interesting."

"Gardyloo!" came the customary warning from the upper story of a wooden house that morning, one of the dozens of houses along the rows of Cross Creek's look-alike houses.

Nimbly Jacob dodged the pail of slop dumped from above. He threaded his way through the housewives and servants, replenishing the family water supply from the pumps lining the street, and grinned at the sight of the tykes cavorting in the water.

He continued past the blacksmith's shop and on several streets farther to the modest clapboard home of John Lillington. The roan tied to its oaken hitching post signaled a visitor. Tom Brindle. As Jacob had counted on.

After he thudded the brass knocker twice, the door opened, and a fetching woman frowned. A swath of brown hair tumbled from beneath her cap over one eye. She shook the dripping end of her mop at him. "Jacob Dare, you missed our housewarming party last month."

He bussed her on the cheek, "And you missed *me*, Peg Lillington."

She gave him a droll smile. "No denying that. New Bern's maidens have also been mooning since your last visit."

"Is John in the study?"

"Smoking like a chimney with Tom."

Jacob had scouted with Tom Brindle for Peg's husband back in the spring of '71 at the Regulators' Battle of Alamance against the Royal Governor William Tryon. After the patriot's victorious battle of

Moore's Creek Bridge, John Lillington had accepted a position as brigadier general in the colony's militia, based there at the county seat of Campbelton.

Tall and lanky with only a wreath of sandy hair on his balding pate and a nose that looked as if it had lost in more than one fisticuffs, John promptly rose, shifted his long-stemmed pipe to his left hand, and greeted Jacob with a hearty handshake. "So, you decided to come out of hibernation for good? Have a seat."

He took up the thatched bottom chair opposite the slope-shouldered Tom and crossed his rifle over his knees. "No. On my way to Fort Charlotte to do some parlance between the Cherokee Nation and the Continental's Indian Commissioners. Good to see you, Tom."

He could smell the pomade in Tom's hair, but for all that, the man was no city slicking fool. He might consume a bottle of brandy a day, but he could shoot straighter than the soberest of marksmen.

"T'would be better," Tom said, "to see *you* in an officer's Continental uniform."

"I cannot see myself trussed up like a turkey."

"Still refusing to bind yourself to one side or the other?" drawled John. "When English law cannot be trusted?"

"Dropped by to let you know a British warship has been spotted anchored at the mouth of the Cape Fear. Most likely carrying upwards toward three, four hundred Hessians." Those German mercenaries, hired by the English parliament, were feared throughout the American colonies almost as much as the Indians.

His contemplative gaze slid from Tom back to John, and he nodded at the small room's smoky haze. "What is this powwow about?"

As if he did not already know.

John leaned his lanky frame over to tamp his pipe on the brass spittoon next to his desk. "We're in a quandary over what to do about the Loyalists leaders in the area who took part in the Battle of Widow Moore's Creek."

"Some of Cross Creek's good and righteous citizens are eager to tar and feather them as an example," Tom said. "Hot tar singeing the hide off a dissenter, Highlander or otherwise, is hideous enough. We want to avoid that if we can. No use stirring up more resentment. Most of all, we are trying to avoid lynchings here."

"Are you talking about making an example of Ranald

Kincairn?"

"Him, 'mongst other Highlanders who fought against our side."

Jacob's eyes narrowed with apparent thoughtfulness that had, in reality, taken much calculated forethought. Then he allowed a slow smile. "There is a better solution. One that would also benefit your county coffers."

~ ~ ~ ~ ~ ~ ~

Moll King's Coffee House in Cross Creek was a hotbed of commerce and political discourse. The smoky coffee house's convenient location made it a popular stop for the North Carolina's elite and erudite. Here, at the crossroad of commerce, where the Stagecoach and Post Roads bridged the Cape Fear River, men collected to argue politics, talk shop, and fret over the Indian raids.

And in the Coffee House's upstairs tea room, set aside for females, the women customarily gathered to drink their steaming chocolate and discuss the same issues. Well, not exactly.

While the merchants and politicians negotiated deals and forged contacts, the conversations between Anne and Catriona and their mothers meandered that morning around subjects like the games later that afternoon, the *ceilidh* that evening . . . and Jacob Dare.

"The mon talking to ye after your speech yesterday?" Anne asked. She wore a mole patch high on the left side of her forehead, denoting support for the Tories. "I noticed him watching ye. But then who wouldna notice a mon with his wolfish guid looks?"

They sat around one of four maple tables wedged into the small upper room, its rose-trellised wallpaper and heavy timbers sooty from the fireplace. "Aye, 'tis the same mon," Catriona said. "He was naught but full of himself."

She was feeling an unaccustomed edginess. Edgy with the increasing hostilities between the Whigs and Tories, when she considered herself aligned with both, despite Jacob Dare's statement otherwise; she was edgy with his insolent manner; and, most of all, she was edgy with her usually exuberant self for letting thought of him mar the Highland Games festivities.

"And ye are certain ye have never met him," Flora asked before taking a sip of her chocolate with one dainty little finger raised. One would never imagine Flora as bold and brave as the fiercest Highland warrior.

"I am looking forward to meeting the young mon tonight," said Enya. Catriona's mother was as tall and curvaceous as Flora was short and straight-arrow narrow.

"Why, Mam? Whatever can ye find of interest in someone with such boorish manners?" Catriona suspected that what she was really asking was what is it about Jacob Dare that she herself could find of such interest. Aye, he was different from what she was accustomed, but so were the occasional imposing alligators to be found crouching along the river banks.

Her mother smiled and took a swallow of her chocolate that stretched endlessly the moment of query. "I suppose because his actions fit his name – he dares."

"As Da dared abduct ye?"

Her mother's enigmatic smile clearly harbored treasured memories. "Aye, that he did."

"Me own stepfather, One-Eyed Hugh," Flora said, her gaze distant and melancholy, "he abducted and married me widowed mother. Twas not a happy union."

Flora, had been through much. Even now, Catriona could sense Flora was uneasy in the public place. After the Widow Moore's Creek bridge battle, local rebels had looted Flora's family plantation, and she had been forced to flee earlier that week to her daughter's nearby rented home with nothing but what she could carry in her two arms.

Catriona's teeth worried her lower lip. Her mind's eye recalled the man in buckskins that molded his body like the skin of an animal. "How can ye come to love a mon if ye are given no choice?"

"Love is always a choice," Enya said. "Over and over again, until your last breath. It is a willingness to surrender your desire for that of another."

"I can tell ye now," Anne said, "if I am not happy, I canna' make me mon happy. And there ye have the crux of it."

"I canna' but agree," Catriona said. "To surrender, to surrender me own judgement, to another, to a mon, is weak, and I do no' think either ye, Mam, or ye, Flory, are weak women. Both of ye have publicly proclaimed there is no future without the right to self-determination."

"Ahh, but your father and I did surrender," Enya said. "We

pledged our loyalty to the Crown, so that we could survive – so that we could leave Scotland alive and come here with our clan, to the American colonies, to start life again."

Indignation rose in her throat like the aftertaste of an overripe honeydew. "Well, 'tis forge me own destiny, I will, thank ye. I willna let anyone decide for me."

Enya arched a brow and glanced at Flora, who shrugged narrow shoulders set off by her red plaid. Their exchange clearly intimated how little the younger generation knew of life.

Anne flicked Catriona a consoling glance that intimated how staid this older generation was.

The unpleasant taste in Catriona's mouth continued the rest of the morning, as she and the other three attended the daily games.

Dainty and colorful parasols, warding off the sunlight but not the river's humidity, twirled and dipped as they were carried from the weight toss with smooth riverbed rocks to the sheath toss with straw bales; from the wailing of the bagpipe competition to the flapping kilts of the Highland Reel dance competition; and, at last, to the market fair with its candied fruits, spit-roasted turkeys, and sugar cakes, washed down by lemonade.

All the while, Catriona's attention roved among the revelers who jostled and elbowed for room along the grass-worn paths. She was both anxious she would see Jacob Dare and anxious she would not. With a few disdainful words now beforehand, she might just well fend off an awkward spell this evening.

At last, she made the three-mile carriage trip home with her mother and went straight upstairs to the speckled cheval mirror and forced herself to look objectively. The only thing small about her was her waist. Large hands, large feet, large mouth. Built like her mother she was, who had often told her that beauty was how one felt inside, and that it reflected in one's eyes.

She spent the rest of the sultry, sweaty afternoon upstairs, shed of stays and clad only in shift and petticoat, reading *Candide*, although she struggled with her French and struggled with thoughts that strayed to Jacob Dare. Most reluctantly, she dressed for the evening's entertainment . . . or perhaps 'ordeal' would be better, for she had no idea what to expect of the scoundrel.

When Barrett looked into her eyes, she did not have to worry if he saw a large dowry. He was already comfortable with a more than modest inheritance and his profitable investments.

And when Jacob Dare looked in her eyes, what did he see?

She had the unnerving sensation he saw clear through her, while she could see nothing beyond his rustic exterior. With her father and three brothers – aye, Barrett, also – she had never had this feeling when looking into their eyes. She saw straight though to their heart's intentions.

~ ~ ~ ~ ~ ~ ~

"Ye canna be serious about courting me," she told the backwoodsman when she warded him off that evening at the entrance hall of the northeast portico.

The Negro liveried footman glanced questioningly from Jacob Dare, with his rifle stock braced on the floor, then to her. She nodded that all was in order, and he bowed away.

"You are stout of heart and strong of arm," the man replied, affably. He was still dressed in leather britches and wrappers, but this time his muslin shirt had been laundered. His sloe black hair, which fell unbound upon his wide shoulders – but for the hair braided back from his temples – had likewise been washed. "And ye are wide of hip for birthing babies. Most importantly, though, you are book learned."

"God Almighty!" Her words hissed like steam from her throat. The oaf's remark pierced her armor of indifference and bruised her heart. Her contemptuous glare should have been enough to incinerate Jacob Dare into ashes right there on the Brussels carpet. "Your kind dunna belong here."

He fixed her with that direct look that took no heed of society's guardedness. "Neither do you. You belong with me."

Not quite able to believe what she had heard, she simply stared back at that sun-browned face. His eyes were not black or brown as she had expected, but the deepest, darkest blue. Her hiss converted to a very audible exasperated exhalation. "And that will never happen, ye – ye conceited dunderhead!"

His smile was slow to come but cheerful. "You do have a mouth on you."

She whirled to leave him in the entrance hall. With dismay, she thought she heard his moccasins' quiet tread behind her. Surely, the bumpkin would not have the gall to stay after that set down.

As she took her seat at the forefront of the great hall and picked up her dulcimer, she could not help but peer beyond the three score or so of heads into the shadow created by the balcony overhang. She could not see him, but she could feel his sights set on her. She sensed about him an element of danger, a threat, and this agitated her even more so.

Stout of heart and strong of arm? Had he verily said that?

Somehow, she found a smile with which to gift the guests, among them Anne and Flora, and, of course, Barrett. Many had turned out for the *ceilidh*, during which Scottish stories, poems and ballads were recited. Usually long, cold winter nights were good excuses to hold a *ceilidh*, but the Highland Games that drew Scots from afar provided ample opportunity, as well.

For her recital, she had chosen to wear a striped silk ball gown of shell pink and its matching mesh snood of maidenhood – precisely because it was opined that pink was unsuitable for redheads. With the same defiance, she wore high heels to emphasize her inordinate height even more.

With the dulcimer across her lap, she began to pluck the fretted strings in a high-spirited rhythm to engage her audience. She let the lively song roll boisterously from deep inside her.

> *"A song and a whisky before breakfast,*
> *when the coffee takes too long.*
> *Lass, ye've been drinking too long –*
> *Only long enough to sing this song."*

Feet were tapping, and the guests were grinning and clapping along with her refrain.

> *'Whisky here and whisky there,*
> *Whisky, whisky everywhere,*
> *Whisky when you're in despair,*
> *Oh, Lord, preserve and protect us*
> *We've been drinking whiskey*
> *afore breakfast."*

Laughter and applause erupted. She saw her mother and father's loving faces . . . and Barrett's proud one. Aye, here in the bosom of her clan, her heart truly sang. She sorely missed her three brothers loving and teasing, but close kinsmen and caring friends eased the pang.

She finished her performance with a romantic traditional Scottish ballad that required more difficult ascending octaves. Her fingers plunked the dulcimer, and her expression turned mournful, her voice drawing the song's tale with haunting undertones.

> *"T'was in the merry month of May*
> *The green buds were a swelling*
> *Sweet William on his deathbed lay*
> *For the love of Barbara Allen."*

Her eyes searched the shadows once more for Jacob Dare's stolid presence, feeling certain he was still there. Once again, she had the strong sensation of having experienced this once before, a déjà vu. The sensation of being watched and studied from shadows, but when she had turned to look had seen no one. She could not naesay this man's vitality. Her next words were for him alone.

> *"O tis better for me ye'll never be,*
> *Tho your heart's blood were a spilling.*
> *For to ye I'll never come,*
> *Never with me heart unwilling."*

As the last note died away, she allowed her attention to abandon the strings – and found, with relief, that Jacob Dare had also abandoned his position, nowhere to be seen. The coward had slunk away.

"So, ye ken," Angus Selkirk was telling his Afton Manor audience in an age-cracked voice at the next night's *ceilidh*, "when Robert the Bruce became King of Scotland over four-hundred years ago, Edward I of England forced him into hiding."

His gray tufted brows pumping in his seamed face, he continued in a lowered, hushed tone, "At the Bruce's verra lowest ebb, he hid himself in a cave, he did. There, he observed a spider spinning a web from one part of the cave to the other."

The old tallow chandler paused to weave his gnarled fingers, much as Jacob's father had when reciting *Macbeth* on wintery nights. "Twice the spider failed, afore succeeding with her web. Thus inspired to try, try, again, the Bruce carried on fighting and went on to defeat Edward II's armies at Bannockburn in 1314."

Jacob's mother's people would sit around their smoke pit fires in their winter's wooden, round homes and also spin epic stories of their own history and myths. But it was not for story spinning Jacob attended the *ceilidh* held each night of the Highland Games at Afton Manor. It was to court the Lady Catriona.

And off to a poor start, he was. He was used to being alone. When he spoke, his words were direct. Without the floweriness that would woo a maiden of Anglo society.

Thanks to his father own spun stories, Shakespeare's fey tribe in *Midsummer's Night Dream* and Spenser's *Faerie Queen* were vivid in his mind's eye. So, too, were the Cherokee's myths – one, in particular, of the Cardinal, the Daughter of the Sun, who had been banished to the Ghost Country.

But Jacob lent little credence to storytelling. Conversation was as paltry for him as actions were significant.

Catriona sat next to Fairfax. Her mane of fire, topped with a frilly cap, inclined toward his butter-yellow, clubbed hair. He was whispering something. Whatever it was, Jacob had a strong feeling the Tory was not sharing his dealings as a British agent competing with American ones for Indian Nations' allegiances. His lace draped wrist lay on the back of her scrolled chair in a proprietary manner.

Standing at the back of the room, Jacob was surprised by his annoyance. But then he was surprised by much that evening. Both surprised that Afton Manor was able to keep ice that late in the spring and surprised by his strong reaction to the Kincairn maiden. He was well aware of speculative glances cast in his direction by her parents and friends.

When Selkirk finished his tale, Catriona's friend Anne rose to take her place before the admiring group, who listened with pleasure while she sang several Gaelic melodies, though not a word of that bewildering ancient tongue did he understand.

Then, at last, that for which he had been waiting. Catriona pulled a stool into the center, spreading wider her pannier skirts, and beckoned closer several children crouching in front. At last, he could fully see her face. Those clear, expressive dove-gray eyes beneath dark brows. That mobile mouth that betrayed more than she realized. Skin like he had never seen – as luminous as the cypress swamps' fairy-fires.

"Tis true," she was saying, "that back in Scotland trowies, kelpies, and selkies ply the rivers and caves and lochs and braes. These otherworldly creatures seek to play their tricks on unsuspecting wayfarers. But even here in the North Carolina colony there is talk of a wild half-English beast who crouches in the shadows . . . "

Her gaze drifted over the guest heads in his direction. Not even a muscle twitched in his angular face, so intent was he on her next words.

" . . . 'tis a wulver, as is said to have the body of a mon with the head of wolf."

"Oooh," said one little girl with yellow ringlets that jiggled with her shivers of delight.

"Ahhh, but the wulver leaves fresh fish and fowl on the windowsills of poor families. The only tricks he plays are on those who are foolish enough to follow him back into the woods." She possessed a clear and lively voice, rich with color and import.

"What happens then?" asked breathlessly a russet haired boy kneeling close.

"Why, he tickles ye until ye canna breathe." And with that she began to tickle the child's chin and neck. He yelped and, giggling, rolled onto the floor in a protective knot. The other children plowed into the romp, and chortles and chuckles filtered through the room.

"All right, all right, 'tis time for music," she said to settle the children down. She reclaimed her dulcimer laid to one side.

But no sooner had she positioned it on her lap, than the footman, who had grudging admitted Jacob, wound his way through the maze of guest chairs to bow before her father and mother and present a scrolled parchment.

All eyes watched her father read the missive. After he finished, he sat still for a moment more. Then he turned to Catriona's mother and patted the hand she had laid inquiringly on his arm sling. With effort, he pushed his full height erect, bracing his hand on the back of his chair. "It seems that the insurrectionists' North Carolina congress is issuing a proclamation threatening us with the loss of our homes if we dunna take the American Oath of Allegiance."

"That canna be!" old Angus Selkirk shouted.

"Why, we have done nothing but kept our word to the king," remonstrated another.

Some sat in astonished disbelief. Others shot to their feet. Flora MacDonald and her daughter Anne hurried to Ranald Kincairn's side to view the proclamation for themselves.

Silently and efficiently as a descending axe, Jacob took his leave.

~ ~ ~ ~ ~ ~ ~

During the warmer months, the river current was slow and allowed for easy rowing up stream. And slow enough to retain its fishy odor. With April's unusually warm weather, sloops, schooners, and scows could navigate up the Cape Fear's log-and-rock jammed waters more easily.

Dugout canoes, rafts, and commercial periaugers also bobbed alongside Cross Creek's landing. More than the usual number of skiffs and rivercrafts were moored for the last day of the Highland Games.

A couple hours after daybreak, his Brown Betsy cradled in the crook of his arm, Jacob watched from the landing as Fergus scrambled out of the flatboat. The coonskin-capped man hobbled onto the dock and, getting his gait back, wound his way among the early risers up the landing toward him.

Despite Fergus's bowed legs, his upper torso was a mass of muscle. "Got a guid return on the naval stores, I did, lad."

Resin, tar, and turpentine, from a seemingly inexhaustible store of longleaf pines backing Kinsfolk Landing, were the present mainstay of Jacob's efforts to create a township fitting for Dare Plantation. The transporting of naval stores and lumber occurred primarily during the winter and spring when the river level was high and its current swiftest. This would be his last trip downstream to civilization until next winter.

"Doubtlessly your Scotsman's thriftiness finagled the best deal out of our copper and silver. Use the English currency to purchase frying pans, muskets, saws – whatever else the trading post may need. Be ready to pole in eight days' time. And, oh, purchase a tortoiseshell hairbrush for Mary."

Fergus spat a brown stream of chaw into the sandy gravel. "She needs a hairbrush taken to her hide. But ye are certain this be what yewr wanting – this one, the tall lass?"

He grinned. "'Tis only because you are so short, she looks so tall. She will fit me just right."

"Are ye glaikit, lad? Ye don't know if she can make candles, spin wool into thread, or even wring a chicken's neck."

"While I am away, I am counting on you to post the banns at the church."

He found Catriona where he had expected – arm in arm, walking with her friend Anne, their chatty mothers in their wake, as they left the Moll King's Coffee House. The four were bound not this time for their waiting carriages but for the steepled Bluff Presbyterian Church.

Its clanging bells summoned Highlanders, already amassing to seek whatever news might provide direction as to the best course to take in the face of the insurrectionists' threat of confiscation of their homes.

He hung back, keeping the church cemetery between himself and her and the others, but with her easily in his sights. The morning sunlight glinted off her wildly coiling hair, tipping its ends with flaming tongues of molten gold.

Reverend Campbell, the spindly and bewigged minister who gave sermons in both English and Gaelic every Sunday and served as school master during the week, stood on the church's top step and spoke solemnly.

"Troublous times lay ahead, I ween. Our governor has been forced to flee aboard the sloop-of-war *Cruiser* anchored at the mouth of the Cape Fear. From there he is administering headquarter orders. Tis said that a shipment of arms, as well as royal troops, will shortly arrive to our aid. Yet I ask ye. Are we to fight neighbor against neighbor, brother against brother, once again? Did not our losses at Widow Moore's Creek, at least, warrant we remain neutral?"

"And will you settle for having your homes seized if you do not side with the insurrectionists?" Barrett Fairfax asked in a compelling voice that reached to the crowd's far edges. He stood with outraged dissenters beneath the shade of a large oak dripping with Spanish Moss. "What then is next?" he demanded. "Tar and feathering? Outright lynching?"

He took five swift strides to stand next to the Reverend Campbell. Fairfax's lace cuffs and frothy jabot contrasted with the minister's more sober, black knee-length coat. "Already many of your men are either dead or imprisoned. Twice before – in Fifteen and Forty-five – you rebelled against the Crown, and we disastrously defeated you, yet offered you protection. I ask if you are men of honor? If *you* remain loyal to the country for which you swore your fealty, King George *will* protect his children."

The persuasive Fairfax made sense. If one knew not of other machinations. "As King George protected the Scottish frontier settlement of Innes Corners?" Jacob heard himself ask. Like barn owls, heads swiveled in his direction at the back of the assembly. "Every man, woman and child of Innes Corners, eighty-three colonists, was massacred last week."

Fairfax waved dismissive beringed fingers. "This, from a bumpkin who knows nothing of official policy and their ramifications? Tell me, sir, can you even read or write?"

"Official policy and their ramifications are not important to me – whether they be Whig or Tory, Loyalist or Patriot, colonists or crown. My neighbors and my holdings at Kinsfolk Landing are what is important to me. And my future wife."

Stepping away from the collection of gravestones, he shouldered through several people. The rest in his path shunned him as if he had small pox. He reached Catriona and her friend. Catriona's fan fluttered, hiding her expression. Did the fan's silk material, painted with some kind of pastoral scene, conceal an embarrassed blush or a stifled yawn or a revolted choke? Fear, though, he was certain, she would not ever evidence.

"I have courted you for nigh a week now. Will you or will you not be my wife?"

A leaf could be heard falling, so stunned was the group. Gray eyes as large as silver dollars blistered him over the top of her rapidly oscillating fan. She snapped it shut, and he glimpsed her generous mouth moving like a beached bass.

At last, she croaked in a Scottish accent that had grown broader, "Ye call that courting, ye scullion? Sitting as doltish as a dunce in me parents' parlor? Why ye would be laughed out of Versailles."

"I come seeking not a courtesan but a wife."

Breaths jammed like corks in throats. Her brows popped up. So, his erudition had surprised her and the other Highlanders.

By now, Fairfax had elbowed his way through the human logjam to reach her side. "What could you possibly offer that she would want?" he asked, indolently taking a black enameled snuff box from his deep pocket.

Heads canted to better hear the response.

With lapped hands, he braced his long rifle on its stock and, ignoring Fairfax, looked at her squarely. "I offer my home and my protection."

Her fist, clutching her painted fan, lay knotted against her chest. Gray eyes, as hard as flint, sparked. "I already have that – a home and protection!"

"You will not for long. Even as we speak, North Carolina's Provincial Congress is writing a declaration of independence."

His gaze swept the assembled Highlanders, listening intently. He lowered his voice and riveted his attention now on her mother to one side of Catriona and slightly behind. "As my wedding gift, Mrs. Kincairn, I pledge Afton Manor will remain yours without abjuring your oath to the Crown."

The noblewoman, majestically beautiful, even with middle-age thickening her waist and silvering her mass of ginger locks, raised a skeptical brow. "Ye are able do this?"

He could well appreciate her skepticism. "Yes."

"You cannot be serious?" Fairfax scoffed, echoing Catriona's same response several nights before at Afton Manor.

He ignored the man and looked down at Catriona. The pulse was beating visibly in the hollow of her throat, and he took advantage while she was off-kilter. "I return in eight days. We can wed here at the church at noon, then begin the journey back to Kinsfolk Landing."

Eight days? Could he make the journey and return in that short of time? But to extend the time would be taking a chance on a change of her mind. Or other turn of events. Cursing his blind obstinacy in seeking a woman who clearly found him without civilities, whose fingertips he had yet even to touch, he began to stride away.

Her melodic voice, raised in alarm, reached him and everyone else. "Mister Dare, wait!"

He stopped but did not turn around.

"I havena said I shall marry ye."

"Either you will be here, waiting for me," he said over his shoulder, "Or you will not."

~ ~ ~ ~ ~ ~ ~

Using one of the Great Indian Trading Paths, Jacob traveled afoot much of the pressing journey. He was able to make better time in some cases by cutting across country through unbroken forests, rough terrain, and swampy creeks than had he relied solely on the King's Road and horses and stagecoaches, or, worse, dugouts.

Nevertheless, he was fatigued and famished when he stumbled through the sally port of Fort Charlotte just hours before the summoned meeting.

Constructed essentially of granite, the fort's four-feet thick walls soared twenty feet with bastions at every corner. As a supply depot of guns, powder, cannon, bullets, and grapeshot, it hopefully demonstrated the Patriots' might to Chief Corn Tassel and his Cherokee counsel who had agreed to meet with the five representatives of the Continental Congress.

Purposefully, Jacob has chosen to sit cross-legged on the floor in the parlor of the commandant's house. This established him as merely a negotiator rather than adversary of either party.

On one side of him, old Chief Corn Tassel and the hostile Dragging Canoe sat on chairs draped with deerskins. With the two, sat sub chiefs of the Creek Nation.

On the other, Colonel Dinsmore and the five Patriot commissioners, led by middle-aged Walter Mathew, esquire, of Philadelphia, sat either in wheel-back chairs or on the maroon broadcloth-covered divan.

The meeting began with the exchanging of white wampum belts and the smoking of tobacco Jacob had brought from Archie Rutherford's farm. The ceremonial smoking would be an attempt at reinforcing the concept of peace.

This tedious process required infinite patience for the white man. Jacob was accustomed to waiting fifteen minutes with his hand in frigid river water just to snag a shad or tickle the belly of a speckled trout. This should be easy.

However, today impatience itched in his mind like scabies under his skin. Could he make the return journey to Campbelton and arrive by the time he had so impulsively designated? Impulsiveness was a characteristic few, if any, would attribute to him.

And would the haughty Lady Catriona even be waiting for him? He could not remember a person's opinion ever mattering to him. He scowled to himself when he realized how much thought he was giving her.

He relayed to the well-regarded Mathew that Dragging Canoe and his followers had already accepted war belts tendered by northern tribes, probably encouraged by the British, to rid America of the whites. "The Cherokee refuse to support the colonial cause. They view the people over the great water and their brothers here as the same flesh and blood."

Placing a pinch of snuff beneath his nostril and taking a short, sharp sniff, old Matthew appeared to be considering the information. Finally, the crusty lawyer said, "Tell them that should they continue to cross the established border and kill women and children and fall on the King's enemies, as well as his friends, they not only will draw against themselves all the forces intended to be used against the King's troops but also will rouse the resentment of these who otherwise might have been friends."

When Jacob had finished translating the attorney's response to Chief Corn Tassel and his party, the chief blinked solemnly. Placing his withered hands on his knees, he purposefully sighed aloud.

"Brother, we are a poor distressed people that are in great trouble. Your people are daily pushing us out of our lands. We have no place to hunt. We do not want to quarrel with our elder brother. We, therefore, hope our elder brother will not take our lands from us. We are all His children. We are the first people who ever lived on this land. It is ours."

In Jacob's humble opinion, which he knew did not come close to being humble, Corn Tassel's commanding presence combined with his powers of delivery, surpassed Virginia's first orators, Patrick Henry and Richard Henry Lee. But then Jacob had always been of the mindset that the less said the better.

Hopefully, the meeting provided a ground for further communications, a start for amicable relations between the colonists and the Indians. But he noted that Dragging Canoe's skeletal face was as obdurate as the fort's granite walls. And, in truth, what hope did the Indians have, when British and Colonial officials, alike, were distributing small-pox infected blankets to them in the name of peace? The poor dumb bastards.

And he thought of his mother. She had not had a choice.

He had one mission to perform before he made the arduous return to Campbelton. Closeting himself with Walter, he asked the attorney to write a letter for him. Inkhorn, quill, and paper were summoned. He settled on one side of a gate leg table, and the lawyer took a seat opposite him. With harsh scratching of the quill pen, Walter wrote out Jacob's dictated missive to the provincial government at New Bern, then sanded the sheet.

Jacob knowledge of the swamps and back-rivers and his experience with the Cherokee and Hatteras Indians should make this request well worth the Patriot's concession of claim to Afton Manor that he himself had provoked. Aye, scurrilous he was.

He had never asked a soul for anything. Scouting for the North Carolina Minutemen, he had years before saved the shaggy scalp of Caswell, recently elected president of the colony's provincial congress.

Now Jacob was asking.

"Ye dunna' have to do this, *mo ghràidh.*" Enya, bedecked in a high, powdered headdress and a brilliantly colored emerald gown of black lace and ribbons, paced at the back of the kirk's pews.

Outside, Catriona's father, supported by a crutch, mingled with the few and close friends who had been informed of the wedding and had shown up in support of the family.

Catriona, wearing an ivory lawn confection with cascades of ruffled lace at the sleeves and a large shepherd's hat, sat as cold as a gravestone at the kirk's front.

"Back in Ayrshire, we lost Afton Manor, after ruling from it for hundreds of years," her mother said, "and tis none the worse we are for it."

"But Afton Manor here, in the colonies of America, is *me* home." Stirring for the first time in long minutes, Catriona thumped her chest with her fist. "The only home I have ever known. The home I want to raise me bairn in. And fight for it I shall, just as ye and da did in Scotland. Even if it means me marrying. Tis high time I did."

Striding to the front now to halt by the wooden altar, her mother paused, her eyes brimming. "Catriona, Kinsfolk Landing is forty miles away. Forty miles, where few go! Might as well be the moon." She bit her bottom lip to keep it from trembling. "I – I canna imagine life without ye, *mo ghràidh*. I carried ye beneath me heart. I watched ye grow into womanhood with a spirit, a kindness and a wisdom, that does your da and me proud."

She bit the inside of her cheek to hold back a childish wail at the mess she had gotten herself into – or, even worse, the strong impulse to blurt that she had changed her mind regarding her hasty decision to marry. She had not thought it through. The very meaning of a courtship implied a period of time, did it not? More time was needed. Aye, that was it. She would call off the wedding.

Instead, she heard herself say, "I pledge I shall return for Christmastide, Mam."

"What if Mr. Dare does not let ye?"

Her smile was tight. "If Jacob Dare wants a learned helpmate so badly for his bride, then he will. That will be me condition, Mam. That I return in time for Christmastide."

Overhead, the church bells rang out the hour. Her breath caught midway in her throat. Noon – and he had yet to show. Suddenly, her earlier loathing of wedding the man did a turnabout to a new and unhappier direction – the realization he could leave her not merely standing at the altar but leave Afton Manor unprotected from the oath-demanding Provincials and their rabid congress.

"What if he changes his mind, Mam? What if he dunna come? What if 'tis all a cruel jest on his part?"

"He will come. Only a simpleton could miss the hunger in Jacob Dare's eyes when he looks at ye. And the resolution in the set of his jaw is as strong as any Highlander's." Absently, her mother massaged her left temple, a familiar gesture that signaled to Catriona her mother had other things on her mind. "Catriona, the choice of a marriage partner is verra important. It should combine and strengthen the clan families."

"What ye speak of, Mam – this solicitous bond of arranged marriages – should I have expected more? Tis a common enough practice."

"Tis far different than an arranged marriage – this, a crude bartering on Jacob Dare's part."

Aye, as if she were a cow at the market. Indignation and hurt threatened to strangle her. She stared down at her ivory silk pumps. After a deep sigh, she said, "But tis worth it to me if we keep Afton Manor."

"Your father and I, we agreed we would stand by your decision. But what do any of us ken of this man? He professes no allegiance to any country. And what of Barrett? The colony's young women would give their eyeteeth for such a suitor."

"Aye, I find Barrett most enjoyable. There might have grown the bonds of love between us, like you and Da share, but – " She broke off, her fingers listlessly plucking at the lacings of her stomacher. Loyal to the crown and gallant Barrett might be, but he could also be hardnosed and arrogant. In that, they were too much alike. Still . . . .

The door squeaked open. "The scoundrel's here, Missy," Phoebe said, her nut-brown eyes snapping with disgust for the whole mess.

Alarm thudded Catriona's heart like a beating drum. She found it difficult to breathe. To slow her heartbeat. She closed her lids, tapped her fist to her chest once more in resolution, then rose.

"Wait, *Mo ghràidh.*" Enya wedged her wide panier skirt through the pew to reach Catriona. "Remove your hat."

"What?"

"Here, your wedding gift." She held in her gloved palm a simple hair pin, not the long and ornate kind that was usually beaded. But Catriona recognized this one of solid gold. "Part of your dowry," her mother said. "For flight, or what have ye, should ye need it."

She blinked back weakening moisture. The gold hairpin was a valuable and sentimental heirloom bestowed on her mother by no less than Bonnie Prince Charlie himself.

"Mam, this means the world to ye."

"No, ye mean the world to me. Now, remove your hat and let me help clasp it in your curls."

Untying the ribbons of her wide-brimmed hat and sweeping it off, she bent her bared head and gulped. Then, stiffening her spine as straight as a ramrod, she retied the ribbons jauntily to one side of her jaw and, with her mother, sailed out to meet her master-to-be.

At the top of the plank steps, she paused for her vision to adjust to the noonday sun. Oddly, she did not have to search for Jacob Dare. Among all those gathered for the wedding, she felt his presence, heavier than the sultry air.

She let out an audible groan. "Mother of God, help me." Lifting the hem of her quilted petticoat, she descended the steps to approach the wedding party and the minister waiting beneath the canopy of the kirk's enormous oak tree. For a joyless legal bonding as this one was, she had not been able to bring herself to wed within the sacredness of the kirk.

She avoided looking at her intended. Instead, her anxious gaze roamed over the few assembled guests. She glimpsed the distressed expression of her father's face, pale as it had been when recovering from his near fatal wounds. Then the worried one of Anne's, her sparse brows nearly knitted over the bridge of her pert nose. Next, the grumpy, bewhiskered face of the older man in a coonskin cap, who toted both Jacob Dare's long rifle and his own, a bayonetted musket.

And, lastly, Barrett's anguished expression. Her attention honed in on the single detail of his knuckles, as white as bone, clasping the ivory knob of his walking stick.

Drawing a steadying breath, she took her place at the side of her tall bridegroom. Streaks of soot smudged his cheekbones below bloodshot eyes. Dark beard stubbled his squared off jaw. His black hair straggled as badly as Phoebe's. Her nostrils whiffed the odor of pungent tobacco, gunpowder, and male sweat. *Bleah!*

If her parents were dismayed by his appearance, not a muscle flickered or lash batted to give evidence. But, to her, his mud-splattered and ragged attire suggested that this wedding was of the least importance to him.

His long, slender fingers caught her stiff ones. She was

surprised to feel the spider web of raised flesh crisscrossing the back of his hand and even more surprised to find his warm hand damp.

It was encouraging. He was as unsure about this undertaking as she. She had the feeling that if either of them looked at the other, the whole ordeal would be called off, and she could not have that . . . and there was still the pledge she yet meant to extract from him.

Inclining her head toward his shoulder, she whispered, her words wobbling like a wildly yawing top, "I canna go through with – with this. Nae, unless ye let me return to me clan for Christmastide."

Without taking his eyes from the minister, her intended said out of one side of his mouth, "Do not think I am studying to be a fool."

The Reverend Hamilton cleared his throat.

"Will ye?" Catriona pressed her intended, still unable to look up at him.

His strong, lengthy fingers gripped her clammy ones. "Yes."

That single syllable came out clipped but could hold a wealth of meaning. Yes, what? Still, with so little time left, she pressed forward. "And ye understand there is to be no dowry?"

"Yes."

"You are entering into this marriage of your own free will?" the minister asked loudly of her and Jacob Dare.

"Aye," she murmured.

"Yes," the dark stranger beside her affirmed.

"Your witnesses?" the minister asked.

Snatching off his coonskin cap, the man with squinty eyes and bushy hair stepped forward. "Fergus Munroe," he rumbled.

Anne, delivering an artificial smile, left Flora's side to stand at Catriona's. "Anne McLeod."

Catriona feared her knees would surely buckle. Nods were exchanged with the minister, and he launched into the pledge of the marriage rite, first in Gaelic, then in English. "Marriage is the binding of family ties. As are all life passages, marriage is an important event to our colonial community that is more like a close-knit family."

She heard words like "love, honor and protect." Then Jacob Dare's steady affirmative, tolling as solemnly as the church bells had at noon.

Next, from a distance she heard her own chilled voice agreeing to love, honor, and obey.

That was the signal for the ruffian at her side to pledge himself with a wedding ring that would bind them forever in the opinion of the Highlander community as well as in the eyes of God.

When he produced the ring from his fringed leather pouch looped across one wide shoulder, along with his powder horn, she could scarcely believe what she saw. A ring made of common horsehair, braided however ingeniously.

She peered up at him from beneath her hat brim. Her demoralized gaze met his apologetic one. He shrugged. "I had not time for a proper ring."

Disappointment crushed her; but then what had she expected from the backcountry man? Certainly, not what came next as the minister prompted, "You may kiss your bride."

Jacob gripped her shoulders. The muscles along her spine petrified. Her hands knotted. As if to defy everyone there – her parents, the minister, her friends, and most definitely Barrett – his firm lips leisurely explored her suddenly benumbed ones. Mayhap a surface grazing but in no way a superficial one, not with his intensity jolting her senseless.

Her lips tasted the saltiness of sweat, but his mouth had the scent of freshly chewed mint. At last, he released her. She should not have been undone by his impudent, flaunting gesture, but something in its intimacy suggested a kind of familiarity that arrowed to her core. The kiss said, "I see you. I know you."

Her protective façade of haughtiness she had assumed from early on could not ward off the dangerously vulnerable feeling. This primitive male might possess the power to unmask the little girl.

'I see your soul's scars from teasing by loving brothers and taunting by heedless kids,' his kiss said. She had outgrown her childhood chubbiness and the ungainliness of her height but not those painful memories.

'I know your heart's secret longing, hidden from those who might interpret it as weakness,' his kiss said. She had donned a mantle of confrontational strength, when she yearned to lay aside her guard and feel at peace.

After the ceremony, a wedding party usually celebrated at the home of the bride's parents, but Jacob had already expressed his intention to get the journey underway to make as much time as possible on the river before breaching the falls where the Hollering Woman Creek tributary flowed into it.

Quickly, too quickly, she hugged Flora, Anne, and Phoebe, who shot Fergus a baleful look. "Riffraff," she graveled.

In return he glowered at her, then spat a stream of tobacco juice.

Phoebe's hooked nose wrinkled and her sagging chin shot up. But her querulous expression softened at the sight of her bonnie charge. "Ye must return, Missy, with a bairn whelped in yewr belly, afore I draw me last breath."

His bairn seeded in her belly? At that moment, Catriona felt so dry, so empty, she could not imagine being impassioned enough to feel desire, much less mild affection for this man — or to feel anything, really. Her whole life, her dreams and plans, were ended. She felt as if she had died on this day. That if she searched, she would find her tombstone among those in the kirk's graveyard.

She could but nod at Phoebe. She could not afford to speak without breaking down entirely before this farce of a loving union, made all the more difficult by the presence of the gallant and brave Barrett.

He bent over her hand, his lip brushing her fingertips exposed by her glove. She could see a wisp of his gold hair peeking from beneath this curlicue wig. He rose to fix her with forceful resolve in his hazel eyes. The muscles at the ends of his narrow mouth tightened. "If you should need me, Catriona, you know I shall come."

"Aye. I ken that, Barrett."

He and Jacob exchanged looks. Barrett's a threat. Jacob's a warning.

Her mother stepped forward, tactfully wedging her closed parasol between them. "Your da and I shall walk the two of ye down to the landing, *mo ghràidh*."

The walk, her father hobbled by his crutch, seemed to take the entire morning. Now that the dastardly deed was done, Catriona wanted only to get on with the mess she had made of her life.

The landing was crowded with travelers, raftsmen, merchants, and hawkers. Jacob and Fergus paused before a planked flatboat buoyed by hollowed-out logs and large enough to sustain a sail and rudder, as well as, dugout canoes lashed at either side.

"Ye will take good care of her," her father said to Jacob. It was not a question but a command.

Why would her husband not? she thought dully. She was his valuable property in terms of production, both farm and familial related.

He passed his long rifle to Fergus, who was already boarding with her trunk, most likely to give them time alone for goodbyes. She felt Jacob's hand touch the small of back, the first physical indication he claimed her as his. That dark blue stare met that of her formidable father's on equal and unflinching terms. They were of the same dominating height. "I pledge to protect your daughter with my life, Kincairn."

He turned his mysterious, forest-dark gaze on her mother. "Lady Kincairn, within the fortnight, a post rider should deliver a document signed by the president of the Provincial Congress himself. It will guarantee that no Oath of Allegiance will be required to secure Afton Manor."

Too overcome with emotion, her mother swallowed and nodded her thanks. But there was still in the set of her mouth the resentment that it had come at the cost of her daughter.

Nevertheless, at that moment, Catriona realized that her choice to marry the backwoodsman had been the right one. A selfish one on her part. Her childhood home represented love and laughter. Stability. Important milestones, like birthdays and clan gatherings and holidays like Hogmanay and Pasch. A site as sacred for her as were the Callanash Stones of Scotland for her father.

So, was the marriage really any different than other marriages arranged to preserve and protect two uniting families?

Realizing there was no time left, she flung her arms around her father's muscled neck. He held her in a bear crush, and when he, at last, released her, she saw his eyes were moist. *"Tha gaol agam ort."*

"I love ye, too." Her lips were wet with her tears.

Her mother and she had already said their good-byes. Her mother only kissed her on her cheek, but whispered in Gaelic, "To survive sometimes, *mo ghràidh,* one must surrender their will. Often we find difficulties create their own kind of beauty."

Proprietarily taking her hand in his large one, a wee less clammy now, Jacob nodded his goodbye to her parents and ushered her aboard the periauger to install her beneath an awning that would protect against sun and rain. Barrels and bags, as well as, a box-like object, almost as large as a shed and covered by a canvas, competed with the awning for space at the periauger's center.

With the pang of parting squeezing her heart, she watched the beloved image of her parents, holding fast to one another on the dock, fade into the distance, until finally out of sight with the curving of the river and its walls of bright green foliage.

A fair breeze cooled the afternoon. From the awning's shade, she could see the landscape flow by. A majestic stag paused to observe them from a clearing in the shoreline. At a sharp bend in the river, waterspider orchids and clusters of ripening grapes dangled overhead. At another bend, birds of every color chorused raucously and took flight in a glorious display of color.

After a while, she covertly studied the man now her husband. Because the upper reaches of the river wound and twisted frequently, he and Fergus were clearly using their utmost exertion to sweep around the choppier curves, steering by long setting poles fixed on fulcrums at either end of the periauger. With all its snags and debris, the river, tea-colored by tannins from decaying vegetation, still provided the best means of travel.

Fergus's bunched shoulders strained with the efforts of paddling upriver against the current. Jacob's wiry upper body moved in a smooth continuous motion, sweeping and steering the paddles to avoid sandbars, sunken logs and snags, while his long legs braced for the pitch and yaw of the raft. His smock was soaked with sweat that clung the homespun material to the ropy muscles of his arms.

At one point, he yelled out to her, "Hold on."

Immediately, heavy turbulence bobbled her, and roiling water drenched her back. She latched onto the handle of her red camelback trunk. But even it went sliding, and only a set of barrels secured by twisted withes saved it – and her – from going overboard.

After that, they passed three more sections of rapids without another incident. As the sun was tipping the tree line in the western sky, Jacob aligned the raft with a stretch of clearing in the river birches that banked the river.

Rope in hand, Fergus leaped ashore to tie off the periauger around one gargantuan tree trunk. Then Jacob tossed out another rope, and the old codger hustled to secure the raft's other end to another stout tree.

Jacob collected his long rifle, and, for the first time in the hours afloat, he strode across the deck to speak to her. The glint of fading sunlight turned his long hair into liquid lacquered jade. She rose, wanting to meet him on equal footing. But, muscle-cramped after sitting so long, she lurched and tripped over a coil of rope.

His hand shot out, grabbing her forearm just below its sleeve's lace. Steadied, she glanced down at those fingers, dark rust against her fair skin. They were callused, and the puckered flesh on the backs of his hands gave evidence they had been horribly burned. Not at all the hands of a nobleman she might have married.

At her gaping stare, he released his hold. "We are putting in here for the night. If you wish to – uhh – have some privacy, don't stray too far." Had his ears actually reddened? "And don't step off the beaten path. You could disappear in one of the bogs. Fergus will see to your needs."

"Why are we laying over?"

"Ahead, at the confluence with Hollering Woman Creek, are the falls."

Listening now, she could barely detect them. "Are they dangerous?"

"Only a couple of feet in height. But this spring the river runs low."

Trying to glean information from this man was like pulling teeth. "So, you are going alone upriver? Why?"

"Best most of the periauger's bulk is transported by canoe trips. Tomorrow morning, we warp the periauger over the falls and then reload."

Fergus said, "Here ye go, Lady Ca – Mistress Dare." The dour man had laid a plank ramp from raft to shoreline.

She realized that was her first time to be addressed by her married name. "Catriona, please." She was not sure if he liked her or, maybe, for that matter, anyone. Within that grizzly beard, a smile never showed.

The clearing had been often used, indicated by a number of scorched rings of rocks, discarded corncobs and bones, and a forgotten battered brass cup. After Jacob made a scouting tour of the clearing, he returned to help Fergus unlatch a canoe. They began rolling barrels noisily down the raft's ramp to be transferred to the canoe.

She took the opportunity to follow one of the more trampled paths that wound back into the deep, nigh impenetrable woods. Reluctant to advance any further, she paused at a dark green grotto of holly trees. Sighting no snakes, spiders, or other creatures, she lifted her voluminous skirts. She happened to glance down at her horsehair wedding ring. *Mother of God, what had she gotten herself into?*

Upon her return, she caught sight of Jacob's broad back, the muscles straining beneath his sweat dampened smock, as he rowed one of the two canoes away from shore. Instantly, her taut shoulders relaxed. Confrontation with the barbarian was postponed.

Fergus knelt on one knee, digging into a small camp chest. Naturally, his musket, loaded and primed, lay within reach. He balanced a board between two flat rocks. On it, he portioned out strawberries and plums, shelled walnuts, a small loaf of bread and sheaths of wilted arugula, along with a cold pork shoulder roast.

Her stomach growled audibly. So nervous had she been, she had forgotten about eating. "Ye think of everything," she complimented him and eased down to sit on the most comfortable looking stone.

"Nope," he said, squatting off to one side. Using his dirk's less than clean blade, he applied his hunter's skill at slicing the roast. Not once did he glance at her. "Yewr mam thought of it. Had it been only Jacob and meself, we would have portaged the goods and traveled straight through."

"Oh." Already she was a hindrance. She reached for the tin plate he wordlessly thrust out and helped herself to the strawberries and a palm full of walnuts. "I suppose . . . me husband . . . will be staying above the falls with the supplies tonight." How long could she put off the consummation of their marriage?

"Nope. I'll make the second canoe trip upriver and stay to guard them. Jacob is returning here to guard ye." He got out his flint and steel and set about starting a small fire with cedar knots and splinters.

Arggh! The strawberry's sweet juice turned as tart as a pickle. "Guard me? Against what? The Indians? He is one, is he not?"

"Couldn't rightly say he's aught but one. As far as guarding ye from the injuns, the feral hogs and mountain lions are more liable to make mincemeat of yew than the injuns."

"Then he *is* an Indian?" she pressed, knowing that she was talking in order to ignore unwanted thoughts. An obscure dread she had. To be a nervous bride was not unusual, but this was fear she felt. She feared Jacob Dare himself, because he was unpredictable . . . whereas she felt he knew her, knew her kind, and that made her feel vulnerable.

Fergus spat out a plum seed. "He is. And he isn't. Either way, most likely, his people were here lang before us."

"His people? The Indians or the whites?" Surely, Jacob Dare did not claim relationship to the first English child born in the colonies, Virginia Dare?

"Both. His people might be English colonists. Might be the Hatteras Indians." For the first time, Fergus's baleful gaze met hers. Crumbs flecked his salt-and-pepper beard. "Ye know, the English Lost Colony on Roanoke Island mysteriously disappeared. Some say the Hatteras tribe absorbed them."

"Bah." She put down a half-eaten plum. Her stomach was churning. How much time before Jacob returned? "Ye should be spinning tales at one of our *ceilidhs*. A fairytale it is – something that happened almost two hundred years ago."

He shrugged shoulders humped with muscles. "Who knows fer sure? What I do know is you've got the stick by the wrong end. He plumb tuckered himself out to get back from Fort Charlotte in time for his wedding."

She eyed him suspiciously. "What was he doing so far away – in South Carolina?"

"Negotiating for the Cherokee and the Continental Congress, he was."

Behind her, the forest birds chattered among themselves restlessly. "Which side is he on?"

"Neither. He is his own – "

He broke off, as if alerted to something she could not detect. Then, she heard it, a faint, sloshing sound. She strained to see in the twilight that filtered through the overarching trees of the far bank. Then a canoe came around a leafy curve into view. Jacob Dare, on his knees, shifted the paddle in a rhythmical stroke from one side of the canoe to the other.

She shot to her feet. The tin plate with its remnants of strawberries and walnuts and plumbs tumbled from her lap to clatter on the beach pebbles. Her throat tightened. Her fingers dug crescents into her palms. She forced her limbs to relax. There was no time left . . . what had her mother said about surrender? Something about 'there must be a willingness to surrender in order to live.' No, in order to love.

But this wild man . . . could she ever come to love him? She reminded herself the respite of Christmastide was only seven months away. Seven long months.

Fergus rose, swiped his greasy hands on his pants, and trotted down to the shoreline to help load the last of the raft's supplies into the canoe

Three quarters of an hour of daylight remained. Three quarters or more before the stranger who was now her husband bedded her.

Long rifle in one hand, Jacob dragged the empty canoe ashore with the other, the gravel crunching beneath the canoe's weight. Even at the distance of a dozen yards, he could see his bride tense. As if fortifying herself to endure his presence.

He should not have expected any other reaction. But he had hoped. Fergus paddled a canoe as good as the next riverman and could have made both trips, but Jacob had opted for taking the first supply load upriver himself. He wanted to give Catriona time to get accustomed to her surroundings before she had to get accustomed to him.

"Lad, come git yeself some vittles," Fergus called, "while I finish the loading."

Sand gave way beneath footsteps that took him closer to the flame. She backed a step, then another. She spun toward the board of food. "Sit. I shall fix your plate."

He refrained from smiling. Laying aside his long rifle, he seated his bone-weary frame on a larger rock. Palms braced on his knees, he watched her hands flit over the victuals. He liked how they moved. With a light and levity not peculiar to earthly forces.

She passed him the plate. Their fingers touched and she withdrew hers as hastily as if flames had licked them. "Thank you," he said gravely.

She backed away once more. "Ye must be worn ragged. A solid

meal will have ye right as rain. After me da was wounded, he would have none of that broth and water they give the sickly. Nae, he bellowed for beef, washed down by whisky. Course, when me mam poured it on his open wounds willy-nilly, he cursed her for witchery. Said she'd kill him if his wounds did not. She threatened to set the leeches on him. Mighty scared she was that he was going to up and die. They were both yelling at one another, and then afore I knew it, I could hear them giggling like children."

Her tumble of words faltered. Her fingers began to twist the beige ribbons of her checkered straw hat. "Well, ye need to get on with your supper." Her hand swatted at a swarm of gnats, and she sauntered to the clearing's far side, exceedingly interested it would seem in examining the fern, a mossy stone, and then a salamander scurrying across a rotten log.

Never taking his stare off her tall, shapely figure, he wolfed down his food. The roast was too heavily seasoned for his taste. But she was right. He was both famished and exhausted. After the last week of sustained traveling, he was ready to fall face forward on the feathered bed. Their feathered bed.

Seeking shelter for the night, a yellow slider turtle plodded past his rifle stock, over the gravel, toward the shoreline. Fergus and the supply-laden canoe vanished around the thickly wooded edge of the river. With his departure, the forest creatures at once quietened. Not so, his bride.

"Oh, look, a firefly!"

"Is it now?" He set aside the tin plate.

She turned to face him. Her generous lips stretched into an attempt at pleasantry. "Did ye know fireflies are a part of the faerie world? Because they are iridescent, they can make others see what they want them to see."

"The Cherokee believe in Little People. They can only be seen when they want to be seen."

"For truth?"

The obvious delight his remark elicited made him want to tell her more. That the Little People had really long hair and often helped lost or sad children. Which he had been.

"When I was a wee one," she said, bestowing a genuine smile, "well, I was never a wee one — but as a child, I had an imaginary friend, Rupert, and he was by far my favorite family member."

He smiled.

Screaming silence. Her eyes darted around. As if to find something on which to comment.

He cleared his throat, hearing the deepening of his voice. "I mean you no harm. But we must start this bridal journey somewhere."

Her chin came up. In the shadowy forest beyond, tree frogs and locusts had struck up a lullaby in recognition of the day's ebbing.

"Come here, Wife."

She made no move, if he discounted the way her pupils dilated to the size of dimes.

He beckoned with his fingers.

Her sigh may well have been as light as the soughing of the river breeze, then her measured steps toward him cracked upon the gravel like gunshots. When she was near enough, he held out his palm. Waiting, as if waiting for a firefly to alight.

When she placed her hand in his, he realized he had had been holding his breath. He drew her to sit upon his knee. The flair of her nostrils told him he most likely stank worse than a stomach-turning muskrat.

She was no small weight but solid, built for giving and taking. The fragrances he had detected when she had stood at his side during their wedding ceremony — orange flower, cinnamon, and jasmine — was fainter now but still just as embarrassingly arousing to him. His body betrayed him, and her eyes betrayed their alarm.

He shifted her on his knee. "We both agreed to this marriage because we wanted something. You, to protect Afton Manor. I, to ennoble Dare Plantation."

While he talked, the fingers of his right hand at the back of her waist just naturally followed her dress's multitude of small hooks to find the muscles aligning her spine. Lightly he trailed his fingers up and down in the soothing way he did when gentling Red Rover. And Catriona was as much a wild creature as the young mountain lioness, despite Catriona's veneer of civilization. It was that veneer he wanted her to bring to Dare Plantation and Kinsfolk Landing.

Her back relaxed ever so little. "Aye, a bargain – that we have made."

His fingers lingered over the soft warm flesh of her nape and focused pressure there. Her head tilted back slightly at the pleasure, and a portion of her hair spilled loose from her wide-brim hat to tickle the back of his scarred hand. "Not a bargain," he corrected, "but a lifelong pledge. And I pledge to you, Wife, that I shall never hurt you."

She looked askance at him. "Ye canna pledge such a thing. Mayhap, physically. But sometimes I have heard even my parents, who love each other beyond measuring, why, they have spit spiteful words that hurt the heart."

He left off massaging her neck to scratch the back of his. "I admit I am a novice at this. I have not lived with another woman for any length of time." Or for that matter, anyone. Least ways, since he was a boy.

She squirmed on his knee to look at him, and once more his body treacherously responded, but this time she did not appear to notice. Her expression was earnest. "Living with someone, 'tis a matter of give and take. Of compromise. Not sacrifice but compromise, ye understand. An untainted willingness."

He was not sure he did. He did understand he wanted her badly at that moment. Had wanted her since he had first beheld her. His left hand itched to feel her thigh's smooth flesh beneath the layers of her skirt's scratchy material, but he kept his fingers anchored on his own knee. "And tonight? Is it a matter of give and take?"

In the rapid dimming light, her eyes were luminous. "I confess I have no experience whatsoever in that area."

He nodded. "Well, why do we not let nature take its course, then?" He nodded over his shoulder, toward the raft. "Yonder, beneath the canvas, is a bed I had ordered made for you. Made for tall people. I had wanted to surprise you with it. It was loading it after I returned from Fort Charlotte that made me late for our wedding."

She was silent, and he wondered if it was because he still had to address what really fretted her. "I am accustomed to sleeping on the ground. And there I shall sleep. Well, in this case, on the periauger itself. Until," he cleared his throat again, "you should feel that need for me."

One thick russet brow arched, and he noted the finer hairs that swept up from its tip. A moment of silence passed in which he feared she could hear his heart beat, strong, steady and with a passion that might not be in line with her own needs.

"And if I never do? Feel the need for you?"

He fought back a grunt of severe disappointment. "I was hoping to beget a child. Children. To hear their laughter at Dare Plantation."

She tilted her heat to better study him from beneath her hat's brim. A mistake on her part because it put her mouth in a dangerous position for his own to claim. "Have there been other women for ye?"

"A man would be a fool to answer that question. But I shall this once. There have been other women. A Tuscarora maiden. An apothecary's daughter. And, oh, yes, a watchmaker's wife."

Both brows shot up in disbelief.

Could he blame her?

"That is it? No others?"

"That is it."

"It is said ye are part Indian."

"My mother is Cherokee." He wanted to close off further discussion on that subject and asked abruptly. "Any other questions?"

"Aye. Ye are fairly dusky as it is."

"That is not a question." He would keep her talking, sitting on his knee long after it went numb, if possible.

Her lips quivered at one end, as if attempting to break free in a smile. "Still, do the tips of your ears always redden even more their natural coloring when ye talk about coupling?"

He could feel the blush that, indeed, heated his ears. "Only with you."

"Why?"

"Because we do not know each other well enough yet."

"Did ye know them . . . those three women?"

The crickets had begun their evening serenade. "Two of them. That is why you need to know me. And I you. Like how you came by that scar just beneath your lower lip."

She grinned. "Me oldest brother Robbie clipped me chin while doing a cartwheel. Knocked out an already loose bottom tooth and saved me da from having to pull it."

Without meaning to, he raised his forefinger to trace the scar, and her chin dodged him. He held back a sigh. Setting her on her feet, he stood. "Time I washed off a week of travel."

He pulled the smock over his head. Might as well get it over with now. She would need to get used to his knife-scarred and bullet-pitted flesh. "Do you want to bathe, also?" he mumbled into the shroud of his shirt.

"Uhh, had me bath this morning, I did."

By the time he had removed the smock, he found her gaze glued to the blue tattoo etched between the broad span between his nipples. Her fingertips reached out to trace the design incised in his flesh, then instantly retracted.

His entire body quivered. He almost grabbed her upper arms to yank her to him, so badly did he want her at that moment. He had been waiting for her so long. Patient beyond even his enormous capacity for patience.

"What it is?" she asked, still staring at his breastbones, so that he could feel his nipples growing taut.

"Cherokee writing. Inscribed there when I was ten."

"For the love of God! That must have hurt. And I thought having the cowpox inoculation when I was but eleven hurt unbearably. Was it a coming of age rite or something?"

Her sympathy wounded him nearly as much. "You might put it that way."

"What does it say?"

"*Gvgeyu.* It does not translate easily into English," he evaded before she could ask.

He bent over to unknot the rawhide thongs about his damp wrappers and shrug off his moccasins so that she could not see his expression. By the time he straightened, it was inscrutable. Purposefully, he slithered out of his filthy leather britches to bare what he had been trying to suppress earlier, and it sprang free with a will of its own.

Her perfect mouth formed a perfect O. Skirts in hand, she swerved away, heading for the ramp. "Guid night," she flung over her shoulder.

Moonlight silvered the blue-black water as he waded into the Cape Fear. But the relief of its chill did nothing to cool his heated blood.

~ ~ ~ ~ ~ ~ ~

Restless, Catriona flopped from her side to her back to face-down on the feathered mattress, seeking the sweet nirvana of sleep. The gently rocking barge should have lulled her.

But how could she sleep when she was so disturbingly aware that a naked Jacob Dare lay on a bearskin pallet spread next to the great canopied and curtained four-poster?

She had so many questions about her new husband. The burns on his hands, the inscription across his chest, his parentage, his wealth of knowledge. And the women with whom he had coupled.

Barrett had been a known quantity, a comfortable familiarity to which no readjusting was required when he had returned to the Colonies from Oxford and military service. But Jacob Dare kept her on her toes, ever in the moment.

At one point, long after midnight, after hours of rolling from one side to the other in fretful half-sleep, she flung out one arm . . . and gasped as a hand claimed her dangling one. Instantly, she went still, ceased breathing, ceased any movement.

Gently, ever so softly, the fingers rubbed the mounds of her palm, massaged its hollow, and kneaded every knuckle of each finger. Much like milking the cow's teats, as she had in her youth. Only now she was the recipient . . . and such an exquisite feeling. She left her hand dangling in that vulnerable position and ever so gradually surrendered to the pleasure Jacob was giving her. She muffled her soft groan into her feathered pillow.

Yet her sleeplessness did not abate. Instead, a growing need pulsed low within her belly. After a while, his fingers stilled, but he continued to hold her hand, his fingers interlocked with hers. "Dunna stop," she rusked.

The hypnotizing kneading resumed. And she did not know what was worse, the sleeplessness or the yearning for something more. Something that would take over her entire body. Desperately, she wanted those fingers to explore past her hand, past her wrist and elbow. But their magic worked its wonder, and, weakened by both physical and emotional fatigue, she gave over to his touch and slipped into a deep slumber.

With the streaming light of daybreak came the crisp smell of sizzling meat to awaken her. She yawned, stretched, and opened her gritty lids to find dark blue eyes studying her intensely.

Jacob was sitting next to her on the bed. "We have a long, hard haul ahead of us," he was saying in that precise British accent of his. "I want to reach Kinsfolk Landing before nightfall." He proffered her a tin plate of fried pork.

She shoved up onto her elbows, only to realize that the coverlet had slipped to reveal breasts fairly bobbing like autumn apples at the lace edge of her chemise.

She yanked up the coverlet to her chin. "You should not be hiding yourself," he chided gently. "Not from my eyes."

"Lad," Fergus called out, "'tis time to be up and at 'em."

At the thump of Fergus's canoe against the graveled beach, Jacob sighed and stood. He wore only his britches, and his long hair fell damply onto his chest, telling her he had taken a morning plunge. He was obviously fastidious about cleanliness. His smooth jawline also told her he had shaved frontier style, without a mirror.

After he joined Fergus ashore, she scrambled to dress, donning once more the gown she had worn for her wedding. Now was not the time to plow through her trunk, searching for something more appropriate for hinter country. Her gown was badly wrinkled. Her silk pumps were clammy from the moist night air. And her hair. Sweet Jesus! The river's humidity had transformed it into a bubbling mass of kinky curls.

With but a nod did Fergus acknowledge her. Only a minimum exchange of words occurred between him and Jacob, and then they got the raft under way, with her perched on the marriage bed, still lashed to the raft.

For nearly a quarter of an hour the trip was pleasant. A squirrel scampered along an overhanging branch, and a blue jay cawed out a warning the furry-tailed intruder was not welcome. Morning sunlight dappled the water and a green-barred perch arced, spraying droplets. Here and there boulders signaled of the falls to come and of the blue mountains beyond.

Both the soaring of the bank to sheer rock cliffs fifty or more feet in height and the amplifying sloshing of tumbling water warned the raft was fast approaching the falls. The current grew swifter where Hollering Woman Creek flowed into it.

Without any noticeably given signal, Fergus took over at Jacob's position, and Jacob slipped into and set loose one of the two canoes. "Hold tight to the bedpost," he told her.

At his feet was coiled rope that played out as he rapidly paddled toward shore. The remainder of the rope in hand, he jumped from the canoe to the bank. His black hair streaming, he sprinted forward along it toward a series of ascending rock ledges.

As he leaped agilely from one ledge to the next, she could not take her sight from his lanky frame. There was an iron in it, in his nature. She knew in those precarious moments he was the human fulcrum, the essential part that determined life or death for her and Fergus

The water swirled turbulently, reclaiming her attention. Directly ahead, the river was now choked with boulders. A drenched Fergus struggled with the setting pole. His shoulders bunched as he tried to steer the raft toward the inside of the river's bend, where the heavy current was less choppy and there were fewer boulders. Obviously, the mass and weight of the bed frame, being harshly bounced, added danger to the raft capsizing.

She looked again and sighted Jacob. He was rapidly bounding one end of the rope around a sturdy tree. Quickly, he set to warping the raft. As Fergus steered it up and over the first rise of the white water's rocky shelf, the raft bobbled and swerved. Her anxious gaze swiveled forward, up the bank. Jacob pulled hand over hand, yanking the raft over another rise. The raft popped up and crashed back into river.

She was jarred, then frothy water soaked her. She gasped, her vision momentarily obscured. Loosening her grip, she wiped her eyes – saw Jacob winching hard on the rope – and next felt a tremendous thud that toppled her from the bed.

Her flailing body slammed against the planking. She felt her ribs bow with the impact and tasted with surprise coppery blood. She grabbed for the bed's scrolled foot, only to feel it slide as the bed itself was tussled between its bindings and the inexorable pull of gravity.

She rolled and tumbled toward the low end of the raft. Out of the corner of her eye, she saw the rear steering pole hurtling past her field of vision. She lurched sidewise for its fulcrum. Her lower torso, hampered by her skirts, went over the raft's edge first. She latched on and held tight. Splinters jammed into her palms. Rocks punched and gouged her water-tossed shins and thighs.

Wind turbulence whipped off her hat. Water rushed in to fill its crown, causing its ribbons to garrote her throat. Her scream was strangled. It was as if the water were a living thing, bent on sucking her from the raft. Her grip was slipping. Yet, foolishly, her fear was that the water might snatch from her hair her precious gold hairpin.

A hand manacled her upper arm. Hauled her, heavy skirts and all, back aboard. Prone, she managed to turn her face up to see Fergus, his bowed legs shifting to balance counterpoint with the pitching of the raft. His sour expression was a welcome sight.

"Jacob would ne'r forgive me if l let ye go overboard. Hold fast to the fulcrum." Then he rotated and hustled back to the front steering pole.

Doing as he said, she lay there, gasping, hurting all over, and wanting to cry.

At last, the raft stabilized, bobbing only slightly with the current. Ribs protesting, she crawled toward the bed. Too tired to stand, she sat with her back against its wooden frame, head pressed against her updrawn knees. She could almost smell the acrid scent of her fright in her mushy clothing and in the hair plastered to her face.

She did not know how much time passed, but she heard Jacob's voice, calling out something to Fergus. She raised her head. Saw Jacob's canoe bump alongside the raft while the two men exchanged words, then pass it as he paddled ahead toward the shallow water of a bend. Fergus followed suit with the raft. She was too worn out to do more than peer through her soggy hair as they jumped ashore to beach both crafts at a slate-like clearing stacked with crates and barrels and bags.

Jacob boarded and strode across the raft to hunker in front of her. "Damn, that scared the devil out of me, Wife. I thought I might lose our bed, too."

"What?" she spat. And then saw that he was fighting back a smile. She shoved a sore palm at his shoulder, then grinned despite her harrowing experience. Only at that point did she notice the nail of her little finger had been torn off. So cleanly, that as to be practically bloodless.

Inexplicably, her hands masked her face, and she unraveled.

Crying. Embarrassingly copious sobs. So unlike her. This weakness. But her once solid world was crumbling.

The hurried marriage . . . to a man she would not have chosen under ordinary circumstances . . . giving up her home and family and friends . . . combined with the imprisonment of her brothers and her father's near mortal wounds . . . and now this, a too-close brush with drowning.

He dropped to sit next to her, looping his arm around her and gathering her against his side. "What it is?"

Face still buried in her hands, she shook her head, feeling miserably like a weakling. She was trembling, whether from her sodden clothes or her mishap or both, she did not know. But his welcoming body heat eased her somewhat.

Without raising her head, she flourished her little finger. "This," she wailed.

He captured her hand. "Ahh, I see. But it will grow back."

She huddled closer, seeking his strength, his power, and raised her head to look at him. His eyes, rimmed with river-wet lashes, studied her intently. She noted he had missed shaving a spot at one side of his upper lip that morning. That negligence on his part made him seem more human and made easier her confession.

"'Tis, also, the unknown," she whispered. "So bewildering. I feel as if I dinnae come equipped for this trip, for this marriage."

"It is not the unknown. It is what you and I together can make of it. It can be an adventure."

She gulped and sniffled. "This is one adventure I had rather bypass."

His lips lost their mobility, tightened ever so little. "The bridal journey or the marriage or both?"

She met his darkened stare, so close to her own. So close she could feel the tension that coursed through his body. "This is not how I envisioned me life playing out. But I have only meself to blame. Pledged me troth to ye I did and will keep that pledge to the best of me ability."

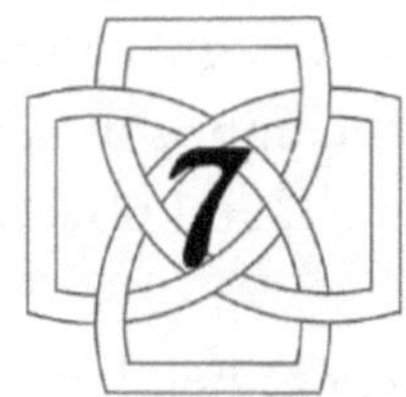

The bridal journey, as Jacob had termed it, seemed to have had a hex placed on it throughout that day. After he and Fergus reloaded the periauger, the rafting appeared to be going smoothly. Then, to avoid colliding with a freshly built beaver dam, the two had been forced to pole into a maze of weedy marshes, primeval remnants of the Great Dismal Swamp.

It had required a good two hours, accompanied by Fergus's colorful oaths, to break the heavy raft free of the reeds and back into the buoyancy of the river. Later in the morning, the raft's rudder had broken on a sunken tree, and the last five miles of the trip had taken all afternoon.

At last, a sign of civilization came into view. A winding wagon road with a gradual gradient had been carved into a slope ascending from the shipping wharf to the top of a steep seventy-foot-high cliff sculpted by water and wind. Atop it resided the settlement of Kinsfolk Landing.

The view looking out from its cliff top wrested the breath from Catriona. She pressed her the pads of fingers at her throat's pulse. Her gaze was drawn to the majestic beauty of the mist-wreathed blue ridges that rolled into the far distance. At eye level, a great blue heron's wide wings soared on an updraft of warm air.

For some seconds, she stood thus, at once rooted in a heady absorption that was nigh overwhelming and yet marveling at the grandness of nature. The awe she experienced left her feeling as she had when viewing the Highland Games' pyrotechnical display. The need to share the experience in order to keep at bay the solitude that could at times be spirit crippling.

A pine-scented breeze whisked tendrils of her dried hair across her cheeks and swished the hem of her skirts across her badly torn silk stockinged feet. Somewhere, most likely snared by river brush, resided her silk wedding pumps. She sighed, consoling herself with the thought they would be impractical here in this wilderness.

Her soul's reverence extinguished, she pivoted to examine the far-flung settlement behind her. No brick paved streets. No handsome brick houses. No white picket fences with their neatly trimmed and ordered hexagonal hedges and fragrant blooming gardens. No shops or coffeehouses. Nae, not even a kirk.

A scattering of maybe three-score crude log cabins with their accompanying field plots occupied an extensive meadow. Cows, chickens, and dogs wandered freely. A somewhat larger structure that she surmised was Fergus's trading post squatted in the meadow's forefront, and what looked to be a couple of mills of sorts topped the cabins at the meadow's distant rear. All this was backed in the far distance by dark, dismal woods.

Long rifle in hand, Jacob stood next to the wagon that had conveyed them and the marriage bed to the bluff top. She knew he was watching for her reaction. She hated to trample his pride in his settlement. "Tis . . . nice," she managed with a pasted smile but suspected she had not fooled him.

Settlers had turned out to greet the wagon of supplies that Fergus had driven up the bluff road. But one by one the settlers drifted now toward Jacob's wagon to ogle the bed with its brocade and damask counterpane – and ogle her.

"Jacob!" grinned a walleyed, brown-haired man of maybe thirty, "glad you ran the rapids without running aground." All the while, the man's eyes, she wasn't sure which one, perused her with curiosity.

"You are just glad, Esau, that I did not lose your hogshead of tobacco overboard."

"And ye bought that bag of barley whiskey?" asked a stout man with merry green eyes that flicked over her with speculation.

"To be sure, Mick. But, alas, the cork fell out. Nothing I could do but to drink the whiskey."

"Aww, go on with yerself, Jacob," the robust man said, jabbing a fist to Jacob's bicep.

A young woman with honey-brown hair straying from its knot and splayed feet, bare and dusty, joined them. She had a boy in tow. Though her attitude was standoffish, her eyes, pale brown and quick with intelligence in a pinched face, never left Jacob.

"Mary," he told her, "I brought something back for you."

"And what's that?" Her eyes, hard as acorns, softened momentarily.

"You will just have to wait. Meanwhile, this is my bride, Catriona."

Now, all attention focused solely on her with astonishment. She imagined she must look as worn out as she felt. Not at all like a bride. She was not certain what to do. Managing a smile, she glanced from Esau to Mick to Mary. "Tis pleased to meet ye, I am."

Immediately, Mick swept off his cap, disclosing thinning red hair and small, shell-like ears that contrasted with his large head and body. He made a deep bow and gave her a jovial smile. "Milady. Mick MacGillivray at yewr service."

Esau bobbed his head and tugged at his lanky forelock.

Above a dingy white collar, Mary squinted at her, then gave a small dip of her pointed chin and hiked only slightly the skirts of her patched homespun in what could – or could not – be interpreted as a curtsey.

"Come along," Jacob said, his hand firmly at Catriona's elbow, turning her back to the wagon with its cargo of her trunk and the novelty, the canopied wedding bed.

When his hands spanned her waist to assist her up onto the bench seat, her breath was whisked from her as surely as it had been moments earlier when viewing the awe-inspiring panorama of the Blue Ridge Mountains. But this she could also attribute to the battering her ribs had taken on the rafts.

"I will show you to your new home."

No, in her heart her home would always be Afton Manor. That place of her birth that called to her heart.

New was about the only positive thing she could say about his log cabin – and that it was slightly larger than the cluster of cabins in the meadow. Dear God in heaven, this was Dare Plantation?

Recently constructed, the story-and-a-half house stood alone a good mile farther west along the bluff and was reached by a long avenue cut through the trees. In a clearing, it was sheltered by a windbreak of black cherry saplings and skirted behind by crop fields. It was not much bigger or better than its barn with an accompanying corn crib, off to one side.

The house's forefront featured a deep porch, from which, she grudgingly admitted, there was a splendid view of the shimmering, magical mountains.

With her red trunk braced on his wide shoulder, Jacob, followed her into the shadowy main room.

She paused, her eyes adjusting to the room's dimness. Its stuffiness, having been closed up for who knew how long, was redolent with the sharp resinous scent of recently sawed pine. It was dizzying. She braced a palm against the adzed door jamb to steady herself, then moved further into the room. At each step, the split-log floor, resembling barrel staves before they were shaved, snagged her already scruffy thread stockings.

As she glanced around, she heard his footsteps depart – a wee relief from the tension she was feeling between them. She surveyed the raised hearth of river rock and its fireplace, large enough to take at least a six-foot log. Shelves were built into the wall on one side of it. On them, kettles, pans, and plates were stored in an orderly fashion.

To the other side of the fireplace was built a bake oven. And she was supposed to cook for him? She, who had never cooked a day in her life. If only Phoebe were here.

A metal bucket held tongs, poker, hatchet, spade and bellows. Another held kindling. The man was clearly and obsessively neat.

A pine cupboard stood along one wall. A trestle table with benches, two split-bottom chairs, and a three-legged stool were the only other pieces in the room – if she discounted the spinning wheel off in a far corner. Had Jacob purchased that with a wife in mind? She knew less about spinning than she did cooking.

Unburdened by her trunk now, Jacob cradled his long rifle on the hooks above the doorway, then crossed to the shutters to throw them open. No windowpanes. Not even oiled paper. A wash of sunlight played on the room's still-green log walls.

He turned back to her. Once again, he presented her with that inscrutable countenance, but she knew by now that a question mark lurked behind that narrow face sculpted with a rock-hard chin and high bluffs for cheekbones – and eyes as dark and mysterious as the wilderness.

She could only nod, hoping her countenance did not betray her disappointment. The silence, as taut as her dulcimer's catgut strings but far more fragile, made her uncomfortable, but she would not be the one to break it.

She turned away to wander into the adjoining room. Remnants of sunlight from the main room illuminated motes flittering like faerie dust throughout the bedchamber. Hesitantly, she entered farther.

Other than her trunk, deposited near the doorway, the room contained only a rough-hewn chest of drawers on high legs. Atop it rested a rusty tin candle holder with drip pan, a wash basin, pitcher, and chamber pot. A work shirt and other garments hung from wall hooks – and a blanket-and-bearskin bedroll reposed on the floor next to the chest.

The jail cells at Halifax, where Robbie, Andrew, and Jaime were imprisoned, were doubtlessly more indulgent.

A framed out but as yet unfinished loft reached by a ladder ran the length of the back of the room. "For storage?" she asked as a way to refrain from commenting on the room's austerity.

"No," he said, so close behind her now she could feel his breath on her nape. "For a child, children, to sleep in."

"Oh." Then she saw it, in the corner's shadow – a baby cradle, its wood appearing green, so freshly cut it must have been. It was small, but not at all insignificant. She shivered. She felt like a mare or heifer bought for breeding.

His large hands splayed on her shoulders, and she flinched. Turning her to face him, he backed her against her trunk and pressed her to sit. Terribly nervous, she stared up into that damned impassive visage he could so easily assume.

What was this about? They had met two weeks ago, been in each other's presence, mayhap, five or six times, and were now expected to profess adoration and consummate their vows as hastily as two rabbits coupling?

He hunkered before her and lifted her skirts. Reflexively, she tried to snatch them from his grasp. His hands easily evaded hers and held up the blood-splotched hem for her to see. "Look. Your scratches and gashes need to be tended to."

So much had happened in the past twenty-four hours that she supposed she was benumbed. "If ye have a salve, I – "

"Wait."

He rose and padded on soft moccasins to the high chest and returned to sit cross-legged before her. He nestled a small leather pouch against the fall flap of his crotch. Once again he lifted her skirts past her ankles and draped them over her knees. Suffused with embarrassment, she snapped her lids shut as quickly as she would her fan.

Almost reverently, as if on some holy pilgrimage, his hands slid oh so slowly up one white stockinged calf to pause just above her knee. Beneath her tattered silk stocking, her flesh tingled with the trail left by the passage of his perceptible fingers. As delicately as a spider weaving a web, he gently rolled her garter and then her hose down over the myriad bruises and scratches and cuts, some of which had already dried and peeled it from her foot.

"Good," he pronounced in a satisfied voice and laid aside the rolled stocking. "No cuts will need stitching."

His examining touch was tender. Yet he was close enough that she could breathe in the inflexible strength in him – and that hint, always, of some unknown threat. Nevertheless, her battered body eased into loose limbs, her gaze drifted upward to the timbered rafters, and she sighed – until a dried scab peeled away with the other hose. "Ouch," she gasped. Her lids flew open. "Ye said ye would never hurt me."

"Not intentionally." She could make out the faint squint lines at the outer corner of his eyes that marked those men who could read the life story told in a opossum's paw prints. His top lip, marked by a faint mustache shadow, curled upward at the ends. "You can pummel *me* after I finish."

"That I shall." But, and she did not know why, she trusted him. She relaxed once more against the rough wall with its clay-daubed chinks. From beneath half-lowered lids, she watched the man, this man to whom she was now legally bound.

From the weathered pouch, he fished out a handful of what looked to be dried, crushed leaves. He spat into his palm and with his other fist pulverized the leaves into a paste.

Her eyes widened. "Ye are no' going to be putting that mush on me, are ye now?"

"Yarrow," he said, without looking up as he smoothed it onto one of her limbs. "A remedy used by my mother's people. Good for wounds and bruises."

"But your spittle?"

From between the thicket of black lashes he was regarding her closely. "It would be much the same as if I kissed you."

"You have." Her mouth twitched peevishly. "At the wedding."

"Thoroughly kissed you."

A faint thrill ran through her. Her stomach dropped and heat burned its way up her throat and cheeks. No suitor had ever talked to her like that. So directly, without regard for social conventions. "You mentioned your mother's people. Is she still alive?" she inquired, evading his close regard with nervous prattle.

"No." He, released her left limb to give his attention to her other. "The yarrow – and my spittle – will heal you fast."

The way he chose his words, the way he spaced them, created a great intimacy in that cabin on the edge of the world.

She marveled at how much smaller her bare foot looked in the palm of his long hand. Such an intimate task, what he was doing. In her nether regions, and she was not certain exactly where, she felt a tightening, like the torqueing of a wrench. Painful yet also inexplicably pleasant.

He stood, swiping the paste remnants from his palms, and looked down at her. "There is a small looking glass in the highboy's top right drawer. The necessary and rain barrel are behind the cabin."

Could she blush any more than she had already? She swallowed, nodded.

After he left her, she crossed to red lacquered chest in springy steps, "Ouching!" with each, because the split log floor scoured her soles. No wonder, the French word for 'pricking', *puncheon*, was used for such primitive floors. Off came her ruined ball gown, her panniers, her pockets, stays, and her petticoats.

She pulled out a serviceable blue gingham daydress with split sleeves, one of four she had brought, and a pair of cotton stockings and low-heeled leather patents. Almost reverently, she removed her gold hairpin and tucked it beneath her dulcimer, wrapped protectively in her red plaid.

Clothes in one arm, she padded across the bedroom to that other chest, the plain and simply made highboy. The top right drawer contained an accoutrement of toiletries: razor, chipped shaving mug, cake of lye soap, leather strap, and a small mottled mirror. She sighed at her wrath of red hair reflected in it.

Curiosity got the better of her. She should not – but she did. She justified she had a right to find out what kind of man this was she had married. She dropped her clothes and opened another drawer. In it were neatly folded a couple of drab homespun smocks, woolen stockings, and durable breeches.

However, another drawer contained a fine set of dress clothes, all newly made – a lawn shirt with a stock and narrow cuffs, a buff linen jacket, matching waistcoat, doeskin breeches, and a pair of low heeled, leather shoes fastened with gilt buckles. Conservative but quite elegant for the rustic Jacob Dare.

Yet it was the next drawer that piqued her imagination. Calf-bound books. *Robinson Crusoe, Gulliver's Travels, Aesop's Fables* and *Johnson's Dictionary.* Even a copy of *The Decameron* in Italian. She picked up one, *The History of Tom Jones.* Like the others, it appeared to have been little read, if at all.

What a paradox this man was.

The tantalizing aroma of bubbling meat galvanized her into closing the drawer and changing quickly. Use of the chamber pot was not even a consideration. Not with Jacob in the next room, so close. Instead, she retreated behind the cabin to the clapboard necessary. It was midway between the cabin and cornfield. The last rays of the sun were already gilding the tops of maples and pines.

While not of brick with stately cut-stone windows like some of those in Campbelton, still the necessary could have been a cesspool or much worse. Stepping from the necessary onto pine needles, she looked directly into the slitted stare of a mountain lion. She screamed. Backed a step up against the necessary's closed door. The mountain lion snarled, baring glistening fangs. She screamed again.

Abruptly, it turned-tail and bounded back through the corn field, past the barn and corncrib, and into the dense forest.

Trembling badly, she took a blind step forward – and collided with Jacob, his long rifle in hand. One arm encircled her waist to keep her from collapsing. "A – a mountain lion," she whispered.

"A reddish-brown beast of a cat?"

She nodded. Her chin was quivering. Her heart was pounding in her ears.

"Red Rover." He enfolded her into the shelter of his arms and chest, so that his chin rested on her head and his long rifle girded her back. She could smell his throat's heat and the charged male scent she identified particularly with her brothers. "She will not harm you. She only needs to get accustomed to you."

Catriona had been the frightened one, but she could feel his heart thudding against her shoulder. She opened her eyes to stare at the bone button of his smock. "As I need to get accustomed to you," she muttered into the coarse homespun. Had it only been thirty-six hours since she had wed? It seemed like weeks.

"There ye be," Fergus said coming up from behind Jacob. "What's all the ruckus?"

Still holding her, Jacob said over her head, "Red Rover paid her a visit. Come on," he told her, taking her by the hand.

Esau met them at the door with his wide, loopy grin, his walleyes alight. "Here you go, Mistress Dare," he said passing her a horn cup. "A welcome home gift."

She could smell its strong brew and noted peripherally the brown stoneware bottle on the table alongside the oil lamp. Hands still shaking, she accepted the cup. "Well, thank ye now, Esau."

"Me and Fergus jist stopped by to help Jacob unload the bed."

She had expected beer or ale, but it was rum she swigged. She had to choke back a cough at the cost of a tear-blurred vision. Jacob watched her with wicked amusement. At that moment, she was unsure as to which was more potent – the burning rum or his dangerous energy.

"Esau is our cooper," he told her. "He makes the barrels to transport our rosin and turpentine." And then to Esau, "My wife plays the dulcimer with some skill. Mayhap, you would show her yours with the fiddle tomorrow night?"

"Tomorrow night?" she croaked, her still misty eyes moving from him to Esau to Fergus and back to him.

"Kinsfolk Landing wants to stage a celebration of sorts for us."

"A celebration would be wonderful." A celebration was the last thing she wanted.

She sat aside her cup and turned her attention to the fireplace. The run in with the mountain cat combined with her run in with the rum had left her with little appetite. Nevertheless, she was, indeed, mistress of the house, and she set about shoveling the Dutch oven's gruel and the skillet's pemmican that Jacob had warmed with goose fat onto three wooden plates for the men.

Jacob lit the oil lamp. Seated at the table, the three men conversed about the community's resin distillery, a visitation by five Catawba, and Jacob's meeting with the Cherokee and the Patriots' Indian commissioners.

"Chief Corn Tassel is straddling the fence," he said, his muscled forearms braced on the table and one scarred hand engulfing his horn cup. "Dragging Canoe has most likely made up his mind to go on the warpath."

"What with British ships at Wilmington and the Cherokees at our backs," Esau drawled, "I'd venture out on a limb to say we're facing an odds-against-us fight."

When she placed plates before Jacob and the other two, he glanced up at her, and she detected something between gratitude and relief in his expression. Never had she waited on another human being, but apparently she had passed muster. Taking the crock of butter she had found in the cupboard, she set it beside the jug of rum.

"*Och*," Fergus grumbled, "they said we could no' earn a living running barrels of tar and resin from this far upriver down to Wilmington." He spat a plug of tobacco in the crack between the floor's log's that he was using as a spittoon. "Well, by God, we've done it. And we'll lick the Redcoats, the Cherokees, and the Tories, if we have to."

At last the two men took their leave, and Jacob settled on his haunches before the fireplace to rake its embers. Their soft, glimmering light played like stars twinkling on the black sky that was his long hair. "I shall scrape the dishes," he told her, capping the embers with a copper curfew. "Go to bed."

"Aye, tis tired I am beyond belief." She waited for a reply but he was replacing the tongs and curfew in the bucket. "Well, guid night to you, then."

"Good night." He had not even bothered to turn and smile.

How soon before he bored her beyond endurance?

More tired than she could remember being in a long time and a wee bit woozy from the rum, she retreated into what would be their bridal chamber. She removed her leather patents and carefully peeled off her cotton stockings, sticky with remnants of Jacob's unguent. Next her daydress. Longing for a lady's maid, she struggled on her own with loosening the strings at the back of her stays.

She disregarded her new and hastily-made lace nightrail and, clad only in her chemise, crawled between the snowy linens of the bed. Never had a mattress felt so heavenly, her bridal bed though it might be.

The room went dark, and she realized Jacob had lowered the kitchen's lamp wick. Lids squeezed closed, she waited. Would he want that night to assert his rights to her that came with their vows? She heard him pad across the puncheon into the bedchamber. Heard his clothing slip to the floor. And then heard the sliding swish of the soft bearskin pallet being laid out. Her breath surged from her in relief and gratitude. He would not make demands upon her tonight.

After a few moments, as she felt herself sliding into sleep, she draped her hand over the marriage bed and sighed again, this time at peace, as his fingers intertwined with hers.

From the north, a spring breeze riffled the oak and hickory leaves, flitted the cornstalks' silvery silk, and wiggled the small mirror suspended from a hook at the rear of the cabin, near the woodpile.

The rising sun and twittering birds found Jacob sitting in his breech cloth cross legged before the tarnished mirror. On his left was a small, wooden-stave tub filled with water from the rain barrel. On his right lay Red Rover, her head in his lap. The mountain cat was wide in the chest and wide between the eyes, and her jaws were sharp enough to snap a man's neck.

The summer before last, he had found her at the spring back in the forest, where he did his daily bathing. A cub, she had gotten stuck partway between two large rocks. She was starving and dehydrated. He had brought her to his home, cradled in one forearm – she was that small – and had nursed her back to health.

When the day came he carried her back into the woods, he expected never to see her again. But occasionally she would return to watch from the safety of the forest as he shaved in the morning or worked the fields in the evenings.

Gradually, she began to approach the house but never let him near enough to stroke her russet fur. Then one day, as he was shaving, just as he was now, Red Rover padded over to plop down next to him. He made not a move to touch her. Only continued with his shaving. A few weeks later, she felt safe enough to lay her head in his lap and nap while he shaved.

He stretched his mouth to one side to better hedge his morning scruff. Mayhap, he thought, it would work the same with his new wife. Cat. This gentling of her. Holding her hand, until his own went numb. Yet, despite his hand's throbbing, throughout the night he held that hand that fit his so perfectly. It was only reasonable that she shared his uncertainty about their state of matrimony.

Red Rover yawned, and he had to smile. That was about the same response he was getting from his wife these first two nights of their marriage. He supposed he now had two Cats.

He heard her before she came around the corner of the cabin. At the same instant, Red Rover's ears pricked up.

His wife came to an abrupt halt, then stood hands on hips, watching him – and Red Rover – cautiously. Pins attempted to restrain her shock of red curls beneath a lace-edged cap. Today, she had foregone her wide paniers. Good.

Attempting to ignore the brevity of his attire, she stared only at his masterful face. "Ye keep missing the same spot."

He proffered his razor and smiled. "You can do better?"

Dubiously, she eyed Red Rover.

"Walk toward me naturally. Let her make up her mind whether to stay or go."

The tentative steps his wife took were not at all natural. Then several more at a sedate pace. At that point, Red Rover pushed upright, whisked her tail, and trotted off toward the corn field and the forest beyond.

Catriona let out the breath she had been holding and closed the distance between them to take up his razor. With excessive attention, she stropped the razor on the wide leather strap affixed to the same hook as the mirror, then turned to kneel before him, her skirt unfurling around her.

He watched as she carefully stroked along his jawline. "I am trusting you will not take it into your head to put a swift end to our marriage," he muttered, "and my life?"

With a grin, she raised her eyes to this. That close, he could see the slight half-moon crease that appeared above her upper lip whenever she smiled. "Dunna tempt me. And no more talking. I dunna want blood to spoil me few dresses I have left."

"Neither do I. Especially since it may be my own blood." Not that he had to worry about talking. She did most of it. Would he ever get used to a female's chatter?

Squinting in concentration, she caught his jaw between her fingers, tipping it. "I used to watch me father and brothers shave. I was fascinated by their strained expressions. I believed I could do it better. So, I practiced on our cat's whiskers." Dimples dented her cheeks. "Got a few scratches from Furball and a whipping from me mam for all me efforts, I did."

He chuckled. "Just do not practice on Red Rover."

She had that look of otherness, of imagination that wondered beyond the edge of frontiers, much as did his moccasins. Her lips grew serious. "I tried to warm the gruel for breakfast, but I must confess I made a – "

"I know. You burnt it. I could smell it from here."

She groaned and rolled her eyes. He was completely captivated by her lack of artifice. "'Tis a disappointment ye have when ye bargained for a – "

He shot out one hand to capture the hand that wielded the razor, silencing her abruptly. The other hand latched onto the rifle, always within easy reach.

A moment later, Mary Barger walked around the corner of the cabin. Clinging to her skirt was her five-year-old son, Billy, his hair as blond as sweet corn. Two years before, her husband Clem had been murdered by the Cherokee.

Mountain poor whites, they had grown little more than required to feed and clothe themselves. But they knew the ways of the wilderness, and so he had given them a lot in exchange for Clem's doing guard patrol around the settlement once a week.

In one hand she held a cloth draped plate, the other a cork-stoppered jug. She hesitated, startled by the intimate act she had come upon, then said, "I reckoned yuhr wife wouldn't be up to baking, Jacob. Brought yuh a mite of leftover hoecake I baked freshet this morning and ale I had brewed a while back."

"Now confess," he teased. "You came for your gift, did you not, Mary?"

He knew, as a widow, she was lonely and only a year or so older than he. She was more accustomed to the wilderness ways than most and would have made for a good help mate. But she was not the refined and cultured woman he had sought to make a silk purse out of a sow's ear. And there were times when he did not know if the sow's ear was Dare Plantation, himself, or both.

"I'm not frettin' none over a gift, mind yuh, if yuh didn't brang me one." Her gaze swept over his naked torso.

Catriona must have seen the raw hunger in the young woman's eyes. Passing him his razor, Catriona stood, skirted him, and took the plate and jug from Mary. "Why, thank ye, Mary. Come on inside, both of ye." She glanced down at the reticent boy. "Me name is Catriona. What is yours?"

Billy said nothing, which was not unusual. Withdrawn, he seemed a little slower than the settlement's other children. "No' the full shilling," Fergus said of the kid.

Ignoring the boy's silence, Catriona went right on talking and walking. "Did ye know that when I was about your age, both wee people and giants visited me upstairs nursery?"

The boy hung back, sucking his thumb, while Mary was forced to tug him along with her and follow Catriona.

"They appeared on me bed at night," Catriona continued lightly, as she rounded the cabin. "Well, the wee people did. And the giants, there were three of them, they would take turns talking to me through me upstairs window, they were that tall."

Sighing, he swiped his razor dry. He stored it with the rest of his shaving gear and rose to join the women. He had the unhappy feeling that his days of peace and quiet were about to be turned topsy-turvy.

"God Awmighty," Mary said, stepping inside and getting her first whiff of the burnt breakfast. She grabbed the culprit kettle handle and shouldered past him.

Looking abashed, Catriona gaze's ricocheted from Mary to him and back to Mary. Then like sprinkles giving way to a hurricane, Catriona started after her. "I will do that meself, Mary," she called at the stiff spine of the departing woman.

He grasped her arm. "Take care of Billy. I will take care of Mary."

She stared at his hand on her sleeve, then glanced up at him. Her expression said she would yield. This once, at least. He could not blame her for resenting the other woman's presumptuousness.

He made a detour into the bedchamber and his high chest, then caught up with Mary behind the house. She was stooped over the wooden tub and scouring at the brass kettle's burnt food. Obviously, she knew he was there, but she ignored him. He proffered the tortoiseshell hairbrush within her line of vision.

She ignored it, also, but her chapped and roughened hand ceased its scrubbing. The thin points of her shoulders hunkered even further over the tub. She tried unsuccessfully to push her drooping hair back over her shoulder. "She doesn't suit yuh, Jacob Dare. Nor you her. She'll go back to her own people, I warn yuh. Her clan'll call her back."

"But what is a man without dreams, Mary? You need your own. I cannot be a part of them."

When she did not accept the brush, he ran it through the length of hair tied back at her nape by a leather string. Instantly, she stilled, her eyes closed. With a twist of his wrist, he anchored the brush in her hair and left, returning to the cabin.

Catriona sat on one of table's benches. Before her was a book, from which she was reading aloud. One of his father's books. Ordered for a son who was to learn to make out only a smattering of written words in the English language.

He looked around for Billy; spotted him hiding behind the spinning wheel. But the boy was, indeed, listening. As was he.

"'A wolf, who was out searching for a meal, saw a goat feeding on grass on top of a high cliff. Wishing to get the goat to climb down from the rock and into his grasp, he called out to her.

'Excuse me, dear Goat,' he said in a friendly voice, 'It is verra dangerous for ye to be at such a height. Do come down before ye injure yeself. Besides, the grass is much greener and thicker down here. Take me advice, and please come down from that high cliff.'

"But the goat knew too well of the wolf's intent. 'Ye dunna care if I injure meself or not. Ye dunna care if I eat good grass or bad. What ye care about is eating me.'"

With a bright smile, she glanced from the page to the spinning wheel in the far corner and the boy. "So the moral of Aesop's fable, Billy, is to beware of friendly advice from an enemy."

Jacob shook his head, ensnared by the enchantment her voice wove like a shimmering sunlit web. This was exactly as his mind had envisioned for Dare Plantation; yet Mary's remark had cast its seeds of doubt.

Retreating to the bedchamber, he donned his clothes and left. While he had made many a mistake, he was not fool enough to think he could understand females. Especially white ones. Best he left the two of them alone to sort out their differences. He turned his steps in the direction of his mill.

With a multitude of longleaf pines, the sandhill region of the Upper Cape Fear Valley was a perfect location for those hardy souls willing to risk the rapids in getting the pine's by-products – resin, turpentine, and pitch – to market in Wilmington throughout harsh winters and turbulent springs.

Just before the Cherokee campaign of 1755, Jacob's father had resigned his colonel's commission at Fort Dobbs. In order to receive the grant of 600 acres of land on the Upper Cape Fear, he had been required to build a mill of some kind. Since Great Britain offered a bounty for naval stores, a lumber mill it had been, built alongside the falls of Hollering Woman Creek, some distance back of the settlement. While lacking a ready access to a market for its mast, spars, and staves, the lumber mill had attracted settlers to whom he had sold land.

But Jacob had seen something more in the dead pine – tar. Years after his father died in an accidental fire at the mill, Jacob returned from living with his mother's people to rebuild not only the lumber mill but also to include along with it a distillery for spirits of turpentine and rosin, operated in the same way whisky was distilled.

He climbed the split-log stairs to the mill's second story, open but for the shingle roof. Smoking kilns were extracting sap from fragments of dead pines and processing it over a slow oak fire. Barrels filled with pine resin were lined up before a ramp that conveyed them down to a wagon waiting below.

Bypassing his clapboard desk, Jacob sought out his stiller, Mick. The stout man had helped himself to a British magistrate's purse and escaped the gallows by becoming an indentured servant for seven years. Jacob had bought his papers and freed him in return for a year's free labor at the mill, room and board included. Mick had stayed on, and Jacob had promoted him to mill manager.

He hunkered near one of the large copper kettles, talking to young Jethro Smythe, the sixteen-year-old-son of a Kinsfolk Landing swine raiser. Sweat sheened both their faces and darkened their grungy smocks under their arm pits. Between the morning's humidity and the heat from the fires, the place was a sweat bath.

The eight-month dipping season for distilling crude turpentine was the most rigorous, and going into the peak of distilling activity, the summer season, hired help was always welcome. Working at both his father's farm and the distillery, Jethro was a hard worker but not necessarily a hard thinker.

When he spotted Jacob, his tanned face with its peach fuzz lit up. He stood and waved a hand. "Me and Mick were just talking about the pretty new bride."

"Telling him about the celebration tonight at the trading post," Mick said, the light in his green eyes dancing. "All of Kinsfolk Landing as well as the backcountry settlers are agog to meet her. Especially, our Fair-of-Face here."

A splash of cherry red suffused the youth's handsome features but his grin was good natured. "I'm of half a mind to make the raft trip down river with your next shipment out. Maybe fetch me back a pretty wife for myself."

"Easy as falling off a log," Jacob said drily. Then to Mick, "Dragging Canoe refused to smoke the peace pipe."

Mick's round cheeks blanched of all color. Jacob knew he was vividly remembering when last a small band of roving Shawnee had attacked the Barger's outlying cabin and murdered Mary's husband. It had been Mick who had noted the plume of smoke and had rushed to the rescue. "You be thinking he will come this far? Attack Kinsfolk Landing again?"

"I am thinking we should form a county militia." He dragged fingers through long, sweat-dampened hair as black as the pitch they distilled. He had managed to live peacefully with the Catawba and Tuscarora, but his own Cherokee's matrilineal clan gave him no recognition as one of their own. "We could muster the men between sixteen and sixty bimonthly. Say next month here at Kinsfolk Landing. They provide their own guns and ammunition."

Mulling over this, Mick tugged at one small ear. "I will get the word out. Tonight will be a good opportunity."

Jacob finished his rounds of the distillery and should have seen to more practical matters – fences that needed repairing or fields that needed manuring. Then, too, he needed to hunt and fish to feed the family.

Family.

And with that thought his footsteps took him back home. Mary was gone. Catriona was sweeping the floor with a broom he had fashioned from a pine stave and straw. Sawdust flurried furiously.

Sunshine pouring through the open shutters gilded her hour-glass body and warmed her beauty to a startling glow. He tried to look away, but he could not. He wanted *her* sunshine. But if her mumbling was any indication of her spirit, a sunny smile would not be happening soon. He stood in the doorway, eavesdropping.

"A bloody pox upon this scabby floor with it scurvy pricks!" Then, even more furiously something mumbled in Gaelic. "*Agus daoine aig nach eil a 'cur luach leabhraichean!*"

His fingers twitched with a need unfamiliar to him. The need to knot them in her untamable hair. The need to graze that soft skin of her throat, as white as cream. The need to thrust her against the stone fireplace and kiss her so hard she hurt as much as he did. Instead, he clamped his fingers on the top rail of the nearest chair. "The floor is not to your liking?"

Caught by surprise, she whirled, fist to her chest. Did he make her that skittish? Soot striped one high cheekbone. "Well now, if I had me likes, I would like to have a smooth, shining fine-grain floor of pine, like that in the colony's capitol in New Bern."

Lodging his long rifle in the hooks over the front door, he mimicked her brogue and her very retort on the first day of the Highland Games. "Ye might as well petition the wee people for a pot of gold."

"Och, go on with yeself, Jacob Dare!" She made a playful swipe at him with the broom as he turned back to her.

He latched onto either end of its handle and deftly captured her between it and himself. Lids wide, she watched as, with the broom as leverage, he pressed her ever closer until her palms were flat against his chest.

Her cheeks were the natural rosy pink of a redhead, not the artifice of a city woman's rouge. She tilted her head, and her lips made a moue. "Now that ye have me, what will ye do with me, husband o' mine?"

Had he been among his mother's people, he would have done the most natural thing and mated his body with hers. But he did the next best thing, what his father's people with their incomprehensible culture called courting. A chaste kiss. Well, he had intended it as such but on its own accord his mouth more or less mated with hers. He could feel her tense, but it was too late for gentleness.

He dropped the broom, hearing it clatter on the floor she

despised. His arm wrapped around her waist, drawing her flush with him. Aligning her face with a long palm, he thumbed away the smear of soot.

Her lips rounded in a tiny 'o'.

That small response was his undoing. He could not help himself. He kissed her with a ferocity of which he had not known himself capable. He had wanted her for so long. Waited so long. Even before their meeting at the Highland Games.

His teeth gnashed hers. His tongue was his scout. It would, if it could, search out her sunshine and her shadows. Her affections, her desires, her regrets and her sharp disappointments. All of her, leaving nothing undiscovered, not even when he knew for certain her regrets and disappointments were of his making.

For a moment, she stood as if paralyzed, hands trapped between her chest and his. In his ears, he could hear his heart beating a drum. Could hear a soft moan, a purring at the back of her throat. Dimly, he was aware that her fingers had slinked from his chest up the column of his neck, then slid around to ensnare the roots of his long hair at the base of his skull.

He would take her, then and there on the rough puncheon, but something quick and intense within him, an inner force, strove for sanity, for logic and reasoning. He suspected this imaginative and passionate creature would turn from his baser instincts. She deserved to be fully wooed as a gentleman of high birth would do. Or should do.

Before he released her, he could not help but bury his nose in the swath of burnt red curls mantling the hollow created by her neck and collarbone. Her perspiration-damp hair smelled of salt and jasmine and cinnamon. Her palms, cradling the back of his head, held him fast. He doubted if she realized her very feminine mound saddled his thrusting thigh in what was evidently a pleasurably rhythmic ride for her.

It was all he could do to set her from him. With the wedding celebration only hours away, he did not want to abbreviate this important moment, turning it into something as common as a mere romp.

Her almost inaudible sigh was the lonely wind on the many dark nights he had lain alone. His voice creaked like the chicken pen's rusty gate hinge. "Tonight, after the celebration at Fergus's, we will most likely receive visitors."

A russet eyebrow raised, and then comprehension showed in the slate-colored eyes. "I see. A belated chivaree?"

"The backwoodsmen can get a bit bawdy. Especially after sampling Fergus's whiskey brew." He picked up the broom and handed it to her. "So you know what is expected of us on a night of a chivaree?"

She returned to sweeping industriously. She avoided looking at him. "Aye. They hope to catch us . . . occupied in our bed, right?"

"Yes." A dry lump stoppered the back of his throat. He collected the double-sided axe from the mantel and a whetstone from the fireplace utensils neatly stored in the copper pail. Sitting on the raised hearth, he studiously stroked the axe head with it. He felt as awkward as he had as a child at Fort Dobbs, and he suspected they were both at a loss as how to rechannel their passion.

"Tonight, the community will turn out in full force. They will inspect you like they would a horse at auction time. Once they get liquored up, they may forget their manners."

"I can handle them," she said. "Me brothers and da can swill with the best of men. I dunna ken if I can handle Mary."

"Why? You did not talk this morning?" He had been hoping the two might become friends. In the wild backcountry, a friend could make the difference between life or death. Occasionally, scouting for Caswell called him away from Kinsfolk Landing. Now that he was married, he had the safety of a wife for which to be concerned.

She waved a hand at the books she had stacked haphazardly on the shelving at one side of the hearth. His meticulous nature niggled him to arrange the books in an orderly, upright fashion on the mantle.

"I was reading to Billy – he appeared to pay no attention – but his mother, she was listening with an expression of pure hunger, Jacob."

By no way did his expression betray his pleasure at hearing her use his given name.

"Pass me that book, will ye? *Robinson Crusoe.*"

He could only guess.

She accepted the one he proffered, paused, glanced at him, then idly riffled through a few pages. "I could tell Mary dinnae ken how to read. That is when I offered to teach her – in exchange for teaching me how to spin. Ye ken what she said? 'Read? What for?' And she took Billy in hand and stomped away."

So, that was what had put Catriona in such a huff that she had been taking it out on the split-log floor when he entered. "Mary is clever. Only she has never had motivation." Until he showed up with a wife who read. His fingers detected a burr on the underside of the axe head, and he flipped it over to attack it. "Give her time."

He was acutely aware of the quiet in the room, with the loud sawing of the locusts outside to accentuate his wife's strained silence. He paused in filing and looked up at her. She stood, broom in one hand, the book in the other. "What?"

"She would have made ye a better wife?"

First Fergus, now his wife, begged the question of him. Was this something he should have heeded? Far too late for that now. "Aye."

"And yet you married me."

"I saw you. I wanted you."

The old comic folk song already had maybe two dozen or so children giggling. With their parents and the entirety of the Piedmont frontier, or so it seemed to Catriona, they had gathered for the wedding celebration at Fergus's trading post, which also served as the town hall.

As a child, she had much more preferred the witches of Shakespeare's *Macbeth* with their "Double, double, toil and trouble; fire burn and cauldron bubble" to the "The Wedding of the Frogge and the Mouse." Nevertheless, at Esau's request earlier that evening, she now sat on a three-legged stool and regaled the children, while also keeping an eye on Jacob.

"It was the Frogge in the well,
humble dum, humble dum,
And the merrie Mouse in the Mill,
tweedle, tweedle twino.

The Frogge would a wooing ride,
humble dum, humble dum,
Sword and buckler by his side,
tweedle, tweedle twino.

When he was upon his high horse set,
humble dum, humble dum,
His boots they shone as black as jet.
tweedle, tweedle twino."

Aye, like Frogge's boots, Jacob's shoulder-length hair gleamed black as polished jet. Given his height, he was the easiest to spot among the four score merrymakers who crowded inside the trading post or, perforce, spilled outside on that lovely spring night.

The trading post's counter and dark-stained shelves of smaller goods and wares – pallets of mink and otter pelts, beaver traps, farm tools, and barrels of rice and bags of sugar– had been pushed back to the far walls or stored in the loft.

After the fresh air of the river and forest, the smells of the trading post – of ladled soft soap made of grease and ashes, of drying hides and brine barrels and wet dogs –overwhelmed her. Outside in the yard, maybe two or three dozen more merrymakers danced and capered within sight of a sawhorse table laden with a whiskey barrel.

In a far corner of the trading post, Jacob stood talking with Fergus, Esau and the settlement's flour miller, the bespectacled Humphrey MacGregor. All four smoked either clay or corncob pipes.

Just before the celebration, the four had convened at Jacob's cabin. While she strove to master the frustrating technique of skewering a rabbit on the spit with hawthorn spikes, she had eaves-dropped on the four. They were discussing a response to imminent Redcoat and Indian threats. Sucking a pricked fingertip, she had listened as Jacob laid out the need to build a powder magazine and stockade for the community.

That was when Esau had cajoled her to play her dulcimer for the celebration later. She had plucked it from her trunk, biting her lower lip at the sight of the red plaid and her mother's gold hairpin. Few outside a clan could understand its ancestral draw. Christmastide. How could she abide being so far away from her home until then?

When she finished her folk song, Esau joined her with his fiddle and together they launched into a fast-paced duel of the Scottish ditty, "I Loved a Lass." Esau's walleyes danced almost as fast as his bow. He was truly a master fiddler.

"When I saw my love to the church go,
W' bride an' bride-maidens, they made a fine show;
An' I followed them on wi' a heart fu' o' woe,
For she's gaun to be wed to anither."

The revelers clapped and stomped, and some sang along with her.

> *'When I saw my love sit down to dine,*
> *I sat down beside her and poured out the wine,*
> *An' I drank to the lass that suld ha' been mine,*
> *An' now she is wed to anither.'*

Applause from both children and grownups thundered throughout the large room. Laughing and breathless, she accepted Esau's hand and stood. Tucking the bow and fiddle under his arm, he said, "Tis a gift yew have, Mistress Dare. Yewr way with music and words."

She laid her dulcimer on the stool. Smiling at the guests and, spreading the skirts of her bronze striped taffeta, she dipped a quick curtsey. "I fear me gift is not worth a farthing here," she murmured. "Alas, me domestic skills fall far short."

But had her music pleased Jacob? From beneath her lashes, her inquiring eyes sought out his dark ones. He had changed into a clean white cambric shirt, with drawstrings at the neck, that emphasized the breadth of his chest.

Welcoming any excuse to congregate, crofters, trappers, and other pioneers had come by way of the Wilderness Road, little more than an accidental linking of game trails, from as far as the Blue Ridge.

Among the merrymakers, she felt the intense attention of both Mary Barger and young blond Jethro Smythe. Making a friend of Mary, who kept her distance, would be difficult. And keeping the youthful Jethro at a distance might prove to be even more so.

Already that evening, the lad had fetched her rum-laced punch, its cup sticky with the gummy pine sap his workman's hand prints had left. He was now traipsing behind her like a love-sick puppy.

Why, she could not imagine. She was already married with no dowry to gain. And she was no great beauty, not at her height. She supposed it was her singularity, her definite difference from the Kinsfolk Landing females. Then, too, Kinsfolk Landing's male population appeared to exceed its female one.

All were curious about her. One withered old woman with a toothless grin squinted up at her from beneath her faded sunbonnet. "They say yewr a viscountess in your own right." Mother McGee leaned on her hickory cane toward her and added in a rusky whisper, "That yewr running away from an enforced marriage in Scotland."

She had to smile. "To be sure. I ran right into a marriage with Jacob Dare."

"Poppycock!" the crone cackled, delighted to be let in on a good joke.

Middle-aged and fair-haired Polly MacGregor, the flour miller's wife, cornered her. Head tilted like a plump partridge's, Polly 's inquisitive eyes regarded her with curiosity. "We speculated amongst us what kind of female it would take to capture Jacob Dare."

She managed an affable smile. "Ye are looking at her."

"And spunk it is you have," she said approvingly. "Me thinks he would be sadly remiss had he let such a fine lass as yourself escape him."

Escape? No, she had committed herself to this marriage and would see it through. In truth, she had thought to be bored by him but, instead, discovered him to be a confounding contradiction. A man of few words but the words he chose were often eloquent. A man who was both white and Indian. A man who was both gentle and fierce.

She did escape – toward the rear of the trading post – and the opportunity to withdraw for a few moments from eyes that measured her and doubtlessly found her lacking. A young Indian woman squatted in front of the brick oven. All bones with braids, she was removing with a long wooden paddle a skillet of cornbread. Shifting awkwardly, she stood, and Catriona realized her left foot was twisted.

Catriona introduced herself, and the young Indian woman smiled shyly, disclosing a missing front tooth. "Coowee – Fergus's woman," she returned. Pleasant looking, she was wearing a worn but a clean calf-length leather dress and high-topped moccasins. She nodded at the skillet. "You eat?"

Shaking her head, she declined with a smile. "I have already eaten." If one could deem a charcoaled rabbit eatable. It was so damnably difficult to judge how fast the coals could char.

Drawing a fortifying breath, she forced herself to circulate among the rest of the settlers, most of them slightly inebriated, at the least. Few had taken their leave, despite the advancing hour.

Square from his head to his torso to his hands, Robert Cameron cornered her. The blacksmith looked her over as if preparing to buy a mare, then smiled congenially.

"Ye do possess a mighty fine conformation to withstand the rigors of the backwoods, Mistress Dare."

She smiled brightly. "I would hope I could give my husband a run for his money."

Without her being aware of his approach, Jacob was at her side. "They are waiting on us," he said, cupping her elbow just above her sleeve's flounce of lace.

"Oh?" She felt that puzzling throb of excitement, similar to what one felt when facing the sharp fangs of Red Rover.

He leaned closer, those disturbingly sensual lips brushing the curls at her ear. "They are waiting on us to consummate our marriage."

"Ohhh." She turned her head toward his lowered one, the top of hers grazing his ear. She caught the teasing, clashing smells of tobacco, hay, honey, and rum. "I remember now. The chivaree."

"Thank you for the reception, all." Waving a hand in farewell, he collected his long rifle at the counter and her dulcimer on the stool. Passing her dulcimer to her, he propelled her toward the door.

Goodbyes, ribald shouts, and hoots were hurled after their departing backs. She felt a hot blush rise from her throat to burn her cheeks.

Once under the canopy of winking stars, the muscles between her shoulders eased. Only a little. He offered her his forearm. Her gaze flew up to his profile, with its long nose and strong jawline. She tucked her hand in the crook of his elbow. The spring night was cool with just a nip to give her an excuse to cling close to him. "Where did you learn such a gallant gesture. Proffering your elbow?"

His hand capped her fingers, still healing from their latest wounds, her shoddy attempt at sewing. In a show of wifely duty mixed with self-pity that day, she had cut up her ruined wedding gown for curtains. He smiled back at her dryly. "I ape my betters."

Well, that put her in her place, if nothing did. His sardonic tone clearly indicated he felt those 'betters' would do well to ape him. She tried to think of something ameliorating to say. "Your tobacco smoke. I like it. It smells sweetly, of sherry."

They were following the mile-long wagon road back to their cabin. A white-hot moon illuminated wild-flower patches of violets, mountain laurel and cowslips that bordered the path.

"Does it now?" He guided her around a wagon rut deep enough to twist an ankle.

"Aye. It reminds me of me parents. Especially, me mam. She would hide in the family necessary to smoke her pipe. So, I would purposefully follow her in after she had left. Well, ye can well imagine, the heavy smell fairly toppled me over. But the necessary was not a good place for a wee lass to topple."

He chuckled softly.

"Not that I was ever a wee lass." She tossed off the remark lightly, so only someone who listened carefully to the words and not the statement itself might detect an undertone of something other than flippancy.

She ached to stop her tongue's blathering. But on it went. "I tried smoking the pipe meself. Hid in the necessary, I did. I became so sick to me stomach that, after heaving so much, it ached for two days. Nonetheless, the necessary's tobacco smoke is a guid antidote for the – well, ye ken, that other odor."

Where a red maple grew almost horizontally over rhododendron bushes she spotted a ghostly pair of yellow eyes just beyond, within the dense foliage. She shivered and gripped her husband's arm. "Uhhh, Jacob," she whispered, "we have a visitor."

"Red Rover. She accompanied us all the way to the trading post."

Would she ever become accustomed to the lurking dangers of her new home? They strolled on in silence. Unbearable silence for her. She knew what still lay ahead. The crunch of last year's leaves and pine needles punctuated their mutual reticence as they drew ever nearer. Could he be as nervous as she? She doubted it. He had experience in coupling.

And that reminded her of the young Indian woman she had met earlier. "How long has Coowee been . . . uhh . . . Fergus's woman?"

"Eight years. Since she was fourteen."

"Fourteen?"

"As a young man, he traded with her tribe, the Tuscarora."

"And he traded with them for a wife?"

"No. He took her in. Coowee had stepped in a bear trap."

"But . . . but . . . ."

"What?"

"She is too young for him, is she not? She must be only half his age."

Those white teeth flashed again. "She does not think so. He

could not get shet of her. Coowee has hounded him over the years to keep her with him."

At last, they arrived at their darkened cabin, and he relieved her of her dulcimer. Unerringly he strode to the oil lamp on the table. Moments later, its soft yellow glow spread across the puncheon. Careful that the hem of her skirts did not snag on its splintery surface, she turned from his attentive stare and entered their bedchamber. She heard him restore his long rifle on its hooks over the door.

Moonlight from the open shutters burnished the four-poster with a patina of old gold, and a night draft wafted her hastily and poorly made curtains at either side of the window. Quickly, she stripped and slipped into her white lace nightrail, as virginal as she. She slid beneath the bedclothing and lay rigid on her back, hands clasped as if for burial.

Moments later, she heard the pad of Jacob's bare feet. Felt the shift in the mattress. Felt his body heat as the bedcover gave way to his lengthy frame. She could tell he lay facing her, yet touching her not. Her heart was galloping. Aye, she was nervous about the unknown, but was excited by it . . . and by him. She longed for him to kiss her again. That part she liked.

"How lang do ye think we have . . . afore they come?"

His hand covered her clasped ones. "A half hour or maybe more." His voice was low with a catch in it. "Do I make you nervous, Wife? I do not want that."

Her head turned toward him. In the room's dimness, she could make out his dark head cradled on one crooked arm, could see by a shaft of moonlight the ambient glow of his eyes. "Aye, ye do make me nervous but in a guid way," she whispered, although there was no reason to do so. Her whisper seemed to reinforce the intimacy of the moment.

"And what way is a good way?" He whispered, as well, but there was an odd note in his tone. It was weighted with . . . with an unidentifiable force . . . but made more perceptible by the darkness encompassing them

"Ye make me feel like thunder and lightning are storming me. Like gale winds are swirling around me."

"It can be like what you feel when you look from the bluff — this thing that happens between a man and a woman when coupling."

"I wouldna ken. This is . . . " she rolled on her side to face him fully, his hands still clasping hers. This is the first time I have ever felt this feeling . . . like hurricane-tossed waves in me belly." She moved his wide hand to palm her stomach and felt the tingling of his touch through her gown. That tingling goose bumped her skin, beginning with her upper arms and creeping down to her wrists.

His hand remained, splayed across her stomach, and unmoving. "And this is good?"

She could hear the ragged edge in his voice. "Aye. But . . . "

"But . . . but what?"

"But tis no' enough. Tis something more that I be wanting." She could feel her brows furrowing in puzzlement. "Something like . . . ."

"Like this?" He moved his hand lower, so that his long fingers cupped that furred curvature beneath her nightrail.

She nodded several times in succession, not even sure he could see her, but her throat was too clogged with raw emotion to make a noise that might resemble speech.

He slipped the arm on which his head had been resting under her neck, his hand fisting her hair, and pulled her across the intervening space to him. She gasped with the feel of his length of muscular nakedness pressed against her.

The long fingers that pleasured her lower region, now hiked her night rail and found that very private – and very moist – place that not even she had touched. Not like that. Never like what he was doing. She was surprised at the sound that came from the back of her throat.

His fingers paused. "What do you feel now?"

"Tis verra guid, what I am feeling." Her hand plowed downward through her bunched nightrail to find his large-boned wrist. "Dunna stop."

His laugh was low and husky and satisfied.

She sighed, and her hand dropped away from his wrist only to graze that distinctively fleshy but rigid length of body part pressed insistently against her. She inhaled sharply. She was not so ignorant about coupling that she did not comprehend human anatomy. Intrigued, her fingertips lingered.

"Do not stop," he parroted her but in a corrugated masculine voice.

Tentatively, her fingers began their own exploration, at its base, and he groaned. Her breath stuttered. "Am I . . . am I hurting ye?"

He chuckled, and his breath fanned her cheeks. "Hardly." He

tugged on the back of her head, drawing her even closer to him. Raising his head over hers, his long hair curtained their faces. Their lips meshed in a kiss that made her stomach flip flop. His stubble abraded her cheek, then her jaw and her throat, as his raiding mouth blazed a foraging trail. Next, he nuzzled her ear lobe, and his breath tickled the inside of her ear. Her own breath seized up.

A clanging of cowbells and rattling of bones and banging of pots and pans on the door stopped her short. Both she and Jacob stiffened. "What do we do?" she whispered in pillowed words.

"Pray they go away," he growled.

But, no, they did not. After a few moments, the nerve-wracking, ear-shattering procession circled around to the side of the cabin. Drunken exclamations pierced the night, followed by the sloshing of water and the thumping noise of something being rolled. After that, a clattering against the side of the cabin. Then a head poked through the window. That of Mick's reddish-wreathed pate.

" – off the rain barrel," someone ordered. Then another – Robert Cameron's square head – took Mick's in the window. "Hey, mon," he shouted over the hooting and howling, "is this any way to treat yore neighbors?"

Jacob sighed, rolled from her, and shucked on his breeches. "Meet me around front," he told them.

She yanked the covers up to her chin. This was not the gentle spoofing of newlyweds she had expected from a chivaree. As he made his way to the main room, moonlight danced on his black mane and the rippling muscles of his broad back, scarred and pitted by battles won or lost. Battles he may have lost, but she strongly suspected he never lost a war.

She heard him lift the latch's bar, and it seemed a horde of men's shoes trampled through the doorway along with their loud noise makers. She listened and could barely detect Jacob 's low voice, offering them swigs from either of their first wedding gifts – Mary's jug of home brewed ale or Esau's jug of rum.

At that point, the conviction steadily took root in Catriona that she was the mistress of the house and that she would not appear as if she were cowering in the bedroom.

Foregoing her stays, she stepped over her pile of paniers and struggled once again into the taffeta dress with all its bothersome lacings. She wrestled her rat's nest of curls into a haphazard knot at her nape, wrapped her red plaid around her modestly, and, barefoot but with a smile on her face, went out to greet the merry makers.

There had to be close to a dozen inebriated males in the room, joking, laughing, and slapping one another on the back. " . . . put her hand on me codpiece, she did."

"Yuh remember Maude? Well she took me member by the . ."

Over their heads, she spotted Jacob. Saw the blue tattooing between his nipples that he made no effort to hide.

At the sight of her, his brows popped up like a jack-in-the-box. She cleared her throat. "Eh-hmmm. Gentlemen."

Those closest to her turned in surprise. One by one others pivoted toward her. The room went silent. She saw Fergus, Esau, Humphrey, who was in the act of passing the jug to Mick — and the slightly weaving Jethro, his lips parted, his bleary-eyed stare nigh goggling her.

She flushed. It was clear to them she had come directly from bed, what with her mussed hair and beard-burnt cheeks. Hands on her hips, she faced them with a smile, she felt, that stretched as wide as the Cape Fear. "As me and me husband are truly grateful for your . . . well-wishes, I would like to gift each of ye with a song — before we send ye on your way."

She wove through the men, reeking of rum, ale, and ever-present musky male odor, to collect her dulcimer where Jacob had placed it in his orderly fashion on one of the shelves. She stood on the hearth's raised river stone. With her added height, she was now on level with her husband.

She directed her gaze first at bespectacled Humphrey. "When were you born, sire?

His brows pumped and lowered. "Well, July of 1729, Mistress."

She smiled, struck a few chords, and sang:

> *"In the year 1729,*
> *the devil got stuff to make a swine*
> *and made a pact with a beggar*
> *to call the swine Humphrey MacGregor."*

Guffaws filled the room. With a nod, she acknowledged their laughter and hoots for her improvisation. She turned to Jethro. "And your birthdate?"

He blushed as fiercely as her clan's red tartan. "May, 1760," he stammered.

Borrowing partly from Shakespeare, she sang:

> *"T'was the merry month of May,*
> *when a maiden did say,*
> *Jethro, if ye'll but be my mon*
> *'tis my heart ye will have won."*

Others pushed forward to hear songs expressly made for them, but hangdog Jethro would not yield his place before her. She was weary, deliciously disoriented by Jacob's dalliance a half hour earlier, and all too aware he was now lounging against the bookcase, arms folded and watching her with an edginess that was disconcerting.

Every so often he accepted the jug passed him. Hoisting it over his forearm, he would quaff the ale.

She wrapped up her performance for the men remaining and, after making a half curtsey to their whoops and applause, went to step down from the hearth to usher them out the door – only to step into Jethro's ale-fumed embrace. "My lady, a kiss I would be - bestow in payment of your song."

Before she could dodge him, young Jethro wrapped an arm around her neck, the other around her waist, and bent her sidewise to plaster his lips, not on hers, but upon her cheek that she instantly snapped sidewise. She could smell his young male's rutting odor and stale, hot breath.

Almost immediately his crushing body was separated from hers. A hand steadying her upper arm prevented her from outright falling. "Easy there, Jethro," Jacob said, his voice as expressionless as his countenance, unless one noticed the muscle that ticked in the hollow of his jaw. "Time you all took your leave."

Fergus nodded at Jacob, then latched onto the staggering Jethro and spun him in the direction of the door. Along with those two, the abashed group shuffled toward it.

"Haste ye back," she called after them from the doorway, then shut the door and faced Jacob.

She could feel the heat of ire radiating off him. He turned his bare back to throw a stick of wood onto the fireplace's dying embers.

"Jacob, Jethro dinnae mean anything by the kiss."

One forearm braced on the mantel, he stared into the flare of sparks. "The lad was in his cups. You did not have to encourage him with that verse you sang."

"What? Ye are most definitely in *your* cups. I did not encourage him, Jacob Dare. I merely sang what popped into me mind."

He took the fire iron and nudged the stick, now sizzling in the fire pit. "Exactly what was in *your* mind, Wife?"

She stamped her bare foot and winced at the splinter that stabbed her heel. "Why, ye twally – ye, ye clodhopper, ye ale-stinking churl!"

Although the muscles ridging his shoulder blades tensed, he otherwise appeared to pay her no heed, which sent her blood to boiling. "I dunna take kindly to being ignored." When he continued to poke at the coals, she reached around and grabbed the fire iron from him. "Tis too hot in here already, ye glaikit jackanapes."

He looked over his shoulder and grinned at her wickedly. "Well, now, let me dowse the fire for my wife." He dropped his fall flap and, taking himself in hand, began to piss into the flames.

"Oh! Oh!" she sputtered at the sight of the steam. Despite her ferocious frustration, her mouth, twitching at its corners, betrayed her. Then she burst out laughing.

Tucking himself back in, he flashed her a wicked smirk. He took the fire iron from her and restored it to its proper place. "It is late. We are both tired. Let us go to bed."

Her brow yanked up and her sore feet anchored to the damned puncheon. If he thought that after . . . .

"No, I am not suggesting that." He raised placating palms and smiled sheepishly down at her. "I have lost my lust."

Her pride pricked, she flounced into their bedroom. Clothes shed behind the bed curtain, she tossed them over the far side and collapsed against the pillow. She heard his plush bearskin pallet slap out onto the floor beside the bed. Minutes ticked by. She rolled onto her stomach. Minutes later, she flopped again onto her back and stared up into the darkness. Finally, she rolled back to her side and draped her hand over the bed's edge.

His familiar scarred fingers interlaced with hers. A contented sigh eddied from her, and she slipped into sleep.

Before daybreak, when the temperature had dropped to its coolest, Jacob rose with the intent of bringing down a buck or bagging a duck or turkey. Later that morning, he had a field to clear of stumps. Hobby, the ten-year-old chestnut thoroughbred imported from England that he had won from Tom Brindle in a game of faro, was better suited for racing than plowing.

Just as the young Highlander wife he had acquired in a tradeoff for his services was more accomplished at entertaining than domesticity.

What was it about him that he would feel such an affinity for creatures so ill-fitted for the wild habitat that was his life?

Stealthily, he and Fergus bellied along the foggy south bank of Hollering Woman Creek that cut diagonally through the forest behind Kinsfolk Landing. They halted at either edge of a clearing carpeted with clover and levered their rifles into position to await the dawn and the deer.

Across the clearing from him, Fergus sniffled loudly through one hairy nostril, then lifted a shoulder in an apologetic shrug.

Inches from Jacob's own nose, a snail fatted up on a mushroom. Soon, with sunrise and with luck, deer would come to water. They were so cautious about approaching a watering hole that it could take nearly a good thirty minutes or more to close that last thirty yards.

Fifteen minutes passed, and the dark purple firmament

imperceptibly transmuted to the faintest of pink light. The breath eased from his chest in a long, almost inaudible sigh. His bunched muscles gradually relaxed. He rarely drank, and last night's chivaree was proof he would do well to revert to his usual tendencies.

But then nothing was usual about his life now.

While he readily admitted, if suitability was the criteria, he may have made a mistake in his selection for a wife, he could not deny that he found her endlessly fascinating – her zest, her fearlessness, her imaginative mind – not that he was overlooking her feminine attributes. But as mismatched as he and she were, he did not know if they could fashion a workable relationship between them

Obviously, he had no definitive idea what a workable relationship between a man and woman should be. Only hazy recollections of his parents' brief lives together.

His first five years, he had lived with his mother's people, only visiting his father at Fort Dobbs or his father visiting his mother's village whenever regulations permitted. Then, after his father resigned his commission and built the Kinsfolk Landing's original cabin, they had lived together as a family for a mere four years before his father's death, when Jacob was nine.

Four years in which to learn at such a young age the delicate balance of two adults living intimately. To learn about sacrifices and compromises demanded by a relationship, as his wife had wisely pointed out. To adapt to sharing space, sharing privacy, sharing himself.

The soft, almost inaudible click of Fergus's musket warned Jacob. He eased back his long rifle's cock.

Guardedly, three white-tailed doe and two fawns picked their way uneasily into the clearing, edging closer to the waterline. By tacit accord, he and Fergus held their fire. The doe and fawns were merely decoys, sent ahead by the buck. Soon a spike appeared. Yet, Fergus and he waited. Then two bucks edged into the clearing. Their racks were magnificent and enough fat was on them still, despite the winter.

Time enough to get off only one shot apiece. In the fitful early morning light, black powder flashed and muskets boomed. The two bucks would provide meat for Kinsfolk Landing homes and his own, when he had to be away.

As he and Fergus worked quickly with their hunting knives to skin and quarter the bucks, Fergus said, "Has the mistress rebounded from last night's ruckus?"

"Don't know." He slid his knife blade along a blackstrap of the buck, strung from a hickory branch. "When I left, she was still asleep."

"Ye do know, yewr wifie may be a hearty lass, for all that she spins tales of druids and trolls and faeries. But faeries, mind ye, have a way of disappearing on ye."

He wiped his bloodied blade on his leather breeches. "Out with it, Fergus."

The coonskin-capped man spat a yellow stream of tobacco juice into the bloodied clover. "Only saying to guard yewr heart."

"As if yours does not do a fife and drum tattoo for Coowee?"

But he knew that Fergus's warning was useless. Not now, now that he had lain beside Catriona, had felt her skin, like cream separated from fresh milk, had touched her private place, warm and moist as a mossy bank, and had experienced her eager response to the demanding urging of his own private part.

She was always on his mind. When often so far from help or home, a distraction, such as his wife was, could lead in an instant to disaster or death.

The deer meat divided and distributed to Mary and other settlers who did not come by hunting so easily, he turned his footsteps toward home – not the home his father, a second son of peerage, had all too often painted in vividly descriptive terms about 'Dare Castle' back in England, but nevertheless a start on such a home, now that he had a wife – and one of peerage, no less.

On the covered porch, she was sweeping diligently. Morning's sunlight turned her hair into a hearth's fire that could warm his hands. He glanced disgruntledly at the shriveled skin of his hands, one toting his long rifle, the other the bloodied elk-skin game sack of deer meat slung over his shoulder. Flames had already more than warmed them.

When she finally noticed his approach, and that would have been far too late in case of an Indian raid, the corners of her generous mouth widened even farther. One hand on her hip, the other resting on the upright broom, she watched as he crossed toward her and climbed the steps.

He noted the wooden bowl of water at the base of one timbered pillar and nodded at it. "You were expecting not myself but a certain four-footed wild creature?"

She grimaced. "I tried to entice Red Rover close enough to let me pet her. At least, this time she did not trot away but stayed to watch for a while. I thought if I merely went about me business, she might grow comfortable enough with me here at your home."

"Our home." He sat the sack down next to the pillar with its bowl of water. Time enough yet to par-roast and salt the meat to preserve it before it went rancid. He, a hand braced on his propped-up rifle, and she with hers on the broom, stared at one another across the difference of less than a meter. So much to be said, and yet neither of them knew how to breach the chasm of their cultural differences.

"Do you know how to prime and load a musket?"

"I have watched me father and brothers."

He nodded. How long could this impasse continue? "I shall see what Fergus has on hand at the trading post."

"Aye." Her teeth tugged on her bottom lip.

Bloody hell. He pulled the powder flask's leather strap and bullet pouch up and over his head to drop it, along with his belted tomahawk, pistol, and knife, next to the game sack. He met her uneasy stare. "Give us a bit of help here, Wife."

She understood to what he was referring. Slowly, and hesitantly – as if not altogether certain this was the best course of action – she extended her palm, as though she would invite this wild creature to draw near. "Smell of blood and woods and earth, ye do," she murmured, turning to tug him behind her inside their cabin.

It reeked of god-awful boiling tallow allayed by the sweet smell of nutmeg. On the table sat a candle mold, alongside a pewter cup of wildflowers wilting from the room's heat.

"Coowee was here," he said.

She looked surprised. "How did ye know? She brought the mold over this morning."

The story of the visitor had been plain. The moccasin prints, too light an impression to be that of a warrior's and with the left imprint dug inward and smudged a bit.

Her expression fraught, she sighed, puffing a red curl bobbing over the bridge of her nose. Heat and housekeeping had loosened additional swaths of damp springy hair from her laced cap to tumble onto her shoulders.

"Alas, I dropped a goodly portion of the wick I was braiding into the flames." An embarrassed smile dimpled her blushing cheeks. "Looked like a snake on fire before I stamped it out." At this, she chuckled. "A real Indian war dance I was doing. Then Coowee and I got to laughing. And all thought of candlemaking went out the door."

Setting his long rifle on its hooks, he took the broom from her and tossed it in the corner with the neglected spinning wheel. So much for orderliness. What did it matter, when he was in a fever pitch?

He drew her into the bedchamber. Sitting on the bed, he braced her hips with his hands and pulled her to stand between his spread knees. "God help us, I am in a haste to claim you, Wife. If I knew the civilized way to go about this – the courtly way – the way to woo you gently, I would."

She placed a fingertip on his lips, shushing him. "I do not need wooing, me mon."

His breath caught. Her words had signaled her acquiescence. Yet instinct told him this was a decisive moment. The future course of their marital relationship hinged on this singular act. Strive though he might, good intentions were overridden by the hot flash of desire. His demented gaze deserted her anxious one to fixate on her bastion of clothing. It covered the sunshine his life wanted.

Tentatively, his blood-stained hands reached toward her soot-stained lutestring dress, feeling its crisply light silk bunch, as he slowly drew it upward, over her stockings calves and knees. The sight of her pale thighs and their furred apex told him she had taken care to leave off her drawers. At that, he yanked the skirt to her waist, unbalancing her. She gasped, and her hands gripped his shoulders for support.

Somehow, the single-minded purposefulness of his momentum slowed once again to partake of the pleasure afforded his view and his touch. When he raked an exploring finger through the red-hot springy curls, her head fell back and she moaned.

Conditioned by his father's society, concern nudged him to pause but a fraction of a second.

"If ye stop, Jacob Dare, I swear I shall see your sorry head in the stocks."

This, when he had fought so hard against taking her by force. He looped an arm around her waist, pulling her atop him and simultaneously rolling to mount her. An explosive grunt at his smashing weight escaped those promising lips. With one hand, he abruptly seized hers and hobbled them out of his way, just above her head. In the process, her cap was raked loose and her feisty red locks were trapped beneath his braced forearm.

Primed and engorged, there was no stopping him now, had she even begged. But, thank all the gods that be, she inched her legs wider for him to fumble between them with the buttons of his fall flap.

One last moment of sanity reared its unwanted head. Her eyes were glazed over, and he was not certain she understood the import of his words. "Wife, I had pledged never to hurt you. Least ways, not intentionally. But this time, I must."

With that, he impaled himself inside the tight, wet, warmth of her. Beneath him, she buckled in pain. "Sweet merciful Jesus," she rasped.

His mouth crashed against hers. His tongue stabbed between her lips with the same fast, furious rhythm that his hips' brutal ramming besieged and battered her delicate furrow. Over and over. Seeking the immediate relief that quite apparently only her body could ever fully alleviate.

His heart slammed time and again against his rib cage. Sweat dripped from his forehead, and, when her tongue stole out to wipe it from her lips, he fired off then and there. He roared with his release and, shuddering, sprawled atop her.

The spasming culmination of his frenzy and its aftermath, the payoff of sublime gratification, was short lived. Like withdrawing a wet charge from a rifle, he pulled himself from within her. She lay there, as stiff as a three-hour old corpse.

After a long thunderously silent moment, broken only by his ragged, rapid breathing that was slowly decelerating, he rasped, "So much for gentle wooing."

He was stunned that he, who had superior endurance power, could so quickly lose his restraint. He could rationalize that he had gone so long without a woman, but that innate sense of his did not tolerate lying to others and most certainly not to himself. He knew that it was because this woman had somehow broken through his childhood defenses.

Her hand wedged between them to press against his shoulder in an effort to shove him off. Her hips attempted to scooch away. "No," he said, dragging her back under him. He smoothed her damp hair away from her face. "I took my pleasure foolishly. Now it is time to give it."

"I have had enough, thank ye," she muttered.

A burning sensation flamed inside his chest. "You have not

had any. Yet."

"Ye are insufferable."

"Yes," he said soberly.

"And as heavy as a horse," she gritted.

That savage part of him wanted to conquer her, but some societal urge directed him, after his monumental blunder, toward a more measured inducement. He shifted his torso weight to one side, but one of his thighs thrown diagonally over her hips held her captive.

His arm outstretched and his head resting on one sweaty bicep, he reflectively studied her cameo-like silhouette. The morning sun slanted a faint bar of sunlight across her torso and his, leaving her face in shadows, but his keen vision easily detected the small quivering of her chin, as it worked to hold back betraying gulping, guttural sobs.

"Cat, I behaved like a half-grown boy messing around with himself in the outhouse."

"Aye, that ye did," she said bitterly.

For one unhappy moment, his thoughts floundered, then, like the careful examination of a trail whose signs had gone cold, he discovered where he had gone astray. He spoke the only way he knew how – with the expressiveness he had learned from his father and the simple directness he had acquired from his mother.

"The women I have known – they were either coarsened by the weather or painted with artifice. You have been sheltered. New and unexplored."

His hand sought between their bodies her knotted hand. He worked open her first, finding her ring finger. As he continued speaking, his fingers turned round and round the horsehair ring he had fashioned for her. "When you are not watching, I study you. Your face. Your hands. The texture of your skin. Your entire body." Soft and fresh. Almost translucent yet flushed with health.

He lifted her hand, holding it aloft to look at it, as if for the first time. "Your nails are smooth as stream-polished pebbles." Then he laid her hand across her chest in that now familiar gesture of hers, his palm overlapping her hand, his extended fingers picking up the rapid thumping of her heart.

"You might think because I do not speak or acknowledge you that I am unaware of you. I know your ways and habits. How you carefully clean your mouth after eating, like a cat. I watched you wash your stockings in the pail of water heated by our breakfast coals yesterday. I am fascinated by your graceful movements. The way your fist flits like a hummingbird to your chest."

His hand deserted hers to skim the base of her throat. He touched one broad fingertip upon that delicate hollow and felt her pulse accelerate. "I am fascinated, too, by your ever-changing expressions. Your eyes, yours lips, your entire face. It is as expressive as Esau's most inspired fiddling."

Next, he pressed his fingertip on her lips. "I listen for your voice. Humming as later you hung my wet shirts outside on the line to dry. Or scolding yourself when annoyed with your cooking efforts since you have been here."

He saw the first faint glistening of dampness above her prominent cheekbones and this disturbed him more than anything yet. He lowered his head and licked away each tear.

A soft eddying whimper trembled on her lips. Her fingers slid through his hair draping at either side of his head and pulled it down for her wet and hungry mouth to find his.

He took heed of her body's silent promptings. This time their coupling was an exploration of each other – their bodies, their movements, their minds, their needs – that took the rest of the morning . . . that he hoped would take the rest of their lives. There was just the two of them in the world.

The last words he heard were a sighed, languid utterance in that lyrical voice of hers. "When ye finally make up your mind to talk, me husband . . . ye give it your full attention . . . like ye do everything. I look forward to our next conversation of such length."

He grinned. He gathered her against him spoon-fashion, his arm wrapped possessively around her.

Later, much later, he thought he heard her murmur in her sleep those precious Gaelic words of love she had shared at her leavetaking with her parents. *"Tha gaol agam ort."*

But whom was it she loved?

~ ~ ~ ~ ~ ~ ~

Sleepily stirring, Catriona rolled over, her hand groping for Jacob's long and lean muscled flank – and found nothing. "Och!" She had half forgotten that he left the day before to travel for the revolutionary Governor Caswell into Tuscarora and Creek Indian territory. Friendly territory. For the present, at least.

She could not remember having ever been alone in her house at Campbelton. Always family, friends, business acquaintance, or servants were to be found. Eerie how quite the predawn was.

Strange, how after merely one short week, she could miss her husband. Miss the stroke of his fingers on her forearm, as she passed near where he sat filleting the shad he had caught. Missed the hungry way he looked at her as she sat by candlelight darning one of her cotton stockings, torn once again by the wicked puncheon.

Strange, how she knew his body more intimately than she did her own. The passion that sizzled between them had driven them to couple incessantly and in so many diverse places. On that damned puncheon that had left splinters in her backside; between corn rows, where he had laughingly chased her down; in the barn loft that had left her sneezing and her hair matted with straw; and in the wagon bed, where, for once, his fine arse had ended up with the splinters.

She smiled to herself. No more pallets on the floor.

And no more addressing her as, 'Wife." She had not missed how upon that first time after he had so thoughtlessly and roughly taken her, he had called her "Cat." And called her that ever since.

More strange was how they could be so intensely intimate, when he was lending his services to the rebels, and her loyalist brothers were imprisoned by them. When, in reality, he considered himself allied with neither side, and she considered herself allied with both.

It was a discussion they avoided. But then they avoided other subjects, as well. Subjects his oblique looks and terse comments told her were taboo. Namely his past – the blue tattooing across his chest, his scarred hands. The fact he could not read. Given his articulate speech, when he chose to speak, she found this astonishing.

The afternoon she had asked him to pass her the *Robinson Crusoe* novel, he had handed her, instead, *Johnson's Dictionary*. She ached to offer to teach him to read but strongly suspected it would be better if he came to her with the request – as Mary had most grudgingly done the day before.

She and Billy were to show up that very morning – in exchange, at last, for Catriona's bargained spinning lessons.

Yawning, stretching, she shoved off the mattress, regretting she must now rise before daylight if she hoped to make of herself a good farmer's wife. Well, Jacob was much more than a farmer. An entrepreneur, a linguist, a mediator, a town developer . . . and a rebel.

Chamber pot that needed to be emptied in one hand, she raised the door's latch bar. Above it, Jacob's long rifle was missing but a primed and loaded fowling piece he had added for her use.

She was startled to discover in dawn's half-light Fergus slumped outside against the wall, his long rifle propped on raised knees.

"Damn, Fergus, I almost dumped the pot's bowfing contents on ye." Her eyes narrowed. "Did ye spend the night here"

He struggled to his feet, ran a hand along his jaw's grizzled beard. "Ye dinnae believe Jacob would leave ye unprotected, did ye now?"

"I dunna ken that much about me husband yet." She stepped off the porch, heading around the house for the compost garden. He trailed her. "Honestly" she said over her shoulder, "I have not the slightest idea even what's running through me husband's mind much less what's written across his chest."

"'I love ye.'"

She stopped and whirled, sloshing the pot's contents precariously. "What?"

"'I love ye.' That is what is punctured across the lad's chest."

She blinked. "I love ye?"

"Aye. His mother had it done, so he would never forget her or the words."

Slowly, she turned back in the direction she had been headed and considered this. "That kind of priceless love seems a wee bit of a drastic measure, Fergus. After all, do not actions speak louder than words?" That seemed to be Jacob's creed. "Surely, his mother's actions could have shown Jacob she loved him in a much less painful manner than to tattoo her child's chest."

Her shadow, the sour-faced Fergus, shambled alongside her. "Aye, but love in the Cherokee language means so much more than in ours."

She reached the compost site, between the oats and sweet potato fields. "Such as what?" She spattered the malodorous mound with the night's waste.

Fergus hopped back. "Tis not easily translated into English. It means something like I will give me life for ye – that I willingly surrender me happiness for yours. That ye will eat even if I do not.

That ye will be safe even if I must put meself in danger. That I will protect ye with me verra breath."

She smiled wistfully. "Lovely sentiments, given the circumstances where ye are now espousing them – a manure dump."

But then her husband was in a sense like his manure dump – practical and purposeful. He had not sought a wife out of his heart's longing but out of his prosaic need for a helpmate. He had been most straight-forward about that, alas. But, God Almighty, could the man make a woman's body sing.

Less than an hour later, other visitors stood before the door she kept open for sunlight and the dramatic view of the misty Blue Ridge beyond the bluff. Her visitors included not only Mary and Billy but also Esau.

He doffed his cap. "Morning, Mistress Dare. Mary, here, told me yewr teachin' her to read. I would be glad to trade you a butter churn I made for lessons."

She took a cue from Jacob, the master of the Indian art of tradeoffs. "Make it a tub large enough to fit meself in, Esau, and ye have yeself a deal – I will teach ye to read." Though she worried if his walleyes could follow the printed word. "Come on in, all three of ye."

Stiffly, Mary extended a basket of flax to her and said in a tone laden with exasperation, "'Tis easy enough to do, spinning. But I'll show yuh now, afore the readin' lessons. Even children are spinsters. Billy, hold the basket."

Most reluctantly, the five-year-old released his hold on her homespun skirt, took his thumb out of his mouth, and, head ducked with shoulders scrunched, complied.

Catriona was familiar with the long, tough flax fibers used to make linen thread but had never needed to learn the spinning process. The Kincairns, like other upper-class North Carolina colonists, bought woolen hose from Scotland, linen shirts from Belgium, and bolts of silk from China to be made into dresses by local mantua makers.

While Esau peered through the books she had set out on the trestle table, Mary went through the process of spinning – much too quickly.

" . . . fiber is held in the left hand. Easy, like when yuh hold a newborn's head. See like this. Now, yuh do it"

Pushing up her lace-edged sleeves past her elbows, Catriona seated herself at the spinning wheel to give it a try.

"No, no, no! Hold the fiber at an angle to the spindle to make the twist. And squeeze it tight between yuhr fingers as yuh would a locust. After that, yuhr spun yarn is wound onto the spindle by working the treadle there."

Before Catriona could blurt a blasphemy, she drew in a steadying breath. "I shall practice by meself later, Mary. Tis time for reading."

As there was no parchment paper nor quill to be had, she seated Mary and Esau at the trestle table, on either side of her and the easier to read book she had opened, *Aesop's Fables.* She made a mental note to ask, when Jacob and Fergus next ran a load of resin and turpentine down river, if hornbooks could be purchased.

While she read yet another fable, pausing to point out simple words to Mary and Esau, Billy sat in the corner, his fingers seeming idly to spin the wheel. Mary frowned in concentration. Esau cocked his ear, more attune to sound than his sight was to his page.

"'A Lion once fell in love with a beautiful maiden and proposed marriage to her father, a forester. The man did not know what to say. He did not like to give his daughter to the Lion, yet he did not wish to enrage the King of Beasts. At last the father said: "We feel highly honored by your Majesty's proposal, but ye see me daughter is a tender young thing, and I fear that in the vehemence of your affection ye might possibly do her some injury. Might I venture to suggest that your Majesty should have your claws removed, and your teeth extracted, then I would gladly consider your proposal again." The Lion was so much in love that he had his claws trimmed and his big teeth taken out. But when he came again to the father of the young girl, the father simply laughed in his face and shooed him out.'"

"Aye, right!" Esau snapped.

"The story is not to your liking, now, is it?" she asked. He was a nice-looking man, once she forgot to try to track his eyes.

"Naw. The lion let others change him and looky what happened."

She was actually looking down at flaxen-haired Billy. He had crawled from behind the wheel to scoot beneath the table.

Mary pushed lank hair from her drawn face. "And the moral be?"

Catriona wondered if the young woman had ever bothered to use the brush Jacob had gifted her. She would look so pretty with a pink ribbon wound through her brown hair, brushed to create lustrous curls. "What do ye think?"

"The means may defeat the ends."

Catriona nodded. "Good, Mary." Inside, she felt like cringing, considering her own judgmental attitude. She had sold short her opinion of these backwoods people. Clever, both of them.

After the three left, she went out to stand on the porch. Rubbing her elbows, she stared off into the distant mountains. Somewhere out there was her husband.

She did not exactly hear anything, but it was perhaps that cessation of noise – the noticeable lack of birds singing – that alerted her. With a glacial motion, she rotated her head to her right. At the end of the porch, near where she had daily placed a bowl of fresh water and another one of scrap food, stretched out Red Rover. The mountain lioness's massive head faced the Blue Ridge, as if she, too waited for their wanderer of the forest.

Catriona nodded to herself. Perhaps, she thought, today's fable had another moral – that love could tame the wildest.

But which of them was the wilder, Jacob or herself?

"'Tis a *dreich* day," she said, greeting a drizzled-damp Mary with Billy in tow, followed by Esau, then – oh, Mother of God, no – not Jethro.

"Morning, Mistress." He tugged on his damp, buttermilk-yellow forelock. "I offered Fergus to bring the foolscap you asked for." Eagerly, he fished the wrinkled sheet from the protection of his dingy, leather work smock. "I was hoping you might let me sit in on some of the lessons."

She caught Mary's smirk. Gossip of young Jethro's knight-like adulation of Catriona would most likely spread like the plague throughout the settlement.

She took the foolscap, which, even separated into four squares, was not enough to practice penmanship among her four students. Fortunately, quills were easy enough to come by, what with all the eagle feathers littering the bluff, and ink could readily be supplied by Spring's blueberries and vinegar.

As if reading her mind, Esau thrust out his hand. "Brought birch bark to write on, too."

She smiled. "Thank ye, Esau. Mary, yer hair is drookit and straggling down your neck. Why dunna ye let me tie it up with a ribbon?"

"What fur? It'll jest git wet again."

She sighed and gathered her students at the table. While she read aloud from the first chapter of *Robinson Crusoe*, Billy deserted his refuge behind the spinning wheel and progressively inched his way beneath the table again. A wee step, then, she had made toward winning his confidence.

After reading, she had the three adults toe the crack in the puncheon floor, while she asked them questions about the novel's first chapter. Esau and Jethro chortled at her schoolmistress's approach to the lesson, and Mary's mouth twitched with annoyance.

Book in hand, Catriona stood before Esau. "Where was Mr. Crusoe born?"

He gnawed on one nail before coming up with the answer. 'York. That be it. York!"

She moved in front of Jethro, whose adoring eyes had never left her. "*When* was Mr. Crusoe born?"

"1632," he answered rightly, his chest puffing like a pouter pigeon's.

She did not tarry to congratulate the lad. Moving next to Mary, Catriona asked, "Of what did Mr. Crusoe's father advise him to beware?"

"Never step foot on a ship," she gloated.

"Verra guid. Tomorrow, our lesson will be over Chapter Two," and this next she directed at Billy, crouched beneath the table, "its title being, 'I am Captured by Pirates!'"

After the four left, she sat on the porch step, chin in hand and stared out at the mist-shrouded mountains. She felt lost out here in the wilderness. Lonely. Isolated. Where nothing could be counted on. Where a kid crouched under the table, and a lioness dozed in a shaft of sunlight off to her side, both a wee closer than the day before.

"Och, Red Rover, we are a pair, are we not?"

Its ears pricked, but it never took its fierce gaze off the blue waves of mountains.

The immensity of the forests crushing around her was intimidating. Formal gardens would be heavenly. And a smooth floor like Afton Manor's instead of a puncheon that pricked her bare feet with splinters that festered her flesh.

But, come Christmastide with its shortbread, boughs of holly and evergreen, and black buns, spiced with fruit and almonds, she would once again be home among her clan.

Home.

~ ~ ~ ~ ~ ~ ~

Long rifle in hand and following an old Indian trading path, Jacob sprinted through the dense growth of trees. Traveling at a forced pace for more than twenty miles, his breath labored loudly in his ears. The rainy mist and the last, limpid light of day did not help. One misstep could mean failure to deliver to Caswell at New Bern vital intelligence regarding the opposition's numbers and strength.

The import of what Jacob had learned from the Tuscarora and Creek was ominous. The British had sent thirty pack horses of ammunition into the Cherokee country. Word was they planned to use the Cherokee in a three-pronged attack on the white intruders along the North Carolina, Georgia, and Virginia frontiers that summer. The Cherokee Middle Towns were to attack North Carolina.

Jacob did not aim to render up his information before he made a way stop at Dare Plantation to saddle Hobby for the remainder of the trip . . . and to bed Cat. He could not get enough of her.

While with the Tuscarora, he had encountered the maiden he had coupled with as an untried youth and was dismayed at how bland she was. In contrast, Cat nearly vibrated with an unquenchable fire.

Even with breath labored, a chuckle escaped his cotton-dry mouth at her oft-thwarted endeavors to make his hovel a home – the wilting wildflowers in the pewter tankard, the uneven curtains sewn from an elegant gown she would most likely never have an occasion for again, the puncheon that, no matter how often she swept, was a magnet for dust and dirt clomps, her garments untidily pooled on the bedroom floor rather than neatly hung on the wall pegs, and her woeful attempts at cooking.

He chuckled again. Given her cooking skills, within a year he would, indeed, be nothing more than the hank and bone she had initially described him.

If their marriage lasted that long.

For all the intimacy that transpired in the marriage bed he had ordered made for her – after all, beds were important status symbols to his wife's people – he and Cat were still strangers. The vital news he carried he dared not share with his own wife. Not when she was one of the Royals. If allegiances and loyalties divided them, what hope was there for them – and how in the hell could they forge a meaningful marriage?

He could not wholly blame Cat for their wary regard of one another. For all his articulateness, acquired at the knee of his very learned father, he had yet to stutter out the shameful confession that he could only barely read and write. It went against his grain to confess that he needed someone else – as he needed her to acquire the rudiments of a gentleman.

More worrying to him, would she ever trust him again should she discover the full extent of the measures he had taken to secure her hand in marriage. Was not he guilty of violating her trust?

Despite these serious issues and despite his utter fatigue, his strides increased those last hours remaining until just before dawn he reached home.

Home.

~ ~ ~ ~ ~ ~ ~

Surfacing from sleep, Catriona flicked away the pesky mosquito buzzing her ear – only to have her wrist captured by a single hand and her lips covered by a ravaging mouth.

Instinctively, she rolled toward her crouching subjugator. Her nose wrinkled. He smelled familiarly of forest and fur, and rain and clammy leather. Smells that were at once earthy and wild.

The lips that claimed hers once again tasted of salty sweat. Her free hand, trapped between her breast and his ribs, worked free to slide up over the snug fringed shirt and anchor in his mane of hair.

His throat rumbled like rolling thunder. His arm wrapped around her waist, his hand pressing her hips and contouring her body to his lengthy frame. His other smoothed back her sleep-mussed hair from her cheek. "You have been too much in my thoughts," he said, rubbing his jaw caressingly against her temple.

Oh, *Dia.* "I have missed . . . missed . . . this." She could not bring herself to confess it was him she missed. In his absence, she felt hollow. And when with him, she felt nervous and breathless and so oddly excited it was like being ill.

"Too often I thought of your rounded ivory loveliness." His hands squeezed her buttocks before sliding under her shift.

She should have been embarrassed by her body's sudden gush. But, as she lived and breathed, she could no more prevent that natural response than she could prevent herself from seating, grinding, into his kneading fingers.

Her hand slipped up under his sweat dampened buckskin, her fingertips tracing the line of hair arrowing down the washboard that was his belly – and she screamed, a shrill, ricocheting cry that punctured the still of the dark night.

At once, Jacob rolled into a hunkered protection over her. "What?" he barely breathed.

She shrank from him, her hands palsied. "A . . . a . . . slimy thing . . . something . . . on you!"

"Aww, bleedin'shit." Immediately he reared on his knees and was peeling the buckskin shirt over his head. "Get a candle."

The rusty tin holder's hastily lit candle held aloft, she stared with open mouth at his sun-browned torso, blotched with leeches and a scattering of ticks. Shivers of repulsion convulsed her spine. Goose bumps mottled her upper arms.

Head bent, long hair splashing his tattooed chest, he was already pulling at a tick's body. "That shortcut through the swamp," he muttered. The tick was anchored below his navel, where his leather breeches were slung low over his hipbones. "Here," he said, holding out the tick.

"What?"

He started toward her, and she backed a step. He sighed. "Give me the drip pan, Cat."

She trembled, extending the candle holder as far from her as she could, and he dropped the tick in the pan's wax. Next, he grabbed at a leech attached just below his left nipple. Then, he went after a leech clamped within the hair of his armpit.

Still, a score or more of the bloodsuckers covered his upper body, front and back. He needed help. He needed a wife like Mary.

But Mary was not here, and she was. She shuddered, closed her lids, then opening them, sat the candle holder on the high chest of drawers. She circled behind him. Inwardly flinching and looking away, she squeamishly took hold of a clinging leech. Quickly, she glanced at it, already fat from engorging on his blood, then dropped it in the drip pan.

He looked over his shoulder. His gaze was grave. "You do not have to do this."

Shuddering, she stared back into those dark blue eyes. "Aye, I do. I am your wife."

Her throat gagged reflexively. Somehow she managed to detach another and add it along with the other vermin writhing in the wax.

She tried to think of other things – of Phoebe's sweet pumpkin bread smelling of melted butter and cinnamon, of Anne MacDonald's charming morning patter at Moll King's coffee house, of Afton Manor's mantle clock chiming out the hour, and the feel of her cool, silk pillowcase under her cheek.

One tick's head was left, latched onto the flesh of Jacob's nape, and she shivered with the willies. Once she was able to pry it loose, she told him, "Drop your leggings and breeches."

He glanced over his shoulder again and flashed her a grin. "I thought never to hear you ask that of me, Cat."

With her blood-stained thumb and forefinger circled, she flicked his ear and returned to face him. "Ye strut far too cockily, me husband."

After he shucked his muddy, scruffy breeches, he had good reason to be cocky as she viewed him in the candle's revealing light: Sleek, powerful, with not a pinch of fat anywhere. Long legs, tightly muscled buttocks, a muscle-plated chest, and shoulders wide as a yardstick. And densely lashed eyes that watched her closely, as she knelt to inspect the lower half of his magnificent physique.

"Oh, mercy," she breathed, staring at the visibly stiffening length of flesh. "Now 'tis not the time to rise to the occasion, Jacob Dare."

From above came his groan. "I cannot help myself." His fingers dug into her shoulders. "God, Cat, let us get this removal business over with. I want to get on with what we started."

When her fingers slid tantalizingly slow up the inside of his thigh to locate a leech buried in the hollow of his furred crotch, she felt him tremble and heard his ragged inhalation. Her own inhalation took in his crotch's maleness, and incredibly, under the circumstances, the smell stimulated the flare of wanton craving deep inside her.

With difficulty, she ignored the evidence of his arousal throbbing so close to her cheek, and worked to remove the repulsive leech. There had to be nearly another dozen leeches that clung to his lower body – dotting his thighs and calves, in the crevices behind his knees, and across his buttocks

At last, after all were removed, she rose and, circling in front of him, backed away from his length of reach. "Tis not finished, we are." She nodded at his blood-flecked body. "Those wounds need to be treated. Follow me." She picked up the candle holder. She avoided looking in its drip pan, packed with wax-entrapped vermin.

"By the way," he called after her in a low, heated growl, "did you know the candlelight reveals every wonderful curve of your body beneath your nightrail?

"Those curves were the bane of me life for a lang time," she said, crossing to the shelf to collect the jug of rum.

His eyes were dilated with desire. "Staring at you, as I am at this very moment, I would find that difficult to believe."

Blushing, but feeling pleased, she uncorked the jug and, eking a little rum into her palm, began to pat the lesions. "Clumsy and awkward, a biblical behemoth, I was. When the dance master came to town to give lessons, none of the lads wanted to dance with me. Worse, when there was a shortage of lads, I had to be the male partner."

He captured her hand and brought it to his mouth. His tongue licked the potent rum from the hollow of her palm. Lashes fluttering closed, she shivered, this time from the pure pleasure of the senses. Then she fixed him with a stern look. "Ye are mucking with me, Jacob. Now loose me hand so we can finish here."

She stepped around to his back, feasting her gaze, as she dabbed rum on the welts, bleeding more than normal wounds. Time and again she dabbed the lesions. Treating one at the base of his spine, she noted his fist, braced on one hip. "Your hands. How did you come by those scars, now?"

She felt the muscle ridging his lower backbone tense beneath her fingers. A long moment ticked by. "Trying to rip the ropes that bound my mother."

"Why was she bound?"

"She was being punished. Burned at the stake."

"Why?" she breathed. She circled around to look at him. His eyes were hard as obsidian. A muscle in his jaw flicked like lightning striking.

"Here, in the southern colonies, both bastardy and adultery are punished, you understand."

She could only nod.

His distant gaze slid slowly back to fasten on hers. "When an unmarried woman gives birth outside of wedlock, she is usually trussed up half naked like an animal. Publicly whipped until blood flows freely."

"But you said she was burnt at the stake."

"I am coming to that." He glanced at her, then looked away again, as if he could not stand the sight of her sympathy. "When that first flogging happened at Fort Dobbs, my father resigned his commission. He moved as far from what you call 'civilization' as he could. Here to the western wilderness."

"And then?"

"He died, four years later. My mother was turned out to fend for herself and me."

"And that meant what?"

"With a bastard son, she was not cordially welcomed among either her people or my father's. She was reduced to servicing Fort Dobbs' soldiers. But the army wives, the laundresses, the local squatters . . . those good citizens were offended."

She said nothing, not wanting to interrupt this rare spate of words.

"They decided they were going to flog me, the bastard. My mother interfered. Their anger turned back on her, again. Flogging was not enough for them." He flexed his hands before him, as if testing their suppleness. "I tried to reach her, to save her, but . . . I was only eleven at the time . . . ." He shrugged.

She was appalled, unable to look into that impassive countenance and know the terrible unseen scars that disinclined him to place his trust in anyone or anything other than his own strength and knowledge. She lowered her gaze to the ceramic jug she held then looked at him once more. "And, so, at eleven, where did you go to live?"

His razor-edged smile curled his lips with cynicism. "With her people for a few years. Then, I struck out on my own. Where I belonged – with the other animals of the forest." His hand atop her shoulder nudged her to her knees. "I believe I still have other places that need your attention."

Sobered, she returned to her ministrations, applying the rum in a feathering touch on the lesion at his inner thigh. And yet, she could not but be stirred by the sight of him. Oh, she had seen bulls grazing in the pastures, their huge bollocks swinging lazily. And she had seen a stallion's enormous erection just before he mounted and rutted.

Common occurrences.

But this . . . this man who had suffered and turned his back on civilization . . . she could not but feel longing for who he was and what he had made of himself. Lightly, tenderly, her lips brushed the spot just above his laceration.

"Awww, God, Cat!"

Taking that as an affirmative that she was pleasing him, she nuzzled her nose in the nearby coarse, spiraling hair. What it enwreathed visibly throbbed. She inhaled audibly of his musk.

As if by accident, her fingernails grazed one hard, seamed testicle. His grip on her shoulders tightened vice-like.

She was becoming bolder at the idea of initiating her own desires, too long tamped down like puritan society's pipe tobacco. She moved her head merely a faction to gently lick him, then drew away.

He groaned. "I was right. You do have a mouth on you."

She looked up. His head was thrown back. The muscles of his throat were taut ropes. She feared she could never get enough of this backwoodsman. Best he never learn she was his to do with as he wanted.

Lust and the law bound them, but love?

What a wretched place. Jacob was gone again after being home but a few hours. More and more often, his work for the Continentals demanded his absence.

And Catriona was miserable. Miserable with the miserable chigger bites. Miserable with the hot monotonous days and monotonous food and long, monotonous nights. Miserable with pulling weeds that choked the kitchen garden, toting in split logs for the fireplace, scouring the necessary, scrubbing the chamber pot, and washing clothes on the tub's washboard.

True, she had the morning reading classes with Esau and Jethro and Mary and Billy to look forward to, but those lessons were nowhere as stimulating as a pianoforte recital at Campbelton or a play at nearby Cross Creek.

And true, she had books to read, but candles were a scarce commodity. As was every blasted thing. She was accustomed to adoring servants carrying out her every whim. And now she had no one – unless she counted Fergus, who once again had taken up residency outside the cabin door come nightfall.

She yanked open the door. Fergus jumped to his feet and swung around, musket at the ready. The rising moon's yellow light slanted beneath the porch roof to disclose beneath the coonskin cap the curmudgeon's bleary eyes. "Well, if the bloody mosquitos dunna carry ye off, the Indians will." She slapped at a whining one. "Come on inside."

His bearded chin ducked to his barrel chest, and, peering up at her, his bristly brows wagged warily. "I can better protect ye from outside, lass."

"For the love of God, Fergus, the mosquitos will feast on the Indians first." Her shoulders slumped. "I am just lonely. Come in and have a wee dram and regale me with tales of Scotland – or Ireland, is it?"

The Ulster Scotsman huffed a little but followed her inside on bandy legs. She crossed to the shelf and took down two cups along with the jug of ale. It was running low. She would be better off learning how to brew than spin. Although, she privately was of the opinion that gnat's urine would taste better than Mary's home brew

She plunked the cups on the table and poured a liberal dose for both her and Fergus. Sitting opposite him on the bench, she raised her cup. "Lang live Scotland. Lang live Ireland!"

He clinked his cup against hers. "To Scotland – and Ireland." He took a deep draught of the ale, then sighed. "But tis been a lang time since I laid me eyes on me country's misty mountains and glens and blue lochs."

"What is it about you backwoods people that ye have the gift of the silver tongue when ye make up your mind to talk? Why did ye leave, Fergus?"

He wrapped his hands with their ragged nails around his cup. She tried to imagine him as a younger man, like Jacob, foraging in the wilderness on his own . . . and how he must have seemed to a suffering Coowee like her own savage knight in armor.

The cabin's silence stretched and stretched. Fergus took another swallow from his cup. Then, as if addressing himself to the books piled on the hearth, he said, "Me family were crofters. When the rent was raised to intolerable heights, we were turned off the land."

"Is that how ye came to be here, in the colonies?"

"Nope. We had no passage money. Nowhere to go, ye understand? Two of me brothers had already died from starvation. Me da was being held in a gaol. Me thirteen-year-old sister was selling herself on the streets of Banbridge. And I . . . " his throat worked, and he took a swig from his cup. He wiped his mouth with the back of his furred hand. "And I, I killed me mam I did."

Now she took a swill, nigh choking.

He was swigging another deeper draught. "Foot guards of the Government's 36th army found me mam and me, hiding in a turf-wall cottage. I had escaped."

His tone was low, stony like a cairn. "When a dozen or more foot guards began taking their turns with me mam, when I saw blood gushing from her . . . from there, well, I shot her dead with one of their French muskets."

A grisly smile exposed his teeth, and she knew that for Fergus it was either that or weep uncontrollably.

She reached across the table and placed her hand over his clenched, hoary one.

His mouth worked. He stared down into his cup. He swallowed again. "Everybody's got his own row to hoe."

"After that, what happened?"

"When the opportunity to indenture meself to a mercantile company in the American colonies presented itself, I signed on – and promptly proceeded to lose meself in the Great Smokys."

"How did you meet Jacob?"

"By that time, I was earning me living trading with the Indians, lass. Dinna care to venture often into towns, what with me being an escaped indentured servant and all. Crossed paths with Jacob at one of the Tuscarora camps. Half me age, he nonetheless was able to convince me there was money to be made at Kinsfolk Landing, what with the tar and resin distillery he had jest set up."

"Aye," she sighed, "he can be quite convincing."

~ ~ ~ ~ ~ ~ ~

Skinny Coowee was among the students who showed up for the next reading lesson. And Catriona had to wonder if it was at Fergus's promptings. The Indian woman glanced from the doorway around Jacob's orderly cabin. Well, it was orderly when Jacob was present. Her stolid, swarthy face betrayed nothing, but her eyes, bird-bright, were absorbing everything. She just stood there, waiting.

Collecting the scattered books, Catriona turned and smiled. "Come in, come in."

Tentatively, she limped inside. At Catriona's directive nod, she sat placidly on the bench, saying nothing, as Catriona readied for the lessons. Minutes later, in trooped Mary and Billy with Jethro and Esau.

These days, Catriona was so delighted to see human faces that she bent over backwards to be gracious to tight mouthed Mary. "Are you thirsty? Can I get you water?"

"Nope. Twixt the chores we got to git back to, we'uns don't 'ave time to dawdle."

Catriona was mightily tempted to send the young woman packing, but that would defeat her purpose – to befriend Jacob's community and make herself a part of it.

With everyone eager to begin, she opened *Robinson Crusoe* to read from Chapter Two, where he was captured by the pirates. Of course, she could not help but feel Jethro's adoring gaze, nor Billy's attentive touch on her hose encased ankle, as he crouched beneath the table. She tried not to move and scare him away.

The boy was slowly coming around. Regrettably, the young man, Jethro, was all too quickly coming around.

Later, as she leaned over him, holding his fingers knotted around the quill as she inscribed the letter 'J' for him, he looked up at her as if she had sprouted angel's wings. "So you think if I came oftener, I could learn quick-like?"

"No, Jethro. You need to practice your letters at home more often." She wondered how his parents felt about his coming for the lessons but felt it wiser not to inquire. The less she encouraged familiarity between her and the lad the better.

And of Coowee, she asked, "Should we write your name in English?"

"Little Bird." Esau piped.

"What?"

"Her name means Little Bird in English," he explained. But, as ever, his walleyed gaze was drawn back and forth between his foolscap and Mary. Did he know how she felt about Jacob – her fierce loyalty and love for Catriona's husband?

She drew a small bird on Coowee's birch bark paper and then wrote her name next to it. The young woman's braids bobbed on her breasts with an affirmative nod. She bestowed on Catriona a large gap-toothed grin.

Catriona detained Mary on the porch after the others had left. "Billy is a wee bit behind kids his age, Mary. But he is alert and inquisitive. What happened to make him . . . afraid of life?"

The girl turned those pale brown eyes on her, bleached by sun and life. "Billy and me watched the Injuns scalp his father from our cabin loft."

"Holy Mother of God," she breathed.

"After they set fire to the cabin, me and Billy hid straight away in the safe hole beneath the floorboards. So, he prefers hiding places. But *yuh* can't hide. Fer all yuhr fancy ways, Jacob will see through them soon or later. Just as he did that apothecary's daughter."

Catriona sighed and watched Mary and Billy, hand in hand, trudge off toward Esau, who waited at the line of maples paralleling the long dirt road cut through to the cabin. He reached out and took Billy's other hand.

That simple gesture reinforced how alone and isolated Catriona felt . . . if she discounted Red Rover who lay stretched out at the end of the porch.

As if sensing her regard, Red Rover did something astonishing. The mountain lion rose smoothly to its paws, stretched, and then padded over to Catriona. Dropping down beside her, it rested its head in her lap.

"Well, well, well," she murmured, stroking the cat's spine tentatively – expecting any moment for its noble head to turn and snap off her fingers. "Two converts, I have made – ye and Billy. Now if only your master could see me as something else than merely a helpmate."

And what was this about the apothecary's daughter?

Her forlornness did not improve with the onset of dark, nor did it help when, tossing a stick of wood into the fireplace and poking at it with the fireiron she burned her finger, the very one that was only just growing back its nail, torn off the day she had been swept overboard.

Releasing the hot fireiron, she sank in a puddle of skirts on the stone hearth and sucked on her red-tipped finger. Then she began weeping. A royal pity party she was having. For all that she had lost. For all that would never be.

At that most untimely moment, Jacob chose to walk in in on her. Beard shadowed and tired eyed, he stopped short, long rifle in hand, and stared. His dark visage was expressionless, but she caught that slightest catch of hopefulness in his usually controlled word spacing. "You are with child? Our child?"

"No! I am not your handmaiden, ye churl!"

She shot off the hearth and skirts in hand stormed into the bedroom, where she meant to smash that bloody baby cradle to sawdust. But before she could slam shut the door, his hand stopped it.

She whirled and moved to put the bedpost between them.

He set aside his long rifle and unslung his powder horn and pouch. Purposefully he strode toward her. His expression was fraught with puzzlement. "Handmaiden?"

She sighed impatiently. "Like Hagar." But, of course, the Bible had not been among the books his father had ordered. "A slave woman who serves her master . . . in *all* ways."

His eyes narrowed. "Have I demanded that of you?"

She shook her head. "No. I dunna understand what is wrong with me." Hands lapped around the bedpost, she laid her forehead against it. "I burnt me finger . . . and I . . . I dunna understand ye, me husband."

He took her hands, unclasping their grip on the post, and sat down on the bed, drawing her to sit on his knee. He picked up one hand, looked at it, then the other. "Ahhh, this is the finger that suffered the burn."

She could but nod. She felt both embarrassed by her childish outburst and that wild almost panicky thumping in her heart, a combination of wariness and excitement when suddenly seeing him after an absence of even an hour.

He placed her blistered fingertip in his mouth and gently sucked.

She whimpered.

His midnight blue eyes watched her. Her own closed, partly at the ecstasy of the feeling and partly to avoid what she might see in his eyes when she asked, "How did you meet the apothecary's daughter?"

"What?" He released her fingertip. "Mary has been talking to you."

She opened her eyes and looked at him steadily. She wished she could stop herself from blurting out questions prodded by this ugly fit of jealousy. "What is her name?"

"Pamela Sullivan."

"How did ye meet her?"

"I placed an order for Mother McGee's rheumatism at her father's shop in Wilmington."

"And?"

"We dallied. I left Wilmington two days later."

"And that is all?"

"I did not know she had stolen aboard my periauger – until we were nigh midway to Kinsfolk Landing.”

“Then what happened?”

He sighed. “Eventually, I sent her to stay with Mary until my next trip down river.”

Another fit of jealousy smote her. “For how long? How long did ye two dally at your cabin?”

“You want to hurt?”

“How long?”

“Nine days.”

“And why did ye not take her to wife? Could she neither read nor write?” she asked spitefully.

His gaze turned Indian obdurate. “She was neither strong of arm nor wide of hip for bairns.”

That was the wrong thing to say; not when her confidence was at a low ebb. But then, what had she expected when she had agreed to marry him? It was not in his capacity, raised primarily with the Indians, to allow himself to show the kind of emotion a white man would. “But, at least, I can read – and ye canna, can ye? Nor write.”

He released her hand. His jaw lifted, and she was not sure if it was pride or shame she saw in those eyes, as dark blue now as a candle flame. “I have a head for numbers. I can cipher to the rule of three.”

Remorse seized her. She bit her lower lip. It did not matter that he had initially chosen her for qualities other than affection. He had kept his pledge to save Afton Manor.

For her, and other women, marriage meant that under the law her husband would have absolute control of her and of any property she might own. But he had been good to her, despite her shortcomings as a pioneer wife. And in bed . . . oh mercy, she could well understand why the apothecary’s daughter had followed him to Kinsfolk Landing. Catriona had not had the slightest idea that pleasuring one another could be so intensely potent and gratifying.

He went to set her from his lap, but she refused to budge and framed his lean face with her palms. His ebony hair had come unbraided at the temples, and she threaded her fingers through its long, thick swaths, tangled with leaves and twigs. He must have charged headlong through the forest to get back.

“Listen to me, husband of mine – me wicked tongue ran away with me ire. I ken I am useless to ye as a wife. I feel badly about that, now. Please, let me help in the only way I am able. Your downriver trips and your scouting take you away often. Ye understand, I get lonely. I could learn your resin distillery business and, while ye are away, could help with the orders and keep your business records and correspondence." She looked at him uncertainly, then added in a subdued voice, "And if ye'd like, we could do a wee bit of reading together at night."

His hands captured her palms and brought her fingertips back to his lips. Once more, he kissed her burnt one. Above it, his eyes burned with his fearless passion. But a hint of a smile played at the corners of his mouth. "You are not completely useless, Cat. But I can think of better things to do together at night than reading."

~ ~ ~ ~ ~ ~ ~

That morning Catriona was out back on her knees before the wooden tub. She was washing her mass of curls, kinked by the summer's humidity. She had already skewered the salted slab of venison onto the hearth's spit. She was not sure when her husband would return from his latest sortie, but just in case, she was prepared to feed his hunger, all his hungers, as a dutiful wife should be. Only, his hunger for her was astonishingly equaled by hers for him.

With war imminent with the Mother Country, Caswell had sent Jacob away once again, this time to treatise with the Creeks.

"Catriona?"

In scrambling to her bare feet, she bumped her knees against the tub's wooden staves. "Och!" She tossed her chin, throwing her heavy wet hair back from her face to slap the length of her back, splattering water over her shift and everywhere around her, like a dog shaking water off its wet coat.

Hands on hips, a twitch to his lips and hazel eyes mirthful, Barrett Fairfax stood staring at her. In the morning sunlight, he shone as brilliantly as a field of sunflowers. Wearing soft doeskin breeches that molded his thighs and a buff linen jacket, he looked definitely the Macaroni. A broadsword rode at his side.

He removed his tricorne and executed an urbane bow. "I must say, you are looking resplendent, Catriona."

She clapped her hands in childlike joy. "Barrett! I dunna believe it! What are ye doing here, and did ye walk all the way from – " Hands slapping crisscrossed over her chest in a gesture of modesty, she laughed. "Mercy, I look nothing like a lady."

But she was too excited to bemoan her disheveled state and the fact she wore nothing but her shift. She linked her arm through his. "Come on inside. Let me get ye a drink. Ye must be thirsty."

She plucked her smock off the wall peg and slid it over her head. With eager steps, she crossed to take a pair of cups and the water jug from the shelf. "Please, please tell me what is happening in Campbelton."

He eyed her bare feet, arched a brow, and smiled sardonically. "When in Rome . . . "

Immediately the dusty toes of one bare foot overlapped the others. She poured cups for them both and seated herself on the other side of the table from him. "And please tell me, as well, what ye, of all people, are doing here in this godforsaken wilderness."

He chuckled. "I asked myself the same question when I agreed to accompany the Remingtons on their keelboat."

"Lord Walter Remington?"

"None other. We put into Kinsfolk Landing for provisions. Remington feels, what with conflict escalating daily, it is better to start over farther west, away from the threat of rebel war parties. The Whigs are pillaging and burning Tory homes and farms left and right."

"Alas, this is fearful, what is happening. Tis something, thankfully, I dunna have to worry meself about – Afton Manor."

"Your sacrifice was foolhardy."

"T'was no sacrifice, Barrett. It benefitted me family, and I trust it benefitted me husband."

His hand swept out, a contemptuous gesture that encompassed the sparsity of the cabin. "How do you stand it? The solitude? The deprivations?"

She saw the contempt for the place in his eyes and felt a renewed sense of desolation. She struggled with a smile. "Do tell me now about Campbelton society. Did Jane Killough land the part in *The Beggar's Opera*?"

He rolled his eyes. "The quality of her performances varies from the mediocre to the awful."

She laughed. "How droll. And Anne? What is she doing?"

"I lost a fortune to her at backgammon last week."

"I had forgotten how competitive you two are."

"And old Thomas Brewer broke a leg while foxhunting. But

that did not keep him from attending John Worthington's masked ball – hobbled in on a crutch as King Henry VIII with gout."

Her hands cradled her cup. She swallowed. "Me parents, have ye talked with them?"

"Catriona, they miss you something terrible. What with your brothers in prison – and now, you, the light of their lives, gone from home – well, your mother isn't her usual lively self." He shrugged. "What can I say?"

"Och, there is naught ye can – "

"Yes, there is, damn it all! Listen to me. I am taking you with me. Now. The Remingtons are only going as far upriver as the Piedmont, then Walter is returning to Campbelton for more household goods. Think of it, you could be back in Campbelton within ten days, back with your parents, back from the dead with its deadly doldrums here at Kinsfolk Landing. Do not play the part of Persephone to this lout's Hades."

Her fingers picked listlessly at a table splinter between them. "I – I canna, Barrett. I *am* married to him, to Jacob. I owe him a monumental debt. And he has been good to me."

"An obligatory marriage, if you will. You two are the least fit mates for one another I can envision. A vicar pairing his parishioners could have done better. At least, you and I are cut from the same fabric. Educated bluebloods with no misplaced loyalties. What's more, this man is guilty of sedition."

Agitated, she rose, stared down at him, shook her head, then stepped away. She moved to the hearth on the pretext of raking the bed of embers so the fire would not go out. He followed. Spade in hand, her back to him, she said, "Ye are making this so verra difficult for me. Ye canna possibly realize how much I miss – "

He reached out a hand to cap hers on the spade. A single drop of water, from either her freshly washed hair or her brimming lids, fell on their clasped hands. "Catriona," he husked, "do you care at all for me?"

She pivoted to face him. "Oh, Barrett, ye ken I care about ye. We have been old – "

Instinct made her pause, glance past Barrett's shoulder toward the open door. There stood Jacob. His gaze moved from Barrett to her.

Jerking her hand from Barrett's grasp, she dropped the spade.

Its clattering sound on the hearth was followed by silence. Nervously, she broke it. "Jacob, ye remember Barrett Fairfax. You met him at the Highland Games. And he came to our wedding."

Jacob said nothing, just waited and watched.

Barrett turned slowly, almost casually, toward Jacob. "I was on my way upriver with mutual friends of Lady Catriona's and mine. Most fortunately, we laid over here for provisioning."

"Barrett was sharing with me the entertaining happenings at Campbelton."

Jacob stepped forward then. He hitched his long rifle upright, resting its barrel upon his shoulder carelessly. She knew better than that. Jacob's every move served a purpose. He merely observed her and Barrett pensively.

"And, of course," Barrett added, "to pass along her parents' love and well wi – "

"Her parents' love or yours?"

Eyes firing salvos, she faced off between the two in the eternal lovers' triangle. "Barrett was just leaving." She turned to him but taunted Jacob by saying, "I canna tell ye how much your visit has meant to me."

"I shall let your parents know we talked." He went to collect his Tricorne from the wall peg, but Jacob, standing now, as if by coincidence in front of the wall pegs, did not step aside.

Barrett's eyes slitted. His jaw clenched. His hand drifted to the hilt of his broadsword. But he was no fool. He was in her husband's camp. He reached around Jacob, took his hat, and turned back to her, saying, "How our Good Lord must detest the common people. He made them so . . . common. I trust we shall have the pleasure of meeting again soon, Catriona. Very soon." Then he strode through the open door.

Hands knotted, she whirled on Jacob. "T'was not what ye weened!"

His searching scrutiny was fastened solely on her eyes. "What *did* I think?"

"Admit it, Barrett showed he is far the civilized superior of ye two."

He hung up his powder horn and bullet pouch and looked over his shoulder at her. "Then, it is not too late for you to file for an annulment." He shrugged. "Or mayhap for me to kill your Barrett."

"Ohhh! Ye – ye are, indeed, little better than a savage. And no comparison to Barrett."

He grinned. Actually grinned. "You would do well to remember that."

Then he pivoted, rifle in hand, and headed back outside. Her body folded onto the bench, and, face in her palms, she gulped deep, steadying breaths that rattled her rib cage. Then came the awful thought – was he going after Barrett? Surely not.

Before she could reach the door, she heard the ring of his axe thudding on the block. Then she espied him, now shirtless, his rifle within reaching distance. Splitting fresh curling chips for the fireplace, he swung his axe easily, continuously, as if it were as much a part of his body as it seemed his rifle was.

She detested his utter dispassionate expression, detested his imperturbable composure, detested his maddening self-assurance. But most of all, she detested that he was so sure of her. He had subjugated the wilderness and animals at Kinsfolk Landing, just as he would her, if she would let him.

An infantile anger urged her to charge into the yard, to fling herself at him. To dig her nails into his flesh. To rip his heart out. If he but had one.

Instead, she turned back inside. Listlessly, she tended the fire, dully watching the coals flare frenziedly as from time to time the venison's dripping fat ignited. She should have left with Barrett while she had the chance.

She could hail the next craft headed downriver, but most crafts were headed upriver farther into the wilderness. Besides, with what would she pay for her passage? Her gold hairpin, worth the fare a hundred times over, was of lesser value in the wilderness and a cast iron skillet far more precious.

The irony of her situation was not lost on her, and she chuckled dryly. Like her hairpin, she was, indeed, of lesser value than even an iron skillet. Hairpins, with ornaments hanging from them, had been fashionable for decades. Some elongated pins often doubled as containers for perfume – or poison. And at that moment, the idea of poisoning her husband's coffee did not seem such a poor one.

Spring gave way to summer. Maple leaves deepened their color, young bucks sprouted antlers, grape clusters weighted vines, and wild azaleas blazed on the bluff.

Coowee learned to write her name. Billy perched beside Catriona on the bench while she read aloud. She learned to spin. And Jacob continued to weave his magic on her senses at night, when neither his tribe nor her clan could interpose.

Some afternoons, she would take a respite from her chores. With work-pained palms at the low center of her aching back, she would stand on the roofed porch and look out at the distant blue mountains, wreathed with their mists of mystery. She would inhale the fresh sweet scent of vegetation and listen to the lively chattering of the woodland creatures – the birds and squirrels and frogs – and feel a deep peace. She could honestly say she was far too busy to be bored.

Nevertheless, she counted the days remaining until the Highlanders' Christmas season, with their stories of St. Nicholas and traditions steeped in Viking lore. She missed her family and friends in Campbelton. Terribly. They understood her. They were like her. She was not an oddity there. She wondered what of Barrett's visit he would report back to her family.

One warm summer morning, Mary and Billy did not show for the reading lessons. When Catriona asked Esau why, he merely shrugged, saying, "Told me she was plumb tuckered."

After class, Catriona decided to accompany Jethro, Coowee, and Esau back to the settlement, where she sought out Mary's house.

A dish towel slung over one shoulder, a smoothing iron in hand, she opened the door and gave fuller view to the rude, squalid one-room log cabin with its earthen floor.

Her hostile look still would catch Catriona off guard. "I – I worry that something is wrong when ye or Billy dunna show for class," she said lamely.

"Well, don't. I just got me monthly flux."

When Mary did not invite her in, only stood in the doorway and glared, Catriona lost her initial good will with which she had begun the morning. "Suit yeself, then," she snapped and tramped the mile back to Jacob's cabin and once again isolation.

Periodically, people came and went at Kinsfolk Landing. Fur trappers, hunters, peddlers, people fleeing west over the mountains and out of reach of government interference, to resettle. She rarely saw the visitors. She heard about them from Esau, Jethro, or Fergus – or sometimes Mary, if she was of a mind to converse, which was rarely. Which, could, also, be said of Jacob these days.

So, early one evening, when Fergus appeared on the porch to tell Jacob that no less than Richard Caswell, elected governor by the upstart North Carolina congress, had put in at Kinsfolk Landing, Catriona was determined to meet the man.

As the town had for her, it turned out for the governor and his two staff members, along with a guard of militiamen garbed in their distinctively fringed hunting shirts. "Dare ye trust me to talk with another landed gentleman?" she asked with a half-teasing, half-taunting smile as she and Jacob strolled the mile's distance to the settlement.

Anticipation of the visitation by Tidewater gentry– even if it was the same legislators who had demanded Loyalists sign an oath to the rebels or forfeit their homes – was restoring some of her high spirits. Likewise, Jacob, glad to see his friend again, was in good spirits.

Jacob took her hand, holding it as a lover might do. Except no word of love had ever passed between them. And most likely would not, even if they lived to celebrate their golden anniversary. Theirs was not a marriage of sentimentality but practicality. Still, she repented her sullenness and was determined to make the best of their marriage, which was like a see-saw – some days better than the others and never one side taking complete precedence over the other.

A hint of a smile curled his lips. "You could return down river on his barge on the morrow."

Beneath his other arm he cradled his long rifle. She knew, though his pace appeared leisurely, almost lazy, he was keenly aware of every single woodland movement and in a split second could spring into action.

Her free hand clamped tighter on her dulcimer. "I said me vows. I keep them. Me word is me bond."

Governor Caswell was not at all the pompous, arrogant politician she had expected. In fact, much shorter than Jacob and about Fergus's age, maybe in his mid-forties, he was virtually nondescript, except for the shaggy thatch of hair that covered his brow. A Grand Master Mason, he was also a lawyer and surveyor by training but his clothing for his wilderness traveling was as simple and durable as any backwoodsman.

His remarkably intelligent eyes, continually alive with curiosity, surveyed her now. "So you are the daughter of the famous Highland chieftess, Lady Enya Kincairn."

She curtsied. "And ye are the famous rebel who steals me husband from me far too often."

"Alack, I confess I must steal him yet again." His gaze, while kindly, held a sympathetic aspect that disturbed her.

He looked to Jacob. "The Philadelphia congress has drafted a declaration of our independence from Great Britain. War is officially upon us. I am visiting our backwoods' communities, drumming up volunteers for Washington's new revolutionary army."

Jacob's black brows scowled. "That will leave settlements out here unprotected."

Her cheeks paled. What could the Continentals' outright declaration of war mean for the safety of her parents? "Are British war vessels still anchored offshore of Wilmington?" she asked, trying to keep her voice neutral yet hoping the British presence could maintain some appearance of order while insanity seemed to rule.

"Mrs. Dare, I realize your family is a Loyalist one, while I consider mine a Patriot one. But sometimes we are forced to make a choice for one side or the other, and perhaps later we may regret our choices."

His words had the ring of an apology, and this bothered her even more.

"If I may," he continued with a slight bow, "I would like to speak in private with your husband?"

With an acceding nod, she watched as he drew Jacob aside. Soon, newly lit pipe smoke enveloped the two.

Meanwhile, word of the outright declaration of war had spread throughout the room. She talked to Robert Cameron about forging for her a warning triangle bell.

She listened as Mother McGee complained about how bad it had been on the frontier during the French and Indian War. " . . . poor soldiers would come down with the galloping shakes and only a dose of Peruvian Bark would cure them."

She agreed with plump Polly MacGregor about the need to include the settlement's women folk in drills and exercises against any future Indian raids.

Mick approached her about playing her dulcimer while Esau accompanied her on the fiddle. "Ye understand – to git the mind off the looming shades of war. Mayhap some lively tunes to git the hands clapping and shoes shuffling?"

But, as she collected her dulcimer, Jacob appeared at her side, his grip on her elbow. He bent his head low, murmuring at her ear. "I am called to depart with Caswell by dawn. We make our farewells with the others now."

Something urgent in his voice told her this was not merely another scouting summons. No, not when, once outside the trading post, he turned her toward him, his hands clamping her upper arms, as if to support her. The night was eerily quiet, with but the faint fiddling of the lilting *Green Sleeves* coming from within the log structure. The smell of blossoms from the wild crabapple tree at the corner of the trading post wafted the air.

"What is it?" Her voice sounded faint and far away in her ears.

As usual, his commanding countenance was unreadable and his tone emotionless. "Afton Manor has been burnt to the ground."

~ ~ ~ ~ ~ ~ ~

Overhead, July's hot and full Thunder Moon had waxed, blistering all of Jacob's hopes.

Catriona closed her eyes. A long, shuddering breath wracked her frame. When she opened them, tears pooled there and horrible grief hollowed her eyes. She was trembling violently. "What . . . how did it . . . my parents, are they safe?"

Robert Cameron staggered out the trading post door, and Jacob pulled her within the shadows of the crabapple and waited until the man had urinated against the trading post's log wall and made his way back inside

"Yes. They escaped with the clothes on their backs. They are at the house your friend Anne Macleod is renting. An angry Patriot mob – a group calling itself Sons of Liberty – attacked five days ago. When they learned Congress approved the draft of the declaration for American liberty."

She stiffened. He felt her bones and veins and heart fossilize. The light in her eyes was extinguished. Her accusing words dropped like stones into the Cape Fear, one by one. "Ye – had – pledged – to – protect – me – home."

He fought against shaking her. He wanted to tell her that her home was here, Dare Plantation at Kinsfolk Landing. Instead, he regarded her silently.

"Ye had pledged to keep Afton Manor safe." Her eyes blazed to life. "In return, I had pledged to be your wife." Her hand flicked the muggy night air in an ugly, dismissive gesture. "Both our pledges are now worthless as a counterfeit Continental. I would rather be an Indian whore than be your wife, do ye hear me?!"

He lost the Indian stoicism of which she accused him to have. He shoved her from him so hard that her head slammed against the log wall, her breath whooshed from her lungs, and she slumped to the ground like a rag doll.

But given her strength, he should not have been surprised that she sprang to a crouch and, galvanized by raw fury, hurled her dulcimer up at him. With a mere flick of a movement, his shoulder dodged the instrument. His smile broadened at her helpless fury. "I can arrange your whoring with my Indian brothers if that is what you prefer."

Then, chuckling, he turned away, striding off into the darkness.

~ ~ ~ ~ ~ ~ ~

Over the next week, stockpiles of arms and ammunition and kegs of gunpowder, appeared within the five tiers of fifteen-foot logs that established the parameter of the stockade Jacob had recommended built. When it was finished, the palisade would have a second overhung story with loopholes for musket defense and a platform that ran along the parapet for patrolling.

As Fergus said dryly, "Either the Redcoats are a'coming or the Indians are a'coming."

That morning Catriona had stood barefoot on the breeze-swept bluff, squinting first in the summer's haze to the west, in the direction of Grandfather Mountain, the highest peak in the Blue Ridge, the direction to which Jacob had headed. Then her gaze drifted in the opposite direction, to the southeast and Campbelton. Even she did not understand this longing for her roots, the very soil from which she sprang. How could the simple word 'home' connote so much, so deeply?

But there was no home to which she could return.

She had plenty of time to think. Her strong sense of fairness compelled her to admit that Jacob had given his word to secure Afton Manor against seizure by the colony's new Patriot congress, not the combustible violence of mindless mob fury.

He was a fair and square man. He had kept his part of their bargain, and she would, too, if for no other reason than she believed they were creating something worthwhile here at this untouched outpost of civilization.

She was most reluctant to delve further into her conciliatory motives, to confront the issue that there might be something more to them. Yet it was not like her to skirt such an issue.

Some untapped but dominant part of her had wanted to marry Jacob Dare all along. Chalk it up to his irresistible appeal or whatever, but she found it remarkable, that she had denied it all this time. She had duped herself. Her aggravation could not be greater at that moment.

And it was at that moment she had espied the barge bobbing on the river. Contact with the outside world! She hurried back to the cabin, thrust her feet in her leather patents and a cap on her head and nigh ran the mile to Kinsfolk Landing and the trading post – only to find the barge had continued upriver. Holding to the trading post counter for support, she had fought against bursting into tears.

She could not account for her weepy condition these days. She, who never wept. Counting off on her fingers, she reviewed the weeks since her last menses. No, she was not with child.

Jacob would know this. He knew her body so well. He had his

white man's home for which he had planned with cold precision. She had lost hers, the one she had treasured all her life and carried in her memory and in her heart. He had his white wife he had bargained for. But he did not yet have his wife with child.

"They were going as far west as the Little Tennessee River at its headwaters in North Carolina."

"What?" she asked Fergus. He was hanging an oxen yoke from the trading post's low rafters. Coowee limped between them, toting in two bucketsful of water and smiled good-naturedly at her. "Who? The barge load of people on its way upriver?"

"Nae. Your husband, lass." He reached for a horse collar to hang next. His face wore its habitual grumpy expression. "Into hostile Indian territory, he went."

He glanced at her then, an odd look, and she had to wonder if he knew of the dissension between her and Jacob. Had their parting disagreement been witnessed or overheard at the trading post that evening?

She planted her palms on the counter and lowered her head. She could not remember feeling so desolate, whether it was from the lingering heartache that Afton Manor was no more or, senselessly, from simply being bypassed by the barge. "Most likely me husband went among the Indians to arrange a barter – his worthless wife for garden seeds."

"Och, he would never do sech a thing." He turned aside to spit a judicious wad of tobacco juice between the seams of the floor boards. "He would barter ye fer much, much more than garden seeds. A mink pelt, maybe. Or, hell, you may bring even as much as a pony."

Despite herself she smiled.

Opposite her, the trader braced his paws on the counter. "T'was ye he wanted, lass – and when he wants something he never gives up."

Her mouth twisted to one side. "Aye, he wanted a hale and hearty woman such as meself for labor – both in the field and on the birthing bed."

The next morning, she rose listlessly to do her chores. At least, Jacob had left their larder supplied with salted meats, pickled vegetables, and dried herbs.

The fact she would be holding class later that morning lifted her spirits somewhat. When she saw her student's approaching, she had time enough only to nibble on a biscuit, before stuffing its remnants into her pocket and scurrying to set books, foolscap, quills and inkhorn on the table.

In trooped her students, with Coowee lumbering behind on her twisted foot. Today, the limp was pronounced. It threw her hip out of place so that her thin body angled sharply from her waist up. Nonetheless, she gave her amiable gap-toothed grin and thrust at Catriona a handful of lovely wildflowers.

Esau bestowed his natural loopy grin. 'Mornin', Missus Dare."

"Good morning to ye, Esau – Mary."

Mary nodded. Her gaze inspected Catriona, looking for what? Her horsehair marriage ring? Had she, too, heard about the fight with Jacob?

Doffing his cap, Jethro blushed and stammered when she bade him good morning.

They grouped around the table. Billy had yet to speak in her presence, but, she was elated when he slid closer on the bench to sit beside her and himself open *Johnson's Dictionary*. He leaned over the page to peer at what must appear to him odd markings.

She said, "I thought it would be fun today to have a spelling-."

Shadows filled the doorway and leaped across the puncheon. In that split second, she had a premonition of danger. All heads swiveled in that direction. At the forefront of Indians crowding the door and spilling out into the yard stood one, his head completely shaven but for a warlock draping from his crown. Vermillion war paint striped the cheeks so that his face looked subhuman.

Like all the coastal tribes, which could account for Jacob's excessive height, these Indians were extraordinarily tall. Their very silence was more menacing than any war whoop. There ensued some discussion among them as their obsidian eyes moved from Catriona to Jethro to Coowee to Esau and lastly Mary and Billy.

The leader grunted and stretched out a hand to curl a beckoning finger that encompassed all of them. "Come."

Catriona's gaze flew up to the fowling piece above the doorway.

"Do as Dragging Canoe says," warned Mary beneath her breath. She rose slowly to her feet and, without taking her eyes from the leader, reached for Billy's grubby hand.

A still bloody blond scalp was bound to the lance of one

Indian. To whom had the scalp belonged? She hoped not Polly MacGregor's. Its blood-dripping presence was incentive enough for the captives to keep silent and obey.

Once outside, the warriors surrounded them and were spitting orders in some garbled language. There had to be a dozen in the war party, armed with tomahawks, knives, and muskets.

Catriona glanced questioning at Coowee. "What are they saying?"

Coowee's narrow, nutmeg-colored face was tight with terror. Having chosen to live among the whites, she could expect no leniency at the hands of these warriors. She humped her bony shoulders and only shook her head in the negative.

Catriona glanced uneasily at Esau. His jaw was working as if he were chewing tobacco. "Talking about killing, maybe."

"When last did you hear tell of their burning anyone at the stake?" Jethro choked out.

She had heard only of white people burning their victims at the stake, victims like Jacob's mother. Before she could respond, the leader spat some kind of order, and one of the braves whacked Jethro hard upside his temple with the walnut stock of his Brown Bess.

Jethro staggered, and she sprang to clutch his shoulder as he sagged. But a brave, the lower portion of his face a grotesque mask striped with red and black horizontal bands, stepped between her and Jethro.

Their captors shoved them out of the cabin yard, past the fields, forded Hollering Woman Creek, and herded them into the dense forest on the other side. Mile after mile they trudged. The pace the Indians set was fast, but the hours dragged.

Catriona's leather patents rubbed excruciating blisters on her feet. Branches and brambles scratched her face and arms. Mosquitoes stabbed at her exposed flesh, and spider webs netted her tumbled hair, which had long since lost its cap and pins. A trail left, she knew, Jacob would track. Even the forest birds fell silent at the funeral procession-like forced march.

If she judged the position of the sun correctly, the Indians halted, at last, at midday near a mossy creek. The captives fell at once to their knees to drink the cold, clear water. Their captor's treatment of Jethro, after he had piped up, underscored the case for silence among them.

However, Billy's whimpering and whining were growing louder. His eyes were dark smudges, his hair a thatch of scarecrow straw, his face dirty and briar-scratched. Immediately, Mary slapped her hand over his mouth. "Hush!"

"Here," Catriona whispered, digging into her tied-on pocket to produce her half-eaten biscuit leftover from that morning. She proffered it to the tired child.

Immediately, his grimy hands grabbed it, and he gobbled it in one swallow.

Mary edged closer to Catriona. "Thank yuh. Listen here," she whispered, inclining her brown hair closer to Catriona's red hair. "Dragging Canoe, he's the big wig among the Cherokee Middle House tribes. So, tis odd he would lead a small raiding party. What fer? To capture only the six of us'uns?"

Unless – unless, Jacob had put him up to it, as he had threatened.

At once, she dismissed the thought. Aye, Fergus had said if Jacob wanted something, he never gave up. When he determined a course of action, he held resolutely to it. It was inconceivable, though, he would have her kidnapped to teach her a lesson for her spiteful outburst about preferring to be an Indian's squaw than his wife.

Even more inconceivable that he would risk the lives of others. But he was part Indian, had been raised mostly with the Indians, thought like the Indians. Could she really ever understand the complex man?

When Dragging Canoe stepped closer and motioned with an abrupt jerk of his hand for them to rise and move out, Billy's little mouth curled in a pout, and he said defiantly, "No."

It was the first word Catriona had heard from the child. But now was not the time for him to decide to test his gift of speech. Quickly, Esau bent and scooped up the child to straddle atop his shoulders. "Gotcha, Billy," he said quietly. "We're going for a piggy-back ride."

Only then did Catriona notice Coowee. Her twisted foot, fatigued by the forced march at the rapid pace, did not hold up as she struggled to stand. She fell on her knees. Catriona braced her arm around the woman's waist and hefted her upright. Jethro scrambled to support her other side, but he was not in much better shape, still woozy as he was with the nasty slam his head had taken.

Coowee's knees kept buckling. She shook her head, her braids swishing her nearly non-existent breasts. "Me no . . . no walk." She tugged free of Catriona and Jethro and plopped back down. "Go. Go walk."

"We can do this," Catriona said and knelt to latch an arm once more about Coowee's skinny waist.

A dozen pair of inimical eyes watched. At their grunts and prods, she and Jethro hauled Coowee to her moccasined feet and fell in line behind the others, with warriors both leading and trailing them.

Following the other captives, they plunged through underbrush, down slippery slopes and up brambly knolls. Her arm supporting Coowee raged with the numbing pain. Coowee fought back groans. Jethro swayed with almost every step. The knocking on his noggin had taken the sap out of him.

The trail they took sometimes intertwined and often paralleled the 200-mile-long Wilderness Road, the only way to get back and forth between the settlements of North Carolina and the newer ones in the Virginia territories of Kentucky and Tennessee. The path was, at times, no more than a narrow track. It wound through brush, craggy heights, and boggy bottoms, along which they were pushed single file. It was here, single file, that Catriona worried most for Coowee.

Several hours later, when Catriona stumbled on a rocky incline, slicing her shin on a jutting slab, she lost her footing. She grabbed at a drooping pine branch, but her numbed hand gave way. Jethro grabbed for her, but both she and Coowee went rolling, taking down the Indian directly behind them.

The other Indians leaped out of the way. At the bottom of the ravine, the buck sprang to his feet. The feather thrust through his topknot drooped forlornly. His comrades laughed and yelped taunts that Catriona, lying partially beneath Coowee, did not quite understand. But their obscene gestures comparing the feather with that part of his genitals were obvious, as well as, their motions at the prostrate Coowee and Catriona.

Fury contorted the buck's painted face. His knife blade glittered in the dappled sunlight.

Half-trapped under Coowee, Catriona could only watch the blade gouge downward. In that single instant, before it could scoop out her heart, she saw her parents' loving faces, heard old Phoebe's querulous voice waking her far too early, felt Jacob's callused and fire-scarred hand reaching up in the night from the pallet to clasp hers.

Time blurred. Two, maybe three, days of even more fast-paced traveling, with Dragging Canoe allotting only a few stops for water and periodic rest.

During one of those all-too-brief rest periods, Mary told their captive group, now numbering only five, "They're in a tearin' hurry ta git wherever it is they're headed."

Coowee's grizzly murder was still a nightmare in the backs of Catriona's lids whenever she closed them. She was afraid to sleep, afraid to dream, afraid of their fate. Afraid even to eat, afraid her portion would not be doled out pemmican but a serving of Coowee's eviscerated heart.

Their destination, she learned, was a Cherokee town, Coyate, on the banks of the Little Tennessee River, the area where Fergus had said Jacob and Caswell and staff had been headed.

Her mind had plenty of time to entertain yet again the possibilities that Jacob was behind their capture, that she was a fool to believe he had integrity, much less, a conscience.

Now painfully barefoot, she and the other captives were shoved through a gate. Its solid fortification walls of thick logs surrounded the Indian village. Lookouts were stationed along a wooden walkway at the top.

It seemed the whole town had turned out to taunt the arriving captives. She and the rest stumbled and limped past jeering women and old men and darting children and dogs and into the seven-sided council house built atop an earthen mound.

In the council house, on the far side of the large stone-rimmed hearth, sat a swarthy man on an array of buffalo robes. His long gray braids draped a sagging bare chest that was tattooed. She did not recognize it as being the same design as that of Jacob's. To either side of him sat a couple of other stolid-faced braves.

From behind, unseen hands thrust her to her knees. The same occurred to Mary, Jethro, and Esau, who toted in his arms a spent and nigh unconscious Billy. Dragging Canoe seated himself between them and the old man, with his apparent advisors, and began conversing with him in staccato-like exchanges.

At one point, the old Indian's rheumy eyes fastened on her. Dragging Canoe shot to his feet in one fluid motion, crossed to stand behind her and yank a lock of her filthy red hair up for all to see. The implication was obvious. A shudder of horror rippled through her.

After a moment, the old Indian nodded and muttered something. From what she could fathom, the nod was one more of boredom with the subject than that of agreement to what Dragging Canoe was proposing.

Then, during the rest of Dragging Canoe's diatribe, the old man shifted his intense focus from her to Esau. Regarding their fate, she had no clue as to what the council decided but, at last, an emphatic nod, this time from the chief, sent their captors escorting them – all but Esau – to a small dome-like house sunk into the ground.

"What do you think they could be doing with him?" Jethro asked, dropping down before its fire pit and cautiously glancing around the darkened, malodorous room.

Mary, with Billy now huddled within the loop of her arm, stared across the fire pit at his worried expression. "I'm thinking the chief took a gander at Esau's walleyes and straight-aways up and decided that Esau's the tribe's lucky rabbit's foot."

Catriona nudged aside some small rocks with her bare foot, swollen with suppurating sores, and curled up in the ash-crusted dirt. She yawned. "We can only hope that favorable superstition will extend to us, as his friends, as well." She was fatigued beyond caring. Besides, flight was out of the question in that village of what she estimated to be nearly two thousand or so. If the Indians decided to scalp or kill her, there was nothing to be done about it. She might as well rest while she could.

Which turned out to be a wise consideration, as even before

sunrise the next morning a fat, grumpy squaw entered. A puffed birthmark blemished most of her right cheek. She carried a cane tray with wooden bowls filled with some kind of putrid gruel and prodded them to eat quickly.

Billy's little fist rubbed his sleepy eyes. He glanced at the maggoty food and shook his head back and forth. His dirty mop of yellow hair swished across his brows.

"Yew gotta eat, Billy," Mary coaxed.

"I canna blame him," Catriona said, frowning down at her bowl of moving vermin.

In what seemed mere minutes, the squaw returned and whisked away the tray with two bowls untouched. Mary and Jethro had scarfed the contents of theirs.

Then three braves appeared at the curtained doorway. One swooped up a squirming, yelling Billy, and the second prodded Jethro with the butt of his tomahawk to follow him outside, which he did with alacrity. The remaining Indian motioned for Catriona and Mary to set off in another direction.

He led them outside the gate to a cornfield, where, with a copper disk just tipping the predawn dark outline of a forest on Catriona's right, they were set to work with a few other squaws. They were to gather into baskets harnessed on their backs the windrows of corn cobs, harvested the day before.

Throughout that day, all the women toiled under guard with nary a word permitted exchanged between her and Mary. That copper disk had charred Catriona's pale flesh by the time it dropped behind the mountains on her left. And by that time, painful ant bites dotted her feet and calves. They were a mere aggravation compared to the gripping pain in the muscles ridging her spine. She hobbled like an old woman.

Only near dusk did the squaws return to the village and Mary and she to the hovel. Built of tree branches bent in a circular shape and plastered with mud and clay, its musty dry darkness was a relief. But the moldering beaver pelts suspended from the arched branches were not. Neither were the odors of horse manure, rancid bear meat, and human feces. None of this she had noticed before, so utterly drained had she been from the forced and fast paced march.

At once, she slumped over onto her side. Her stomach growled, but she shrank from what might be in the family cooking pot in the hovel's center – stories were widespread of Indian cuisine containing anything from turtle tails to dog paws to slugs. If this cuisine was the reason for the Cherokee's legendary height, she would settle for her own and forego the delicacies.

Likewise, her sunburned flesh shrank at painful contact with anything. She was totally tortured. And, here she had thought her duties as a frontier wife had been extraordinarily demanding. "Mary, wake me please, if this be a nightmare."

"Yuhr alive," Mary said, stretching out, as well. "Mebbe not so purty anymore."

She might have taken offense, but she could hear tears weighting the woman's next words. "I can only hope me Billy behaved – and the savages haven't bashed out his brains."

She was struck with guilt. Not once, in stooping and collecting along the rows of cornstalks, had she given Billy even a thought. Her thoughts had centered around only how to escape.

Certainly, if not for Jacob's need for a white wife, a strong white wife able to bear children – and read, she would be ensconced in the leaded pane-glass window seat of her bedroom back at Campbelton – and reading.

No, she would not.

Afton Manor was gone. Never more to exist except in memory.

The animal skin curtain lifted, and Jethro slipped inside to plop down with them. As soon as his eyes adjusted to the dimness, he asked, "Esau? Billy?"

Mary shook her head. Her lips crunched into a thin line. Then, she got out, "We don't know nuttin' of 'em."

"They had me hoeing weeds with squaws in a squash garden," Jethro said. "Got the feeling what they're jist biding their time with us."

A short while later, Esau appeared with Billy in hand. The kid was astonishingly at ease. After the horror of witnessing his father's scalping, Catriona would have thought this captivity would have reduced him to a blubbering mess. But, no. Mayhap, Esau had managed to reassure him. Or mayhap, it was as if the child, at that young age, had realized he had seen the worse and could live through anything after that.

"Momma," he yelled, hurtling his thin, little body against Mary, while she struggled upright from her dead-like slumber.

Yet another word from the boy – Momma. Catriona exchanged a significant glance with Mary.

Esau squatted next to Mary but directed his statement at Catriona and Jethro. "Looks as though we may be here for a while."

She pushed to a sitting position and shoveled her filthy, bloody, stinking hair from her sunburned face. "You mean it is possible, though, we might be permitted to leave at some point?"

"That Chief Atakullakulla – the one with the tattooed clan markings on his chest – he didn't rightly say so. But from what I can tell, his son Dragging Canoe and hisself are in opposing camps. Dragging Canoe, he is fer ripping out the beating heart of every white man twixts here and the coast. His father is sidling. Says that while it would seem better for the red men to die like warriors than to dwindle away by inches, their deaths will in the end be for naught. That the white man will take away their homes, their land, and the red man will be no more."

"What's that mean fer us'uns?" Mary demanded, drawing a worn-out Billy into her lap and cradling his head against her meager chest.

"Means we do what they tell us. I was trussed off to follow their medicine man around the day long."

His walleyes sought out Catriona. "Not much difference far as I make out twixts them and yew Highlanders."

"What?" she asked, knowing that her thoughts must be fuzzy, what with lack of sleep and hunger and all the other deprivations.

"The Aniwaya – the Wolf Clan of hunters and warriors – is the largest of the clans here. From what I can figger, their clans are related by blood through a female ancestor. Women preside as chiefs of their own council."

"Well, yuh can be sure," Mary drawled, "that our fat hostess here is gonna make sure she has first rights to us."

"So what happens now?" Catriona asked of Esau. "Can we be ransomed?" That was the best she could hope for the five of them.

"'Pears our fate hinges not on any kind of councilwoman but on a white man what that they are waiting to show up. Reckon he's got hisself some kind of clout with the Indians . . . and is most likely the scurvy swine behind our capture."

Clout with the Indians? That could only be Jacob. God help

her, maybe she was with child, as he had once questioned, because now, although she had not cried since their seizure and during their days of forced march to the Indian village, not even upon Coowee's death, she wanted to weep her heart out at the possibility her husband would commit such a senseless and heartless reprisal.

Yet, that practical part of her nature begged her emotionally ragged side that reigned now under this duress to hold off judgment. She had not wanted to admit that she had come to hold her husband in some high regard, but, indeed she had – and she desperately needed to believe she was wrong about his being responsible for their captivity.

The next day was more of the same, except instead of exposing her skin to a burning, blistering sun in cornfields, she and Mary were sent with a berry picking party to have their skin pricked and gouged by briars.

And yet another day, they were sent out to gather firewood, the heavy loads which they toted strapped by grapevines to their back. The fat squaw with the facial birthmark took great delight in switching their arms and legs with a three-foot-long hickory stick if they moved too slowly. Jethro had dubbed her 'Mole Woman.'

Ultimately, rage boiled over Catriona's tolerance level. She grabbed the switch from the squaw and, staring her directly in the eye, snapped the switch between her hands.

Mary gasped. "Are yuh crazy, Catriona? Yuh'll git us burnt quicker than yuhr bacon."

Mole Woman's caterpillar-thick brows shoved up her low forehead. Her jaw dropped open and puddled her neck with more rings of fat. Then she grinned, and Catriona knew the squaw was anticipating some kind of awful reprisal once they arrived back at the village.

This was one work day whose end Catriona for once wanted to delay.

Luck appeared to be on her side. The captives were not returned to their mud hovel but were escorted to the council house once again. She could tell something of import was about, because their captors were no longer taunting them or joking among themselves. A curious tension electrified the late afternoon's stagnant air.

Inside, Jethro sat, his head resting in exhaustion on forearms braced on raised knees. When she dropped down beside him, he glanced over at her. Gone was his puppy dog gaze when around her, replaced by the reassuring wink of a young knight who over the last week had run the gauntlet and was proud of his wounds.

Beside him, Esau sat cross-legged with an incredibly dirty Billy, who looked more Indian than white, in his lap. At the sight of his mother, the boy jumped and ran to wrap his broomstick arms around her tattered skirt. As tired as she was, she stooped, scooped him up in her arms, then took a seat next to Esau.

The five of them were not the council house's only occupants. On the far side of the central hearth sat Chef Atakullakulla, Dragging Canoe, a couple of older Indians, perhaps one being Esau's medicine man because of the leather pouch suspended from his thick neck. Also, there were three Tory Rangers, distinguished by their green tunics. . . and a serious faced Barrett.

At once, his eyes fastened on her. He said nothing, just waited as the old chief began to speak in a stentorian voice worthy of the House of Burgesses. All the while, he spoke, she tried to make sense of Barrett's presence. He had told her he was traveling upriver with the Remington's but only as far as the Piedmont. So . . . .

Abruptly Chief Atakullakulla ceased speaking. At that point, Barrett unfurled parallel strings of leather about three yards long, belted at intervals by leather pouches.

"A wampum war belt," Jethro muttered.

The Indians spoke back and forth with one another, then Chief Atakullakulla nodded his head in an emphatic gesture.

At that point, Barrett directed his attention at her. He wore not his usual elegant attire but was garbed like a common backwoodsman. Nevertheless, a hint of his distinctive hauteur edged his words. "I have arranged to ransom you."

She should have felt boundless joy. Her fingers flicked toward her companions. "And them?"

Jethro, Mary and Esau's gazes swerved from him to her and back to him.

"Catriona, I can only bend circumstances to fit my purpose to a point without arousing Atakullakulla's suspicion. I have told him you are my chosen one. That we are affianced."

"I am already married."

"A farce of a marriage. You know this. And I have told Chief Atakullakulla this."

"I canna go. Not without them."

His palm thrust out at Dragging Canoe. "You would prefer to be the second wife of some subhuman brave like this and toil the rest of your life like a squaw?"

"How did ye know we had been taken captive?"

"Or would you prefer your red hair hang as a scalp piece from some brave's lance?"

"Catriona," Mary hissed, "don't be a fool. Do it! Oncet yuhr free, mebbe yuh can – "

She shook her head. "No! Dunna you see? They were just waiting for Barrett. They will kill the rest of – "

Her voice was drowned out by the retorts of musket fire. Simultaneously, her nostrils flared with the odor of something burning. Screams and shouts curdled the hot, humid air.

The Indians shot to their feet. She, Jethro, Esau and Mary stumbled to theirs and, on the heels of the stampeding Indians, cleared the Council House rapidly.

Through the haze of smoke, she saw white men loading and firing their flintlocks and rapidly reloading. Others, brandished their axes much as Highlanders did their claymores. And still others, used the cold steel of their bayonets to impale fleeing Indians.

"The river," Jethro shouted at them. "Head for the river."

Her arm was grabbed, and she looked up to see Barrett's fierce expression. "Come with me," he yelled.

Her gaze swung back to Mary, Esau, and the others, but they had disappeared through the roiling, acrid smoke of burning huts. Then Jethro wrenched free her arm and yanked her with him into the smoke's pall. All around shots pinged and gun smoke plumed and tongues of huts' burning flames flared. She lost sight of the others but spotted here and there fringe-shirted militiamen savagely attacking.

She and Jethro made it just outside the palisaded walls to the bank, gray with eddying smoke. Even here, bedlam prevailed. Somehow in the melee they became separated. Off to her right, Mole Woman, waddling as fast as her fat would allow, halted abruptly and swung toward her. The squaw's sudden grin was clearly one of delight for the opportunity for retaliation.

Fear paralyzed Catriona – like in the occasional nightmare, where she wanted to scream and nothing would come out.

Then, a hurtling hatchet cleaved the squaw's low forehead. She toppled like a stone statue. Catriona gaped. Next, the breath was knocked from her as she was tackled, and all her hope for escape was obliterated.

~ ~ ~ ~ ~ ~ ~

The three canoes shot along the river, glistening with the sun's dying light. Jacob, in the stern of the canoe with an exhaustion-drugged Cat bundled in a rough blanket at his knees, paddled in long, deep strokes, as did the other two Catawba Indians toward the prow. Up ahead, Fergus and Esau put their full weight into paddling two other captives. Behind, paddled Tom Brindle and a pair of North Carolina militiamen with yet another captive.

Oars flashed in and out of the water, spraying sparkling gems. Along the banks, the maple leaves were just beginning to redden with the hint of approaching autumn. The fragrance of azaleas was intensified by the late afternoon heat. A big trout broke water alongside the oars' silvery splash.

The Cherokee, in siding with the English, had forfeited their land. American militia forces numbering 2,400 from North Carolina, Georgia, and Virginia, with the aid of Catawba scouts, had coordinated attacks on thirty-six Cherokee towns, destroying their cornfields and livestock. No other choice had existed, not with the Cherokee at the colonists' back door and the English at their front.

South Carolina had offered a bounty of 50 pounds for each Cherokee scalp and 100 pounds for each Cherokee prisoner. The Georgia Militia had vowed to burn out the Cherokee and indiscriminately kill men, women, and children in retaliation for all the innocent white lives cut short.

And he – well, he had taken savage pleasure in cleaving the skull of the squaw who had been persecuting his Cat.

Any chase Barrett Fairfax would be giving was behind, and ahead awaited the falls with their thirty-foot plunge.

And what awaited, Jacob wondered, him and his wife – the garrulous Cat, with her easy smile that had stopped him in his tracks. The sight of her at the Highlander Games had been like picking up a vestige of a trail he had overlooked since childhood. With an intoxicating force, the sight of her had attacked his senses, insulated from polite society.

The boy, Jacob, had been impressionable, not yet molded by

life's unforgiving laws. Laws that set apart the aristocrat from the uncouth, the gentry from the bastard.

He possessed little of his father's eloquence. Jacob had to make his actions speak for his poverty of words. Yet those actions had only worsened his attempts to woo her. She held it against him for taking her in marriage by so practical and expedient an arrangement. Yet she had no idea the full extent to which he had gone – taking advantage of her clan's plight and adding pressure.

But what do you do when you want something so much? Bank on a leprechaun to provide it? At the Highlander Games, he had known not when next his tar and pitch business might bring him to Campbelton. Had he not reached for what he wanted, any other man in his right mind, or not, might have asked her father for her hand. Barrett Fairfax being foremost.

The fair-haired favorite of Tidewater society was an English agent. Doubtlessly, Fairfax would be lauded back in Tory territory, especially in Campbelton.

The roar of water signaled the falls ahead. In unison, the paddlers thrust their oars hard against the churning current and swung the three canoes toward the concealing reeds and, behind them, the large flat rock covered in lichen. He lifted Catriona from the canoe's hard ribs. Tomorrow, he would doubtlessly hear her venting her annoyance with her freshly bruised body. Bone-weary as he was, he could not but feel pleasure at her satisfying weight.

She stirred in half protest, and he set her on her feet in the glade, where Esau and the other rescued captives were already gathering. She turned unnaturally bright eyes up at him. "Go with the others," he told her. "Rest while you can."

With casual proficiency, he made a swift inspecting circuit of the forest margins, then joined Tom and Fergus, palavering with the Catawba and the militiamen. "A smokeless fire – oak bark and green branches – for what is left of the buffalo carcass," Tom was advising.

"Once we eat, best we strike out afoot as soon as possible," Fergus said. The trader's expression had not veered once from its habitually gruffness, despite burying Coowee's desecrated body days earlier.

They were still in enemy country. Jacob set a militiaman to work on the canoes, sinking them with hatchet holes.

With twilight, the marsh wrens' sweet trills gradually

diminished. While the others ate, he sat with his long rifle balanced across his knees and cleaned it. It was damp from the canoe bottom, and he took care to oil its steel at the lock.

Cat left the huddled others and, wrapped in the dirty blanket, crossed the clearing to join him. In all her disarray, her sunburnt cheeks, her filthy tangled mass of hair, and hands and feet pustuled with insect bites and weeping sores, she had never looked more vibrant to him – as if forged by fire.

"How did ye know where to find us?"

"When Coowee did not return from your lessons, Fergus went looking for her." He blew down the muzzle to make sure it was not clogged by partially burnt powder. "He tracked for a distance your trail – your cap, your hair pins, scraps of clothing. When he realized its destination – the Cherokee town of Coyate – he set out after us."

"Barrett, he planned this, dinnae he – taking me captive?"

"Yes."

"And ye persuaded Caswell's militia to attack Dragging Canoe's village?"

"The attack was already planned. Led by Brigadier General Rutherford. His men probably saw the operation as a potential land grab."

"Yet ye still carried me off."

"You are my wife."

She chewed on her lip. He was expecting her to bring up their argument outside the trading post or his rough treatment of her or Afton Manor's destruction – any number of complaints, but she surprised him.

"Ye will admit that what ye did that first time – at the Highlander Games – was no different than Barrett having me kidnapped two weeks ago? Ye also finagled to take me."

He measured out a charge of powder. "Legally."

"But ye would have taken me, legally or illegally, aye?"

"Yes."

"Then are ye no better than Barrett – in taking me?"

"Is that how you think?" It was obvious to him that she believed Barrett to be the more civilized between them, but surely she could not believe that made Barrett the better man.

"I dunna rightly ken," she groaned.

"You have had time to know."

He could see she was trying to reach her own conclusion. He said nothing, only continued with his priming and reloading.

"Back at Kinsfolk Landing, ye had made no objections to me going with Barrett – ye even suggested an annulment if I wanted one. Yet ye came for me at the Indian village. That makes no sense." She looked down at her clenched hands, as if she could not bring herself to look at him.

He waited for the gabble, that torrent of words, white people felt necessary.

"We are so different. If it were only our political loyalties . . . but that is only a wee part of our differences," she said with a great attempt at reasonableness. She risked glancing up at him. "Look at yeself, sitting there, dog-tired, yet, nevertheless, cleaning your rifle. Ye are fastidious. And I – me maid, Phoebe – she calls me Messy Betsy. Ye are as parsimonious as a Scotsman with your words, while for me . . . well, communication, it is everything."

When he continued to say nothing, she paused, then blurted, "Even now, we canna converse. Ye sit there like that slab of stone. What do ye expect of me?"

That was a fool question. Had she anticipated him to gainsay her? "I expect you to be my wife. In all ways."

Indignation flashed across her countenance, only to be replaced by what would seem a supreme effort at tolerance. She was wanting something more from him, he realized. Those words that had been locked away in his childhood. But he should not have to say them. From his point of view, actions counted for everything. He had studied his conviction, and it bore up well under examination.

Prepared to wait for the next conclusion she drew, he began to stuff the patch with the flint into the muzzle. At that moment, Tom chose to join them. He slid the rifle strap from one sloped shoulder, and hunkered before the fire. "I figger we got two, maybe three hours, afore the injuns pick up our trail."

Jacob only nodded. He could smell the singed wool of Tom's trowsers that came from standing too near the fire, drying himself from the river's flight. Tom turned his attention to the blanket-wrapped Cat. "Heard 'bout the bonfire of Afton Manor."

Beyond exhaustion, she only nodded. "Aye."

"Could'a been worse," Tom continued. "Congress was wanting yur father's neck in a noose. Jacob, here, had the idear of swapping yur father's neck fer Afton Manor. Course, Congress gobbled up the idea of adding the revenue of Afton Manor to their coffers. A shame the rabble had to burn it down. Well, I'll see 'bout setting' up a sentry for the hour's respite."

Jacob knew what was coming and braced for it.

Once Tom took his leave, Cat turned on Jacob eyes blazing as hot and sputtering as the fire. So angry was she, she could barely spit out her furious words. "Ye . . . ye knew all along . . . ye wove your web ye did, like some colossal cunning, spider . . . trapping me . . . arranging to give over to the insurrectionists me home . . . taking it from me, so ye could give it back to me . . . bartering the security of me home . . . for a wife stout of heart and strong of arm . . . and able to bare your bairn!"

He hunkered before the fire, shoving dirt to douse its coals. Cat raged on.

"Well, I will no' bear your bairn, do ye hear me?"

She buried her face in her hands. Her shoulders shook, as with fever, and when she lifted her head, he could see she was shattered. Her features struggled to compose themselves. She looked at him scathingly, then spoke slowly, distinctly, as if addressing that Indian part of him that could not conceive words like culture or refinement. "You rescued me today. I owe you that. I am willing to be your helpmate . . . but not your handmaiden. And only until Christmas, when ye pledged your word you would take me home."

As a child, he had never known the word 'home' much less the one, 'Christmas.' Now he wished he had never heard the words, so empty of meaning.

Heat lightning flickered outside the cabin's open doorway. The night was sultry, not a leaf stirred, and the cabin's silence grated on Catriona's nerves

After being in such intimate contact with the other captives, sleeping and eating under the most confined circumstances, she felt the strain of being alone with Jacob that first night back in their cabin. While she sat near the hearth on the stool and shucked corn for supper, he was priming his Doune pistol. The thud of her kitchen knife, the click of the pistol's hammer, only emphasized the silence between them.

Laying aside the pistol, he crossed to hunker in front of the fireplace and ladle out a chunk of the boiled squirrel he had put on earlier. Out of the corner of her eye, she watched him warily. From the ladle, he plucked the steaming chunk between his thumb and forefinger and, blowing on it, held it up to her lips. "Eat."

She shook her head. "I canna," she whispered. Survival that week of captivity had demanded total focus, but now that she was safe, now that her mind had time to ponder – to collide with the cruelty, the brutality and barbarism she had both witnessed and endured – the mere idea of food was repellent.

"Soon, you will look like Mother McGee."

She frowned, but he nevertheless nudged the chunk between her lips. She thought she would choke, but its savory juices whetted her hunger instead.

He fed her another piece, asking quietly, "Were you bedded

against your will?"

She shook her head once more. "No." She shivered. He was asking if she had been violated by the Indians . . . when she felt violated by him. Then, watching him carefully, she asked, "Would it make a difference if I had been?"

"No."

"Why not?"

"The good – the bad, you are still you."

So much for eloquence.

After a taxing, all-night march, the party under his command had arrived at Kinsfolk Landing two days later, just before sundown. Instead of collapsing on the bed, she had spent a full hour, scrunched in the wooden tub, and had scrubbed herself free of Indian taint. Her resentment against the Indians she could not scrub away.

And, yet, here Jacob hunkered before her, those dark eyes watching her with the Indian's blank gaze. Distant thunder murmured its discontent. "Fairfax will want you again."

"No, t'was not me he wanted . . . he wanted to strike out at ye. Ye wounded his pride once too often."

"He cannot have spent time with you – at Afton Manor – or in this cabin – our cabin – and not want you. But it is not what he wants or what you want. It is what I want. I have lived alone too long. Compromise is not my nature. I will take you back to Campbelton come Christmas. Give you over to your people."

Just as the squirrel meat had whetted her hunger, so too had the mention of Campbelton whetted her longing. She was both hungry and longed for her clan. Her fury over Jacob's scurrilous deceit was spent. There was nothing left within her, nothing left for them. "Aye. Tis for the best. For the both of us. We canna go on hurting one another."

Barrett had his pride, but so did her husband. The gauntlet had been thrown down. Or rather the pallet had been unfurled. She would have to come to him. She would have to leave their marriage bed and join him there on the floor. Lady Catriona would have to be his squaw.

"Your feet need attention," he said, rising from the hearth and heading for their bedchamber. He returned with his leather pouch of herbs and hunkered before her. Without waiting for her assent, he began his ministrations, his long fingers gently but firmly applying the healing unguents. Her eyes closed, and she luxuriated in the relief and pleasure those fingers bestowed. The scene was so reminiscence of that first night in his cabin, eons ago, it seemed, when there had been a future and hope for the two of them.

When he left off, only then did her lids open, and she realized her lashes were damp.

The thunderstorm that had threatened all day finally broke at bedtime. It lashed rain and wind against the cabin Jacob had built for himself and the family he planned. As he took care with everything he planned. From the strength and attention to detail with which he had built the cabin – its doors and windows and chimney – to the finesse with which he had cornered her parents and her into a marriage agreement.

Grudgingly, she admitted she was fiercely attracted to him – the very man to whom she had sold herself in exchange for the security of her home, which now was nothing but burnt wood and charred bricks.

Oh, he was clever and conniving. Right from that first day of the Highland Games he had schemed to have her home threatened with seizure if her family did not take the Oath of Allegiance, all so that he could conveniently – and, yes, heroically – intervene to save the day by bargaining her home for her hand.

How she loathed him at that moment. And loathed herself more for wanting him. But attraction was not enough for a misbegotten relationship forged in deception. There had to be something in common. A lifestyle, a position in life, similar interests, and education. And similar values like honesty and openness and, of course, trust.

With the storm raging about them and the thunder rattling the cabin, she could not sleep. The electrified air smelled like gunpowder . . . and their bed smelled of pleasure and pain.

By habit now, her hand slipped to the edge of the mattress. The rustle of the sheets could in no way be heard above the booming thunder. Not even the brilliant flashes of lightning, shafting above and below the thin aperture between the window frame and shutters, could reveal her sun-blistered hand . . . if she should choose to let her fingers crawl their familiar path.

She did not know which she despised more – his deception or her weakness. Her hand slid over . . . and his hand reached up to welcome it.

~ ~ ~ ~ ~ ~ ~ ~

As if mocking the desolation of Catriona's own marriage, a beaming Mary announced her intentions to wed Esau when next the circuit rider rode through – and she asked Catriona to stand with her. "If it hadn't been for yuh showing up," she said, by way of an oblique compliment, "I would have gone on pining fer Jacob and been blind to the gold in Esau."

Esau had quite naturally asked Jacob to stand with him.

Kinsfolk Landing was not shocked by the news. Since returning from captivity with the Indians, it was evident Mary was sweet on Esau and that in turn he loved the widow to distraction.

Near noon one midsummer day, the Methodist saddlebag preacher rode into Kinsfolk Landing on a plug that looked as if it had surely seen its last hours. The clergyman, as bony as his horse, was dressed in a long, dusty and much brushed and threadbare, black broadcloth coat. His wool trousers were rumpled, and he wore a black cravat that made his wash-yellowed shirt look whiter than it was.

Like ants to a lump of sugar, all the townsfolk turned out for the wedding held on the bluff, its field serendipitously arrayed with summer's wildflowers. That high, the bluff offered a breeze to cool brows normally sweating under the intense summer sunlight.

Billy's grin was as bright as a new dollar. He held Catriona and Jacob's hands. They stood just behind the bride and groom. Mary look quite lovely in the pale pink lutestring gown Catriona had given her to make over. As the preacher began the service, Esau wiped the sweat from his brow with the back of his hand, this despite the cooling breeze.

"Mary Barger," the preacher began, "are you marrying of your own free will?"

Listening to the vows that she and Jacob themselves had made scarcely four months before, Catriona had to wonder if he, too, rued the day they had married.

Once the preacher told Esau he could kiss his bride, the entire wedding party decamped to the trading post to celebrate. The men congregated to one side of the large log building, the women to the other.

What with Catriona having willfully destroyed her dulcimer in a fit of childishness and Esau caught up in the duties of the newly married, the merriment of music was lacking. Of course, the corn liquor was not, and the reception soon progressed into that of a bacchanalia.

Gone was Mother McGee's rheumatism as she tried with much floundering of her feet and cane to dance the jig to an imaginary tune harkening back to her youth.

An unsteady Mick held aloft a jug from which he had been swilling. "What do we say to giving the newlyweds a house-raising?" To which the settlers let loose with drunken cheers of agreement.

Polly and Humphrey took turns interrupting one another as they related tales of their own courtship.

"No flowers," Polly said. "Hump came bearing a pair of chickens in a cage on his first courting."

"Her maw and paw were delighted," Humphrey said, a hectic flush of inebriation suffusing his cheeks.

"But of all the infernal nonsense to court yur girl with," Polly declared and tossed back another draught of the corn liquor.

"What did it take?" Catriona asked, genuinely interested.

Humphrey slid his wife a puckish glance. "I was trying to get my surveyor's license at William and Mary and purloined a copy of *Romeo and Juliet*."

"I had no idea who Romeo and Juliet were," Polly said, her dimples deepening in her plump cheeks. "But the way Hump's eyes glowed when he looked at me twixt readin', well, I was plumb his'n from that moment on."

When Catriona and Jacob finally took their leave, the sun was balanced on the Blue Ridge. Neither she nor he spoke. The deficit of words said everything. She did not want to be querulous. She wanted to be reasonable. She and Jacob had made an unwise bargain in marrying one another. But there was no point in throwing good money after bad. It was that simple.

Not that she could ever forgive him. But they could, at least, live together these next few months like two civilized people.

Not that he was civilized

As they reached their cabin, he said, "Go inside. Stay there." His tone, totally devoid of inflection, nevertheless brooked no rebuttal.

Still, she watched suspiciously from the doorway. With long rifle ready, he circled the cabin, slowly and carefully and stealthily. Further out, he prowled the area with the exceptional grace and strength of a ballet. His head – and eyes, she knew from experience – swiveled continuously from top to bottom and left to right. Gradually, his circles of inspection expanded to encompass the trees in front and the fields behind.

A cowardly shiver rippled up and down her spine. Goose bumps prickled her flesh. These days, the fear of a reprisal by Dragging Canoe, who she learned had escaped, was ever present, expending an inordinate amount of her thoughts.

Then she heard the thunderous roar, that of an enraged animal. She waited for the retort of Jacob's rifle. None came. Had he been caught by surprise? No, not Jacob. A misfire then?

She reeled back inside, reached over the door for the fowling piece Fergus had provided for her.

Horsing around with her brothers, she had fired a musket maybe three or four times. And she had taken a few practice shots while Jacob had been away – firing at an old tin plate she had set up atop the log pile and missing each time. But now was too late to worry about her marksman skills.

Shotgun in hand, she sprinted around the back of the cabin. Beyond where the barley field met with the forest, came the rumbling, furious growl of what had to be a bear. She ran through the rows of clumpy plants and headed for the bank of trees. Her chest labored with her panted breathing.

She was guided by the rustling of underbrush and snarls. She nearly collided with Jacob. Tomahawk now in his right hand, he was warily circling a huge black bear. Parallel strips ripped Jacob's bloodied smock at shoulder level. His rifle, its muzzle bent at a deep angle, lay near one tree. A bleeding Red Rover was sprawled some yards farther.

At her appearance, the mammoth, seven feet tall or more on its rear legs, claws as long as a man's fingers, swiveled towards her. "Stay behind me," Jacob warned quietly.

For Jacob to try to use his flintlock pistol, she knew, would be a death wish. Instead, without stepping back, he rotated and threw his entire body into the swinging of his tomahawk. Its glittering blade hurtled through the air and buried itself into the bear's head.

It dropped onto all fours and charged forward with a roar of rage. Jacob pushed her aside and lightly sidestepped the oncoming bear. The tomahawk still buried in its skull, the bear swerved back toward them – then abruptly collapsed.

One moccasined foot anchoring the bear's head, Jacob yanked the tomahawk free. He turned to her, his face a blank page. "I told you to stay inside the cabin."

She would have shot him point blank then and there, except she realized belatedly she had forgotten to prime the fowling piece.

~ ~ ~ ~ ~ ~ ~

Summer's eye-blinding green foliage faded into late summer's drab shades, but Jacob's desire for his wife, rather than fading, intensified.

Two or three times a week, Cat would show up at the resin distillery. While his father may have founded Kinsfolk Landing, he himself had established the distillery, which provided for jobs and ensured Kinsfolk Landing as a permanent settlement. Permanency. That, the permanency of Kinsfolk Landing, was his keystone.

During her visits, undertaken with a resolute detachment, he would explain yet another facet of the distillery's operations. Afterwards she would closet herself with Fergus and the account books. If her quill's slashes and additions and subtractions were any indication, the books were in alarming disorder. To her credit, as the weeks passed, out of chaos she created order.

Not so did she prevail with their personal lives. Each evening, after a usually botched supper indifferently prepared by her, she would read aloud from one of the books ordered by his father, while he – seemingly indifferently – honed his axe or knife, tended the fire, or primed the long rifle he had obtained at the trading post. Sometimes – seemingly indifferently – he would pause near the table and look over her shoulder, as she pointed out each word with her tapered finger.

He would smell the sweet lavender fragrance of her hair and steal a glance at her plump lips, and he would have to fight down the urge of the white man's way to explain, to inveigle, to seduce her with words into his bed. But if his wife did not understand without words, what good was she? Given her imaginative inclination, he had thought she understood this.

But then her words were the way she spun her own web of entrapment.

He examined his decision to return her to her clan. Yes, it was the only way. There she could compare. She needed to know what she wanted.

If it was Fairfax she wanted, his name never passed her lips. Word along the river was that he headed up an irregular unit of Tories and Cherokee who sallied forth from forests and swamps to attack outlying forts and settlements along the Appalachians.

The town hall summons at the trading post that evening appeared to confirm Jacob's gut feeling that his time with Cat was short, indeed.

Important information from one backwoods county to another was transmitted by an express messenger on horseback who braved the corduroyed roads made by laying small trees over muddy paths. A weary post rider had arrived with his letter bag earlier that day. He delivered the news that the Fifth Provincial Congress would be meeting in New Bern in November to approve the first state constitution from among all the colonies.

At the trading post, both pipe smoke and vocal opinions were thick. Maybe thirty or forty men were gathered amid barrels of pitch, stacked coils of rope, mounds of furs, and racks of spars and oars.

Jacob listened from the back of the trading post, near the fireplace, where Coowee had once hovered in service to others. Fergus's gargoyle expression never betrayed any heartbreak he might be suffering. Jacob knew better. Behind the counter, the whiskey keg's spigot lately produced but drops when turned.

As Humphrey was the only man in Kinsfolk Landing with a higher education, he had taken the honors of reading aloud the proclamation delivered by the post rider. When finished, he removed his spectacles and grumbled, "What with the last lickin' our chickenfeed of a national navy took, it's high time New Bern either pissed or got off the pot."

"Now wait just a gol-durned minute," Mick said, "I hear tell New Bern's privateers have been harassing British and Loyalist ships along our Carolina waterways."

"Still, for all our friggin' efforts," Esau interjected, "our raids are more like mosquitos attacking a cow that just flicks its tail at the annoyance. Not that much prize money, according to this here report, is filtering through to our admiralty courts."

"Speakin' of friggin'," Humphrey grinned, "how's the married life, Esau?"

"Hear! Hear!" young Jethro said, elbowing in the ribs the blushing cooper. Other bawdy comments rang out, but Esau only smiled good naturedly.

Fergus pounded a meat mallet on the counter to demand order. "Let's git this politicking business over with."

Discussion over New Bern's summons to appoint a burgess member from the county was resumed. Jacob remained silent while opinions peppered the air. To take sides meant delivering one's allegiance to another. As far as he could determine, people were people, regardless of sides they took.

Maybe that was why he had sought out the fringe of society, taking no sides, except when it served his purpose, like interpreting and scouting for the patriots, for which his services had paid for a marriage bed . . . or throwing his lot in with the patriot militia's attack on the Cherokee – for the sole purpose of reclaiming what was his, his wife.

Mornings, he took delight in watching her stir awake slowly, one arm invariably resting above her head on the pillow. Watching the quiet, steady rise and fall of the slope of her pale breasts above the nightrail. Imagining the small, pink buttons that were her nipples. Listening to her soft indrawn breaths. Smelling her warm, womanly scent in the downy hair that tufted her armpit.

But he would arise just before she became completely conscious of him – and conscious of how much he wanted her. The extent of his wanting was dangerous, a weakness he could ill afford.

She had won Billy's and Red Rover's trust and had earned the respect of Kinsfolk Landing settlers, but abstractions such as those were not enough to hold her rooted in the backcountry. Not when her own roots called her home.

"North Carolina Tories are undermining patriot economy, they are," growled Robert Cameron, between picking his teeth with his thumbnail. "They are printing counterfeit North Carolina notes – even included New Bern's bloody guv'ner's mansion on it."

Fergus's mallet pounded the counter again. "Floor is hereby open for nominations for a burgess to represent our county at the General Assembly at New Bern."

Naturally, the educated Humphrey MacGregor would make a most suitable burgess member. At this point, having heard all the post rider's news, Jacob grabbed his long rifle, propped beside him on the log wall – only to hear his name called aloud.

He, a nominee as a burgess? He, the laconic backwoodsman who could barely read or write, to circulate among the most learned and eloquent statesmen of the Tidewater gentry? He almost laughed aloud. He shook his head. "No."

That one emphatically spoken word and his fierce expression declared his intention.

He strode on toward the door, shouldering his way through the press of men. He reached for the door, only to hear his name called forth again, then taken up in a chant.

"Jacob Dare. Jacob Dare. Jacob Dare."

~ ~ ~ ~ ~ ~ ~ ~

Jacob Dare.

How despicable and devious the backwoodsman was — waiting, as he had, like a fox with patient cunning, for her and her parents, his prey, to take the bait.

But she was worse – weak with her betraying want of him. Day and night. Hourly.

How knackered their lives together were.

Beneath a starlit firmament and full pumpkin-colored moon, both Catriona and Red Rover, healing from its bout with the bear, awaited on the porch Jacob's return from the town hall meeting. Beyond the yard, the avenue of maples blazed a vivid orange, as if to challenge the brilliant moon.

She could smell autumn in the frosty air and gathered her red plaid more securely around her fine lawn and lace nightrail. The smell of drifting wood smoke contented her. Her cold toes lapped over one another. Both the murmur of the river beyond the bluff and the slushing of the falls of Hollering Woman creek near the forest behind the cabin filtered through the trees, beckoning her, by either route, downriver to home.

What news had the post rider brought of civilized society? Time had distorted her memory of its glittering balls and populated coffee houses and crowded river walk strolls. She wanted desperately to attend the town hall meeting rather than wait for its news to be brought to her by a man who could distil its flavorful facts to a few sparing words.

Only the prickling of the mountain cat's ears warned her that something was astir. Her heart beat doubled. "What is it, Red Rover?" she whispered.

When no growling followed, only the beat of is tail on the rough puncheon, she knew that Jacob must be drawing near – so near that she had to wonder how she had failed to notice his presence. One hand braced on the cedar post at the porch's far end, the other hooking his rifle in the crook of his elbow, he was observing her.

She let out her swiftly inhaled gasp. "How long have you been there?"

"Long enough to watch you twist round about the horsehair wedding ring on your finger."

With that lithe, easy grace, he padded toward her as soundlessly as the mountain cat would. Red Rover rose to lick his hand, then settled back onto all fours as Jacob dropped down on its opposite side. He reached to tunnel his accomplished fingers through its thick fur, and the cat purred low.

As her body treacherously nigh did when he but touched her – those long fingers grazing hers when she passed him the water jug he requested or when he handed her the hairbrush she had nervously dropped. But never to hold again her hand at night. She could never forgive him for duping her. She was quite sure that once she was back in Campbelton, she would forget this intense want of him. The excitement she felt when with him would pale.

As if reading her mind, he said, "The day after tomorrow, we are leaving Kinsfolk Landing."

With an effort, she moved her gaze from his kneading fingers to his chiseled profile. His inky hair was drawn back at the temples into a braid that mingled with the rest of his chest-length hair. "Where are we going?"

"To New Bern."

"New Bern?" She frowned. Why?"

"I have been elected to represent our county at the first General Assembly of the State of North Carolina."

Her fist went to her heart. Courtesy required she should congratulate him on the prestigious election. Joy about their leave-taking should have prompted her to hug him. But to show either was a weakness, and this was a man who could not possibly understand weakness. "That's presumptuous, isn't it – that ye will prevail against England's dictums?"

He shrugged, his dark eyes both quick with perception and coldly inscrutable. He smiled consolingly. "It is sometimes the case that the small, pesky gnat unseats the mighty rider from his horse."

She affected a shrug and reached out to stroke Red Rover. Her fingertips touched those of Jacob's. Neither she nor he moved. She fought to control her uneven breath. "Then, ye can drop me off downriver at Cross Creek landing on your way to New Bern."

"Afraid not. We are going by way of a well-traveled game path. It cuts diagonally from here across North Carolina to New Bern. Cross Creek – and Campbelton will be bypassed."

"But . . . but ye said . . . ye promised that – "

"Aye, by Christmas." He rose to his towering height and stared down at her with a sober expression. "The legislature should end the 16th of December. The following week I shall return you to your clan."

Farewells were difficult for Catriona, and so she packed, pretending she was leaving Kinsfolk Landing for six weeks instead of a lifetime. At least, Fergus and Jethro were also to accompany them. As Jacob hefted her camelback trunk, he paused, listening. The cabin door was closed, yet he said, "They are here."

Outside, dawn's chilly and misty light disclosed not only Fergus and Jethro but also Kinsfolk Landing settlers, gathered to send off her and Jacob. At the sight of the couple in the doorway, cowbells began to be rung and pots pounded. Whistles and shouts and cheers went up. She saw the smiling faces of Mary and Esau with Billy on his shoulders, Polly and Humphrey, Mick, Mother McGee, waving her cane, the blockhouse Robert Cameron, and so many others.

Catriona had to blink fast. Her throat ached. Jacob could only nod. In this far, barbaric country, where she had confronted disasters and death, she had also found friends whose loyalty and warmth equaled those of her friends back home.

There it was again . . . that word home. Her home no longer existed, neither here at Kinsfolk Landing nor at Campbelton.

If one considered water a factor, the journey back to Tidewater's civilization was much the same as the one made six months earlier away from civilization. Unlike the foamy waters of the Cape Fear, the water was in the form of a drizzle at the outset of their pilgrimage – and for her, that was what it was, a holy journey back to her roots.

Initially, Jacob's horse trotted along the broad, beaten and now muddy Buffalo Trace, while she sat huddled within her hooded traveling cloak in the wagon, with Jethro at the reins. The wagon freighted not only her trunk but also barrels of pitch. Fergus's four pack horses, loaded with axes, shovels, and sparse camp equipment, followed. Jacob was too practical of a businessman not to take advantage of the trip back East.

The landscape gradually altered, and all too often Hobby, in the lead, had to pick its way through mushy bogs, where cane grew twenty feet high, and up rain-slicked ridges. The rain swept on through, and after that the days of travel were mostly wreathed in a mild autumn haze. The hardwood forest was spectacular with its changing colors

The night before the anticipated arrival, some dozen miles outside the Swiss-settled New Bern, Jacob called a halt for reparations at a countryside tavern. Hot water for a bath, warm ale, and cold chicken were ordered from the tavern's kitchen.

Nervously, she stood by the small room's bed, as he threw some sticks on the coal and ashes in the tiny fireplace. Taking up a candle, he relit it in the steadily growing flames. Between the firelight and the candlelight, he was a shimmering apparition, the wulver that beckoned one to follow him into the deep, dark woods.

Uneasiness mottled her heart like a bad rash would her skin. She was straining away from him and yet toward him. All too easy it would be to succumb to her debilitating attraction to her husband. But, please God, not when her home, her family, were so close, a mere six weeks and a hundred miles or so.

"Fear not, Wife." With no candleholder readily available, he dribbled the wax onto the table and anchored the candle stub to it. "After I pay the tavern bill, I shall sleep in the stables with Jethro and Fergus."

"Nae." Incredibly, she heard herself saying, "I would be contented if ye would stay the night in the room." She was confronted with the unhappy knowledge that it would be their last night together before re-entering the society where she belonged and he was excluded.

Her innate fair-mindedness resented that society could base a man's worth on his education alone, and she worried for her unsophisticated husband, worried how he would fare in the murky and tricky business of New Bern politics. But then, she reminded herself, he was a master of trickery.

At that moment, a Negro boy entered, toting a wooden bucket in each hand. Bobbing his kinky head in greeting, he emptied the steaming water into the wood-rimmed, copper hip tub, then scurried from the room.

Once again, she and Jacob were left alone. They stared at each other. It was as if they were the only two people left in the world.

He circled behind her to remove her dusty traveling cloak from her shoulders. His warm fingers grazed her skin, and she shivered. Not from the delicious feeling his touch imparted, but with the sudden and stark realization of what she had been avoiding acknowledging. Immediately trailing that realization came fear, the fear of blurting those words of love, which over the months had been creeping toward her consciousness stealthily.

She simply could not let herself do this, not when she was so damnably susceptible to his magnetism. A magnetism composed of both dangerous charm and beguiling subterfuge. He had never been the simplistic rustic for which she had taken him. She twisted around to confront him and backed away a step. "I can bathe on me own."

In the candle-lit room his dark features were saturnine. His voice was akin to Red Rover's low, growling purr. "Humor this simpleton if you will."

Too easily, he loosed the eyelets at the back of her gown, sliding it from her shoulders to puddle around her feet. Next he unlaced her stays. Then his deft fingers slid off her chemise. It was not her imagination that his fingers lingered in a stroking fashion along her upper arms.

Only then, turning her to face him, did he address the matter of her drawers. She looked up into his eyes as he unknotted their drawstring. She could have pushed away those dusky fingers, but something deep and treacherous within her wanted to yield this final time to his domination of her.

Arms crossed almost maidenly at her chest and the apex of her limbs, she stood before him, trying to hide her inner trembling. Then, chin lifted, she dropped her arms and bared her body. Bare her soul, she could not. And never would she say those words that made her vulnerable to him.

His gaze slowly perused her, as if to commit her to memory, from her flaming red hair at her head to the thatch at her thighs. "Your bravery was what I first saw. Before your beauty."

"At the Highland Games," she acknowledged wearily. What good would it do to drum up that memory now?

"No." He scooped her in his arms and lowered her into the tub's warm, welcoming water.

She sighed as it lapped at her muscles' kinks and her skin's accumulation of trail dust and wood smoke. Knees jammed to her chest, she reclined her head on the tub's rim. This was nigh as close to heaven as she would ever come. "Then where?" she murmured, peering up at him from between lids that had drifted half closed.

"I saw you once afore," he said, stripping off his travel stained leather tunic. The candlelight glowed on his bronzed chest and arm muscles and blue-black hair. "Years afore the Highland Games even."

She blinked. "Where?"

"At Cross Creek. My father had brought me with him to claim the books he had ordered for me."

He circled behind her, and she tried to twist in the tub's narrow confines to look up at him. "Ye remembered me from that long ago?"

He knelt and wet a scrap of cloth from the ladle of gelatinous brown soap. "You are not one to overlook. Not even then."

The cloth lathed first her face, gently scrubbing the inner and outer rims of her ears, her throat, and her nape. She could feel his steady breath on her shoulders. "I watched you cross the high falls on a fallen timber." His hand gently lifted first one arm, then the other and washed the tufts of her armpits. "Your arms were flung wide for balance. Or to embrace life, I was not sure which."

"I had forgotten that. I couldna been more than seven or so." She half smiled to herself, recalling how perilously high the roaring falls had seemed to her. "I had been pretending I was a pirate."

He discarded the cloth and attacked her scalp, sudsing it clean with his strong fingers and leaving her body limp with the exquisite sensations. "Your friends hung back, afraid."

So, that was the vivid memory that had plagued her all these years of someone watching, someone's intense regard. "The Indian boy. That was ye?" The cloth fixated on her aching breasts, below them, and then most lingeringly rubbing at their centers. At the pleasurable feeling, her lids drifted half closed.

"Yes. The Indian boy." He skimmed the wet cloth down across her stomach and her navel, stopping short.

Next, he shifted his position to hunker at the end of the tub and focused his attention on her feet. "The Indian boy had seen once a flock of cardinals. It was winter. They had winged upon a tree's bare branches. Completely covered them. It was a spectacular sight against the snow. Their red crests were bobbing and they were flexing their wings. They turned the tree into a blinding red jewel."

He rubbed the cloth along her calves and then up her thighs. When, at last, his hand nudged them apart enough to lavish attention at their apex, she thought she would splinter.

"When I saw you at the falls, I knew I wanted that jewel."

Her lids flared. Stunned by this, she could only stare at him, as he used the cloth to caress her folds. "I remember feeling . . . feeling ye watching me," she murmured in a breathless raspy voice. "The feeling had goaded me doubting spirit to . . . walk the plank." To her abject disappointment, once she had reached the safety of the far bank and turned to search out the tall, mahogany-skinned youth, he had vanished.

Two of his fingers, enfolded in the cloth, dipped inside her. As they continued their gentle kneading, she could feel pressure from within building, as if to blow apart her body, much like as a child she had blown apart dandelions.

She tried to hold on to lucidity. She would *not* surrender. Struggling to surface in her pleasure-drugged mind was the conviction of self-determination she had so strongly voiced at Moll King's Coffee House . . . but . . . could she be wrong? Did it have to be either self-determination or surrender? Could it not be the choice to yield . . . to merely take a new position.

At this novel thought, she tried literally, physically, to take a new position, to stand – to move beyond the reach of his inducement. The decision must be hers. Made when clear headed, not when under Jacob's beguilement. But she was trapped, squeezed into the small hip tub as tightly as a bullet in its chamber.

At her flailing, he actually chuckled.

"Ye are intolerable," she fumed.

Somehow, and she was not sure of how exactly he pried her loose so easily, but he lifted her from the tub and, cradling her, crossed the now wet plank floor. His body joined hers on the tavern's rawhide bed with its coarse muslin bedsheets. Her arms wrapped around his neck to hold him, and her thighs spread to welcome him. Already hard, he thrust easily inside her.

Hands braced on his muscle-rigid forearms, she looked up into the dark blue pools of his eyes. "I shall never forget ye, Jacob Dare."

"I mean to make certain of that." His mouth took hers captive. At the same time, he hips thrust against hers. A steady, rhythmic stroking that gradually accelerated until she thought she could not sustain the building sensation another moment longer. It happened to her. Skyrockets flaring and cannons firing and her body blasting into violent shuddering spams.

At last, drenched with sweat, he pumped into her his life force. He bellowed with his culmination, before his weight collapsed upon her. For silent moments, they lay entwined, their hearts pounding in synchronicity. When she found her breath, she murmured into his ear, "But neither can I ever forgive ye."

Then came his confident, whispered retort. "Know this, Cat. If I learn I have gotten you with child, I will find you, no matter where you flee, no matter how long it takes. Even if it takes years."

~ ~ ~ ~ ~ ~ ~

Although the modest, raked-roofed bungalow house Jacob had rented, identical to the other houses fronting Pollock Street, was nothing like Afton Manor had been, it was, however, made of brick, which elevated it above Dare Plantation. With double-hung sashes and sunny, big-windowed rooms, it also had two bedrooms. A full-width veranda fronted it, and a brick scullery squatted amid the herb and vegetable gardens out behind it.

Best, its floor was of maple.

The New Bern house was roughly bounded by the Neuse and Trent Rivers and on the south side by the First Presbyterian Church. She had not realized how much she had missed a church's weekly services and a city's social gatherings, but the latter she would avoid. Her Tory leanings could not but bring discord.

While residing in the state capital, Fergus was to ply the distillery and trading post business. Jethro was to serve as steward, driver, and footman and was to accompany Catriona on errands. These outings she forestalled until long after Jacob left their bedchamber for his daily General Assembly meetings at Tyron Palace. Already, North Carolina had become the first state to vote for independence.

What was there not to like about the unique charm of the

colony's capital? Nae, the state's capital now. North Carolina's largest city was wealthy through plantation agriculture servicing the Triangle Trade with the Caribbean and New England. The trade consisted of slaves, sugar, and other desired goods and infused the town with a rich cultural life.

New Bern's waterfront market offered its colorful and flavorful home-grown crops, its vast array of tantalizing foreign spices and imported linens and laces, and its dispirited indentured servants and slaves.

A recent acquaintance of Catriona's – the lovely, young married Félicité Newell – accompanied her through the market that morning. They had met at First Presbyterian Church, which her husband faithfully attended. Jethro dutifully trailed behind and eyed the saucy Frenchwoman with obvious youthful lust.

A brunette from Bordeaux, she had classic features, and high on her cheek rode a black beauty patch. Her much older husband, a silk merchant and delegate from Raleigh, was not in the best of health. "*Mais bien sur*, your damp and chilly air here, bad eet ees for Oliver's bouts of ague." The salty sea breeze with its briny tang ruffled the tendrils not sleeked beneath Lady Félicité's bergére bonnet.

"Try Peruvian Bark," Catriona offered, vaguely recalling Mother McGee 's mention of it. "The market may have it."

Félicité regarded her fondly. "*Votre homme*, he is *très* . . uh, virile, that ees the word?"

Catriona, who was only passable in French, had to smile. She liked Félicité's champagne-bubbling, utterly capricious manner. "Aye, I think the females of New Bern would say that be the right word to describe me husband."

Félicité led them into the shelter of the slave market hall, a yellow-painted open air building surmounted by a Town Hall and belfry. "If only," the petite beauty said, idly examining the genitals of a short Negro male, "*mon homme* was made *comme ça*." She sighed, "*Mais, non. Davantage comme ça*." She held up her little finger and wiggled it suggestively.

Even Jacob, who understood no French, could translate her gesture of genital comparison. Catriona did not know whether to be shocked more by the young woman's description of her husband or her blatant handling of the slave, one of maybe fifteen or twenty men and women offered for sale that morning.

Turning from the Negro with an indifferent shrug, Félicité cast a surreptitious glance at Jethro and asked of Catriona. "Your young *homme – sa servitude, Il est à vendre?*"

"No," she laughed, handing Jethro the wicker basket of produce she had purchased and keeping the nosegay for herself. "Jethro's papers are not for sale."

He grinned proudly. "I be a free man, Lady Félicité."

"*Hélas!*" she dimpled, "or buy you I would."

Later, as he shepherded Catriona back to the Pollock Street house, she asked, "What do you know of Lady Félicité?" In the short three weeks since their arrival at New Bern, Jethro, with his affable nature, had managed to make friends with everyone in the area, from the minister's milk maid to the pub's barkeeper.

His mouth twitched amiably. "'Tis said she has tumbled every New Bern male twixt sixteen and sixty. Sadly, I cannot attest to that rumor."

She delivered a wan smile. "Give yeself another year, and I would wager the same will be said of yourself and every female twixt sixteen and sixty."

He slid her a sidewise smirk and teased. "Would that include yourself?"

She shook her head in mock despair, then chuckled. "Ye are far too young for me tastes, Jethro Smythe." And immature. But the experiences they had shared in captivity had drawn them closer, creating a bond of sincere friendship.

That evening, Fergus and Jacob, with a sheath of papers tucked under one arm, returned to the Pollock Street quarters. He tossed Jethro his tricorne and buff linen jacket, both of which he had once stored in his chest of drawers. Could what she had suspected was his vision of becoming something more than a blanket Indian have foreseen such a day when he would be a representative of an infant nation?

His weary gaze found her, placing the drooping nosegay in a small china vase on the mahogany table's center. She had already laid the table for the four of them. He arched a brow at the flowers that had somehow gotten crushed when she had unloaded her basket of squash, corn cobs, and apples.

She shrugged and crimped her mouth apologetically. They might share the same bedroom here at New Bern, but they did not share the same bed. Falling back on his upbringing, Jacob once more slept on the floor.

But these days, with her return to her way of life, it was as if she were grounded again, and her hand no longer need seek out the comfort of his in the night. Aye, she could do this – see this through to the bloody final farewell

Rolling the sleeves of his fine lawn shirt to his forearms, he aligned the five heavily noted vellum sheets alongside each other on the sideboard. Peeking over his shoulder, she saw that the sheets were one of the drafts of the state's Declaration of Rights.

He braced his palms at either side of the layout of pages to study them. And from behind she studied him – his long black clubbed hair contrasting with the white of his shirt, his broad shoulders emphasizing the tapering of his wide back to conjunct with the tightly muscled buttocks.

"Each day, I listen to lengthy speeches," he muttered. "Flurries of words. Mouthing sounds. After three weeks, I find their sum is condensed to these five pages. Pages with black markings I can only begin to interpret."

"Hhmmph," Fergus grunted, liberally pouring a pint of bitters from the sideboard's jug, "not even an Oxford College graduate can decipher that rot."

"I need you to interpret this scribbling, Wife." His long hand swept the width of the aligned pages. "I need to decide for myself if we are doing the best for all of us."

So, it was back to 'Wife' rather than 'Cat'? "Us? Meaning the political handshakers and backslappers at Tryon Palace? Your people? Me people?"

"I mean for every person on this continent," he snapped. The meetings were lasting late into the nights. His eyes, red-rimmed from both strain in reading and lack of sleep, indicated his renowned patience was wearing thin.

"Time me and Jethro watered the garden outback," muttered Fergus, latching onto the younger man's elbow and propelling him toward the rear door.

Jethro looked over his shoulder at her, but she nodded that all was right.

After the two retreated through the door, she turned back to Jacob. "Verra well, I shall clarify the words ye dunna understand, but do understand this – I can never side completely with ye."

"I do not want you to side with me. I want you to explain these words."

Drawing a breath, she clarified the ones he pointed out – words like immunities, emolument, and accoutered.

But with her head pressed near his, inhaling his male scent, weakened by the mere sight of his muscle-striated forearms, lightly flecked with his dark hair, and impressed by his perseverance and passion, she was no longer clear of her own allegiances.

What of loyalties? What of deceptions and broken promises? Was blood, truly, thicker than water? This unquenchable want of him distorted her perceptions.

Jacob shook his head in perplexity. His black brows met over his bladed nose. "It would seem simple words could be applied. Words like protections. Rewards and – "

Jethro burst through the doorway. He skidded to a halt and plowed a soot-blackened hand through his lanky blond locks. "Uhhh, smoke – 'tis billowing from the kitchen."

With a sickening feeling in her stomach, she wheeled through the door and down the hall to the kitchen. Fergus was furiously dousing the flames with flour from the keg. The awful stench she recognized at once – the eggs she had been hard boiling. The other burnt odor – it had to be the duck she had been roasting.

"Ye have heard of Félicité's Flaming Duck recipe?" she suggested in a small voice thick with her burr and accompanied by a bright smile.

~ ~ ~ ~ ~ ~ ~

During the month-long legislature session, Catriona had been able to forestall any teas, dinners, or state affairs. reasoning with Jacob that, as a Highlander loyalist, her presence would make for a most uncomfortable event. But the governor was hosting a ball to capitalize on the end of the legislation, ten days away, and attendance was obligatory.

The Assembly Ball would be the highlight of Catriona's social life since marriage. She could cry off with the typical female complaint that she had nothing to wear, which was quite nearly the truth. She had given Mary her last fashionable gown. Now, all she had left were her plaid, the three well-worn day dresses – and the gold hairpin.

Since in a mere fortnight, a couple of days or so after the Assembly Ball, Jacob would be returning her home, she no longer had concern about need-be flight.

She weighed the gold hairpin in her palm. With its rising value against the sinking Continental currency, she could use it to purchase not just a gown for the Assembly Ball but an entire new wardrobe should she so desire . . . or she could use it to purchase something far better.

With Jethro accompanying her, she once again entered the vast Market House. The mid-morning was chilly. The colors of autumn's harvest ran riot in the stalls. The place was loud with the piping of parakeets and squeal of pigs and merchants bargaining. A bootblack boy sang in a patois she did not recognize as he rapidly polished a tradesman's boot.

Among the usual wares being sold, but off to one section, were grouped the slaves and indentured servants. Of the latter, only three women's servitude papers were for sale that day – one a sturdy farm girl from Ireland, the other a middle-aged washwoman whose master was in debt and thereby selling her papers.

But it was the intelligent eyes of the third, an underfed and unkempt lass of maybe sixteen or seventeen, who instantly garnered Catriona's attention. Blessed with an abundance of freckles and unkempt auburn locks, she hostilely stared down her prospective buyers.

"Why are the girl's papers being sold?" Catriona asked of the agent. Agents were known to scour both the European and Continental ports, taverns, and countryside to sign on workers as indentures.

The hefty man peered through his spectacles as he flipped through the girl's deed of trust and accompanying papers. "Murdered her stepmother, she did."

Catriona glanced at the girl, whose heart-shaped chin had shot up. Indenture was often an alternative to the death penalty. "What was the sentence reduced to?"

"Seven years."

She walked back the few steps to the girl, wearing a cheap but sturdy red, short hooded cloak. This very well could have been she had she not been so fortunate to have a loving, prosperous family. "Can ye read and write and cipher?"

"Aye." The brown saucer-wide eyes regarded her hopefully. What redeeming quality she apparently saw in Catriona was unimaginable. For all the girl knew, Catriona thought, she might very well be a harsh task mistress, as devilishly resourceful at tormenting as Mole Woman had been. "Pa's a Quaker missionary in Kentucky."

Catriona heard the faintest hint of an English accent and her attention was riveted now. "Ye are from England?"

"No, but me mum was. Ran away to the colonies with Pa when her father threatened to see him swing at Newgate. Lord Sheriff, her father was."

Lord Sheriff? Catriona grinned. Gentry. This was too good to be true. "Can ye spin and cook?"

"Won more than my share of spinning bees. And been cooking I 'ave since I could stand on a stool – leastwise, I 'ave been until pa up and married again. 'aven't been cooking and spinning since they arrested me, leastwise. But if thou dost buy me, I could cook mighty fine meals for thee and thine."

Catriona hesitated. Tucked away in her skirt's pocket was the gold hairpin. Her fingers rubbed it, taking comfort in its reassuring warmth. Could she bring herself to give up that precious and sentimental heirloom?

But, worse, could she bear this heartache that demanded the unselfish act of giving over her place to another better fit than she? She, who had been cherished and outrageously indulged by her parents and brothers and loved ones – well, discounting irascible Phoebe, who tried, most of the time unsuccessfully, to make her toe the mark.

But did love demand that great of sacrifice, the supreme act of love – wanting what was best for the other, despite one's own vital interest? Was that the act of good judgement, which she so valued?

She glanced at Jethro, seeking his opinion of the prospective purchase. He shrugged. Doubtless, his preoccupation was still caught up with the fair Félicité rather than this wretched looking piece of humanity standing before them.

"Splendid," Catriona told the agent.

'Splendid' was not Jacob's opinion that night. "What? We need a servant for what?"

She planted her hands on her hips. They confronted each other in their bedchamber, she in her nightrail, he still dressed, having returned late yet again from the session. The sessions were running longer in an effort to wrap up loose ends by the December 16th date.

"The girl – Abigail – can read and write. She can do your future chores, like cooking and sewing. Far better than I have." And Abigail had the mettle required by harsh life on the stringent frontier.

"I cannot afford her papers, Cat."

He had yet to see the girl. Catriona had ordered a scouring bath for her and then sent her to bed down on a rope-slung cot in the scullery out back. "I paid for her under a Deed of Trust sale with me gold hairpin."

A soft knock on the door interrupted them. He reached to yank open the door.

Abigail – a sparkling clean and glowing Abigail with an eager smile on her freckled face – stood there, holding a tray with cups. "'eard your late arrival and thought to meself thou and the Mistress would like a hot butter rum toddy to warm thee before bedtime."

He glanced at Catriona and raked a quizzing brow. She was as surprised as he by the voluntarily rendered service but only said, "Jacob, this is Abigail."

"Thank you, Abigail," he said, dismissing her and, taking the tray, placed it on the bureau. Once the door was closed, his dark eyes studied her solemnly. "So, this is the handmaiden to replace you?"

"'Tis me Christmas gift.," she snapped. "Ye will need help . . . once I am gone." No need to tell her husband the girl was a convicted murderess.

Somehow, the good Catriona meant to do had gotten all twisted around. Of all that had happened since setting eyes on Jacob Dare, the worst was the realization of her many inadequacies. Her feckless determination to have her way now exposed her terrifying helplessness – she, who had prided herself on her independence.

They stared across the width of the bed at each other. Her expression, one of frustration. His, of enduring reserve. "I needed no help before I took you as my wife. I need none now. Or in the future."

"Canna ye see? As a Tory wife, I am a handicap." She turned to pick up one of the tray's cups and offered it to him. She was watching carefully his expression. "And 'tis best ye attend the Assembly Ball alone."

Waving off her proffered cup, he gave her an attentive look. Then, he began to unknot his conservative cravat that lacked lace or ruffles. "The opinions of others matter not one whit to me. But if I attend, you shall be at my side. By North Carolina law, we are still husband and wife."

She sat the cup down, sloshing its contents. "Ye forfeited your right to me when Afton Manor went up in flames." She turned to slide beneath the counterpane. The bedclothing was cold, and she could wish for Jacob's heated body drawing her into the curvature of his.

"Ahhh, but I have your Christmas gift, do I not?" he asked, shucking his shirt, then his stockings and breeches.

From beneath half-closed lids, her eyes followed him. With a preternatural grace, he strode unabashedly naked to toss a few sticks on the dying fire and then pinch out the guttering candle. She heard his feet pad to the bedside and the unscrolling of the bedroll.

She strained to keep the waspishness from her voice. But she had paid for his Christmas gift with something so very precious to her, and he had disdained even the gesture, itself. "I assured Abigail she would be emancipated after one year of service."

"As are you now." The finality in his voice was made more emphatic by the darkness.

He had not bedded her since the night at the tavern. In turn, she had not sought out in the confines of their bedchamber the comfort of his hand. Now, her hand, cradled beneath her cheek, was damp. The torment of what might have been grew into a gnawing pain, and she curled into a tight ball.

If only things were different.

If only there was not a war.

If only she were a more worthy homemaker.

If only he had not deceived her.

If only he had it within himself to love her . . . to love her with all her shortcomings.

The day before the Assembly Ball, Catriona stood before the cheval mirror and noted that she looked as poor as the proverbial church mouse, despite Abigail's consummate skill with thimble and needle.

"There's only so much one can do with a dress that looked like it was a ragpicker's leftover," the bond girl mumbled, a sewing needle clamped between her small teeth as she knelt to readjust the folds of the made-over gown. "Not that I 'aven't picked over a 'eap of rags myself, but a lady like thou . . . wife to a 'andsome gent like Master Jacob . . . well, thou needest to look right smart."

Peering down at the girl's bent head, the auburn hair now tidily coiffed beneath her white lace cap, Catriona knew she had made the right decision in purchasing the girl's indenture papers. London born, of gentry parentage, Abigail had grown up on the colonial frontier and been provided with a sound Quaker education. She would be the perfect match for Jacob. But the thought of his bedding her was one Catriona kept thrusting back in the far reaches of her mind.

Another thought surfaced to replace it, which was only little better. "Abigail, why did you murder your stepmother?"

The girl's flitting fingers stilled. She looked up. The needle fell from her lips, and she hastened to reclaim it. "Truly, Mistress, t'was an accident. Of sorts. "

Catriona raised a brow. "Of sorts?"

"Me stepmother was a mean woman. She 'ad a passel of brats and did not want me around. I was cleanin' out the cold coals from the fireplace, when the 'arpy started beating me with 'er broom. I 'ad forgotten to put the butter back in the well, you see, and it 'ad gone rancid. I was only trying to ward off 'er broom's blows with the poker."

At that, Catriona winced.

"The 'arpy tripped on that rag rug, the very one she 'ad me braid. Tripped twice, she did, on me poker. But the third time did her in." Abigail paused reflectively, then flashed her sunny grin. "The Lord doth work in mysterious ways."

Well, the crime was a wee thing when all was considered. And, besides, no handmaiden was perfect. Catriona smiled wanly. "Me thinks if we keep the needle in your hands and not the poker, all will be well with ye."

But she knew all would never be well between herself and Jacob. Nevertheless, within twenty-four hours was the Assembly Ball and then within days thereafter they would leave New Bern. With good weather, it would be a scant three days' travel back to her clan.

Anticipation of reunion with her mother and father and old Phoebe and Angus and all the others made the coming parting with Jacob a wee bit more bearable. She did not want to be the harpy, as Abigail had termed it, that she herself felt she was fast becoming. Neither she nor her husband were happy with this marriage of practicality. Certainly, they could arrange for a civilized termination to their union.

"Abigail, stand up, please."

Puzzled, the girl's head tilted but she released the dress hem and rose to her feet. "Aye, Mistress?"

She took the girl's short, stubby fingers between hers and peered solemnly down at her. "I am . . . I must return to me clan . . . for a while." She choked back tears that nevertheless thickened her voice. "And I want ye to make sure Master Jacob is well cared for . . . not just in the daily chores . . . but . . . but also perhaps in aiding him in reading and writing, if ye see him to be struggling."

"Mistress, tis missing thee we will be, but thy husband is a goodly man. The likes of most of us females wouldn't be fit even to sew his fallflap buttons." She grinned cheerfully. "Count on me to give it my all."

Which was something, Catriona reflected unhappily, she herself had not done.

~ ~ ~ ~ ~ ~ ~

To rebels of the Old North State, the ornate Tryon Palace, rising from the banks of the Trent River, had long been a symbol of British oppression and extravagance. Its heavily levied taxes to pay for its construction further inflamed many backcountry residents. Completed in 1770, it had served as the British colonial government house of the royal governors and capitol of the colony.

Now it served as the capitol of the state of North Carolina.

The mansion was alit with fragrant bayberry candles, welcoming warmth against a chilly darkness, both outside the palace and inside Catriona's heart.

Green boughs wound around the sweep of staircase railing. Garlands of holly and ivy decorated fireplace mantles, and mistletoe tempted couples passing through every doorway. Cinnamon tarts, cranberry-orange cake, and smoked partridge scented the air. Somewhere a harpsichord was playing the lively "God Rest Ye Merry Gentlemen."

Pausing in the Affairs of State Room, Catriona rested her palm lightly on Jacob's forearm. Beneath her gloved fingertips, she could feel his muscles knot. Her stomach knotted, as well. She stared at the array of elegantly dressed guests and was forced to admit how reversed his and her roles and status were now. Jacob was the center of attention, admired and respected.

"Stop biting your lip," he admonished in a low aside to her.

"I canna help meself. I feel like Daniel in the Lion's Den."

Governor Caswell, along with his wife, crossed the crowded floor to greet Jacob with an enthusiastic handshake. Beneath the thatch of brown hair combed low on his forehead, his discerning eyes turned to Catriona. "Good to see you again, Mrs. Dare."

"New Bern has been speculating about the mysterious Mrs. Dare," said his wife. Her powdered hair was swept into a high pile of curls in the shape of, incredibly, a snake – an invention of Ben Franklin's as a symbol for the Revolution along with his penned words, 'Don't Tread on me.' "And you are every bit as beautiful as the rumors say,"

She grinned. "Me fears me husband would describe me as the Mouthy Mistress Dare."

"Well," Caswell said, "Jacob will tell you we have plenty of mouthy legislators. You will fit right in."

She was astounded by her reception. Surely the other guests knew of her leanings to the Mother Country. After all, she was the daughter of the Chieftess of the Afton Clan and the famed Flora MacDonald was her godmother.

But then more than half the state, being comprised of so many Highlander immigrants, felt themselves to be both American and British, subjects of the King.

Like herself, while opposing taxation without representation, they could not break their oath to the King nor imagine taking up arms against him. And like the nearly 400,000 American inhabitants still loyal to the crown, they wanted to take a middle-of-the road position.

They were cautious and afraid that chaos and mob rule would result and were naturally angry when, forced by the Patriots with violence such as burning houses and tarring and feathering, to declare their opposition.

Along the length of the two platter-laden tables, lit by silver candelabra, the sixty-odd guests discussed the war for independence, some leaning more moderately for a constitutional monarchy rather than to wage war.

" . . . remind you that England has a highly trained army, the world's largest navy, and a highly efficient system of public finance that could easily fund the war and defeat our feeble show of thumbing our noses."

Others expressed their preference for a constitutional republic. "England's parliament is seriously handicapped by its misunderstanding of the depth of our support for the Patriot position."

And still a few others were rabid for revolution, now under way officially. "Liberty or Death – Patrick Henry said it best."

Oliver Newell laughed inanely, rising to speak, and boasted, "Since South Carolinians repelled the British attempt to take Charleston, we should have no trouble with the British in our own harbors, what with their tricky waters."

At the far end of the other table, his wife Félicité looked positively bored by the war talk and rolled her eyes at Catriona.

Jacob leaned close to her ear. "While here," he suggested with his low, thrifty and precision-spaced words, "you can petition Caswell for an annulment."

She shrugged her bare shoulders and whispered back, "I can

file at Campbelton's county courthouse."

Throughout the dinner conversations she was feeling a mild pleasure that she had restrained her usually loquacious, opinionated self. These American insurrectionists – she felt allied with them, as well as, with the Loyalists. She was pulled in two directions, like the childhood rope game of Tug-of-War.

To her surprise, Jacob appeared at ease in the discussions that bounced back and forth from guest to guest, from table to table. He said little, true, but his responses were objective and sound. Surprising her even more, he stood to speak. At this, the room went silent, for on those rare occasions when he did choose to speak, people listened.

"Do not expect the war to be a walk in the park. The Lobsterbacks control Boston and New York City. Lord Cornwallis has captured Fort Lee from Nathanael Greene."

He paused. His brief but sobering statement might have put a damper on the festive mood, but for his next words, sparse and spaced.

"However, the colonies do have the tactical experience learned during Indian wars. Striking quickly from behind trees or fences. Then disappearing into the forests."

His gunsight vision scoped the stuffy, crowded room. He smiled sociably. "More, the Continental Army has the popular support. Common people. Ordinary farmers and laborers. They choose to put themselves into the line of fire. Because of this, the war for freedom will prevail."

The woodsman was the rebels' wind of change, the fresh rain sweeping from forest and river, the thunder and lightning that would open the West. The guests shot to their feet. Fervent and sincere applause rang like Philadelphia's freedom bell.

The talk of war escalated, and eventually Sarah, as hostess, intervened. "Mistress Dare, besides your beauty, your musical talents also proceed you. Will you grant us a boon and regal us, please?"

"Well, I dunna have me dulcimer," she demurred and glanced sidewise at Jacob to see if he shared her unpleasant memory of its destruction. As usual, his expression was noncommittal.

"Ahhh, but we have a harpsichord and violin," said Caswell and waved the liveried servant to summon the musicians. From around the table the polite pattering of clapping hands encouraged her somewhat. To further remonstrate could only cloud the cooperative feeling Jacob's speech had accomplished.

She nodded and rose to join the two musicians taking up their positions. She looked out over the expectant faces. She realized something in her was the rebel, also. Grinning, she said, "A favorite song tis, then. 'Yankee Doodle Dandy.'"

Immediately, another round of applause went up. Swishing her skirts, she plied the aisle between the two tables, leaning first over a peruked old man at one table and then next to the comely Lady Félicité at the other, to render up the Patriot version of the song.

> *"Yankee Doodle went to town*
> *A-riding on a pony,*
> *Stuck a feather in his cap*
> *And called it macaroni.*
>
> *Yankee Doodle keep it up,*
> *Yankee Doodle dandy,*
> *Mind the music and the step,*
> *And with the girls be handy."*

Before the guests, clapping in time to the snappy lyrics, could know what she was about, she switched to the British version.

> *"The seventeen of June, at break of day,*
> *The Rebels they supriz'd us,*
> *With their strong works, which they'd thrown up,*
> *To burn the Town and drive us.*
>
> *Yankee Doodle came to town,*
> *For to buy a firelock,*
> *We will tar and feather him,*
> *And so we will John Hancock."*

So engaged were the dinner guests with her theatrics, they little realized the British version until she was well into the chorus. But, at that point, she abruptly switched to a Handel piece, signaling to the musicians to play the festive and all-inclusive Christmas carol, "Joy to the World."

With that, one by one the diners rose to finish the chorus with her. A resounding success she and Jacob were, if she did say so herself. Singularly and in small groups, the guests clustered around to laud her. Over their shoulders she spotted Lady Félicité and her pasty and portly husband Oliver Newell engaged in conversation with the towering Jacob.

He and the man both wore preoccupied expressions. Ever the coquette, Félicité focused her fawning gaze on Jacob. Catriona sighed and disengaged herself to join the three.

Félicité smiled delightedly. "Catriona, *vous étiez magnifique!*"

Her husband, a rather short man, smothered a coughing spasm with his fist, then with another inane laugh, peered at her through his monocle. "I do say, you have a most captivating voice."

She inclined her head. "Thank ye."

"We do hope," he said, his meaningless laugh competing now with a paroxysm of coughing, "that you will grace our home with your songs. Our music room does have the finest selection of instruments to be found in the Carolinas. Europe's most brilliant composers and leading musicians seek us out when touring America. Last year, we hosted a Bach Christmas oratorio."

Jacob, obviously impatient with the man's gasconading, placed a firm hand at Catriona's back and said, "We have much to do before we leave New Bern."

Beneath the vestibule's grand chandelier, he gripped her shoulders and turned her to face him. The heat from the multitude of candles was stifling. Or perhaps it was the uneasiness that suddenly prickled her skin. "There is something you need to know."

She eyed him dubiously. "What?"

"Your Fairfax has been taken captive." He was watching her attentively. "He is being held in the Halifax jail."

Her fist went to her breast. "No! First me brothers. Now Barrett."

At the sight of her stricken expression, his mouth tightened at the edges, the only visible reaction to her desolate reply. Had he expected a less emotional response from her? Following on the heels of that thought came a niggling question accompanied by a stray shiver raveling her backbone.

Could her husband be in any way responsible for Barrett's capture and imprisonment? After all, Jacob was one of those rare men who never gave up.

"You and Fergus leave for Campbelton the day after to-morrow," he said. "I have told Abigail to begin packing."

The keen disappointment surging through her took her by surprise. "Ye willna be taking me to Campbelton then?"

"I am keeping my promise. You will be returned to your clan by Christmas."

His detached gaze, his uncompromising strength, and his stoic calm kindled in her the familiar flare of resentment. "Oh."

She could feel the blade's edge of anger jabbing at her pride. That he could so easily let her go hurt. Absurdly, she wanted to slap him. Or for him to slap her. Just some show of emotion that would indicate he had feelings.

Outside, the frosty air nipped her cheeks as she walked alongside him the few streets over to the Pollock Street house. They could have well been strangers but that their bodies had so often conjoined in ecstasy. And it was his utter self-sufficiency that had helped keep him even more a stranger

Abigail met them at the door. "Got the warmin' pan heated for thy bed," she said merrily. "The nights, they are startin' to turn cold as the King's bloody 'eart."

"Where is Fergus?" he asked.

Her grin displayed her cheek's freckles more prominently. "In the kitchen. Getting a 'ead start he is on the buttered scones I baked for the journey. Always 'appens when I make up a batch."

With a sickening heart, Catriona watched Jacob stride toward through the door and down the hallway to the kitchen beyond. She turned her steps to Jethro and Fergus's room.

Promptly, Jethro answered her knock. At seeing her, his familiar one-sided grin tugged upward. On his narrow, cornhusk bed lay a knapsack. He, too, would be departing. Not for Campbelton but for Kinsfolk Landing, along with Jacob and Abigail. Yet another farewell to make.

"What with the Indian raid . . . we have been through so much together, ye and I . . . well, Jethro, I just come to tell ye goodbye."

Bashfully, he looked down at his feet. One toe poked through the stocking's hole. He looked back up at her. "Now that I can read and write somewhat, do you think t'would be all right iffen I posted a letter to you now and then. You know, tellin' you what's ado at Kinsfolk Landing? Just until you return."

Startled, her spine straightened. So, Jacob had said nothing of the finality of their marriage. When he had broached the annulment earlier, had he been calling her bluff? Was he leaving the door open for her to change her mind?

She tilted her head to kiss Jethro on his peach-fuzzed cheek. "But, of course. I would be delighted to read a letter from ye."

The next two days were a blur. More goodbyes, with Félicité showing up armed with a bottle of French champagne, no less. "*Votre homme*, if you tire of him," she purred with that enchanting smile, "here I am. I help you out, no?"

No.

Félicité did not seem the sort of woman in whom Jacob would be interested. But, then, Catriona knew she could be wrong, since it was distinctly obvious she did not know or understand her husband that well. The image of Jacob and the young Frenchwoman, or Abigail for that matter, entwined in bed nigh squeezed the blood from her heart.

That final night at the Pollock Street house, she realized with a certainty she had to – no, profoundly wanted to – make the effort to give her marriage one last chance. All this time, she had denied to herself that she could love Jacob. She had attributed the strong force that drew them irrevocably to one another, even from that first childhood sighting of one another at the falls, merely as one of powerful attraction.

Rather than seek out her husband in the parlor, where he would most likely be closeted with Fergus, she went on down the hallway to hers and Jacob's bedchamber. She wanted to postpone this difficult admission to him of her submission until they were alone . . . until she could better breathe.

As she drew near their bedchamber, her steps slowed, then stopped abruptly. She could hear his murmured words and Abigail's giggling response.

So, her husband was already seeking the solace of her Christmas gift of the handmaiden.

Catriona pivoted and headed back toward the kitchen. She was shaking clear through to her bones, her hands tremoring and her teeth chattering. Winter's chill shrouded the Pollock Street house. A cup of hot tea was in order. Or, preferably hot coffee. Or mayhap a cup of hot chocolate. Or mayhap several cups of Abigail's hot toddy.

The twin settlements of Cross Creek and Campbelton on opposite sides of the Cape Fear were only a little over a hundred miles as the crow flies from New Bern. Given the unusually good weather, chilly but rain and wind free, the journey home would most likely be completed in a mere three days, with Fergus leading at the head of three of his four pack horses and she following, astride Hobby.

Fergus was as taciturn as ever. The old reprobate's coonskin cap was constantly turning this way and that, his gaze roving the sandy road ahead, scanning the forests on both sides. Not much would he be likely to miss. His rifle lay across his lap, and his knife, tomahawk, and pistol were, as usual, belted at his waist.

It was not until that last evening on the trail that he bothered to say more than warn of a wash-out ahead or that her saddle cinch was loose.

They were camped in a meadow of saplings, their few remaining leaves shimmering gold with twilight's slight of hand. His muscle lumped back to her, he was squatted before the cooking fire he was building. Gathering a few branches, he snapped them into smaller lengths and stacked them in a teepee-like fashion over the tiny flames.

Before hobbling Jacob's chestnut for the night, she stroked the thoroughbred's mane. A stultifying sadness such as she could not recall weighted her shoulders and churned her stomach. Not even when she was leaving her parents and friends behind at Campbelton the day she married or leaving her friends at Kinsfolk Landing had she felt this despondent.

She pressed her cheek against the horse's warm muzzle. Its whinnying breath frosted the air. "Tis missing you I shall be, Hobby." she whispered.

The chestnut nickered softly.

Fergus cleared his throat. "Jacob said I was to let you know right fore I delivered yew 'bout yewr Christmas present."

She spun to look at Fergus. "What? A Christmas present?"

"Yup." He swigged from a tin canteen that she surmised most likely did not contain water. "Jacob wasn't hankering none for ya to have it lang afore hand."

Gathering her cloak about her, she circled a withered brambleberry patch to hunker opposite the fire from Fergus. "He has a Christmas present – for me?"

He corked the canteen, then dug out the sack of maple sugar. He set the coffee pot next to the skillet of bacon on a flat river rock, close to the heat. "Yup. It should git to Campbelton a mite ahead of us, what with any luck."

"What is it?"

"No surprise if I tell ya." His dirty fingers poked bacon inside two of the scones Abigail had baked. He handed Catriona one. Her stomach rebelled against even the thought of eating. Nevertheless, she dutifully accepted the scone.

He peered at her from beneath the fur of his coonskin cap. "Will tell ya, gal, that he sold the distillery to buy ya . . . the present."

"No!" Her fingers dropped the scone in the dirt. "The distillery, it was his down payment for Kinsfolk Landing's future. It will be disastrous for his plans."

"Fortune – misfortune. Far as I kin tell, tis all the same to him. He makes his own luck."

As she considered this, the coffee in the pot on the side nearest the coals began to simmer. What kind of gift could have cost the considerable amount of money the distillery was worth? "Who bought it? The distillery?"

He grunted sourly. "Oliver Newell."

The air whooshed from her lungs. Had that paved the way for an affair between Félicité and Jacob? Had she underestimated the Frenchwoman?

~ ~ ~ ~ ~ ~ ~

The weather, which had held up favorably, gave way to light snow ten miles from Campbelton and slowed them down. – just when feverish anticipation was prodding her to knee Hobby to a faster pace. However, the snow flurries increased, impeding their traveling progress even further.

While Anne Macleod's home outside Campbelton was not as palatial as Afton Manor had been, nor as brilliantly lit, and was only rented, on that cold and dark evening the sight of the pillared, two-story red brick home with its frost-crystalled windows swelled Catriona's chest. Homecoming. Rejoining with ones the heart loved.

As Hobby and the pack horses clip-clopped up the tree-lined drive, crusted with snow, the front door was flung open and Phoebe appeared, hands on hips, leaning forward to better sight who were the late arriving visitors.

Catriona slid down from Hobby. She was cold, saddle sore, and stiff. She wobbled more than walked toward the veranda steps.

"Lord God Awmighty," Phoebe cried and, lifting her black skirt, huffed down the steps to wrap her bony arms around Catriona. "Yewr back, yewr back."

Blinking hard, Catriona hugged the woman, who smelled of old lace and lavender. Catriona could not think of anything better at that moment than being crushed against Phoebe's scrawny bosom.

Phoebe drew back and scrutinized her sharply. "Yewr too thin. They didn't feed ya now, did they?" She shot a scowling look over Catriona's shoulder at Fergus.

"Hrumpph," he grumbled and, muttering a profanity, dubiously eyed the woman up and down. Then, spatting his amber tobacco juice in the snow-blanketed yard, he said, "Yer sack of bones looks like it could use a feedbag."

Phoebe's eyes slitted, but she turned an affectionate gaze on Catriona. "Got to be worn plumb frazzled and hungry as a bear. Come on inside and warm yewrself. We weren't expecting yew until tomorrow, at best."

"But how did ye know we were coming?"

Phoebe looked at her oddly. "Why, the messenger, and then . . . well, come on in and see fer yewrself." She shot a contentious look at Fergus. "Ye kin head for the scullery. A mite of washin' and a mite of food may well 'elp ye look 'uman."

Inside, a warmth and coziness greeted Catriona. Fragrant

evergreen boughs graced doors and windows, and mountain laurel decorated the mantel, where a welcoming fire blazed. Her nostrils flared at the rich scent of holiday cooking – of gingerbread and brown sugared ham, of baked pies and roasted turkey. A Great Highland bagpipe broke off in the midst of "O' Come All Ye Faithful."

But it was the sight of her parents and Flora and Anne and other friends, nae more – the sight of Robbie, Andrew, and Jamie rushing to her – that vanquished her control, imposed with so much difficulty throughout these many months. The clan was all there. Tears cascaded down her cheeks, and she buried her face in her hands, trembling as she loudly sobbed out her heart.

"Me bairn, how I have missed ye." cried her mother, embracing her, one hand cradling Catriona's head against the curve of her neck, the other stroking her back, in the comforting way only a mother could do. "All is well. Ye are home, at last. All my children are here for Christmastide."

Through watery eyes, Catriona saw past her mother, past her delighted father, teary-eyed himself, and a thinner Robbie and Andrew, to a grinning Jamie and Anne and Flora who had now taken up posts near the fireplace – and, incredibly, a weary but smiling Barrett.

With dawning horror, Catriona knew then. Knew that Jacob had ransomed her brothers and Barrett as his Christmas gift for her. She was stricken by the sickening knowledge that she and Jacob had sacrificed for each other their most meaningful treasures to give to one another someone who might better love them.

"Ye are all right, *mo ulaidh*?" her father asked, his deep-set intelligent eyes searching her face intently.

"Aye, Da," she sniffled. "Tis guid to be home."

"It took ye lang enough," called out a tired-looking Andrew. "We expected ye yesterday." Her brother sported a beard, and his strawberry-colored hair was abnormally long from the ten months' imprisonment. "How lang will ye be here?"

She could not bring herself to answer and could only give him an affectionate smile and a tight embrace.

Robbie shouldered through the press of people to bestow a brotherly bear hug. "What was Tryon Palace like?"

She wanted to tell him it paled in comparison with Afton Manor. The Afton Manor that was. "Magnificent," she said, kissing him on his scruffy cheek.

Flora hugged her close, saying, "Here ye are returning, and Anne and I are planning on leaving. Leaving America, if we can arrange for our husbands to be included in a prisoner exchange."

"Oh, Flory, ye canna. Once the war is over – whether King George or General George wins – t'will be easier here, I foreswear."

"Will Jacob be coming later?" asked Anne, pulling her aside.

All Catriona could think was how Anne, so generous of heart, must be hurting, more so at Christmastide, what with her own husband a prisoner – while Catriona's men kinfolk had been freed. "I dunna think so," she said squeezing her friend's hand. "Jacob is caught up in the other camp, that of the Rebels."

Anne looked her full in the eye. "So that is the lay of the land?"

Catriona nodded. She could not risk ruining the evening for everyone by sharing the disheartening news that would only start her blubbering afresh.

"It canna be 'either-or,'" Anne said. "There must be a midway meeting ground for you two, based on love. Love if even for only mankind."

"Ye would think so." But all too often perception and pride barred the way.

At last, she summoned the courage to make her way toward the fireplace, redolent with its aroma of chestnuts roasting in a covered pan. She could recall sitting for hours at other Christmastides, delighting in the pulsating glow of the fireplace's embers and smelling all the lovely candles around her home, particularly the sweet–smelling vanilla and cinnamon ones.

Only after talking with all the others, did she reach Barrett. One hand braced on the mantle, the other planted on his hip beneath the spread of his jacket, he stood before the welcoming blaze of the fire with his customary studied elegance. One of her kind. He appeared to be listening to the crackle of the burning applewood.

He regarded her with a thoughtfulness, which he covered with a quick smile. He and her brothers had arrived scarcely twelve hours ahead of her. His broadcloth jacket, the one he must have worn when captured, looked ready for Abigail's ragpickers.

Ever the consummate gentleman, he executed a short bow. "Is it in poor taste to say," he asked with an attempt at levity, "Welcome home from the land of the dead?"

She came up short. While life on the frontier had been a

difficult and perilous time, and often not a happy period, she had felt more alive than ever she had within the security of her parents' home. And that was what it had been – her parents' home, not really her own.

"Tis guid to see ye, Barrett. When I heard ye had been taken captive, I worried fiercely for ye." Now, here at Christmas, was not the time to confront him about his role at the Cherokee town of Coyate and what part had he played in her own captivity.

Phoebe interrupted to lead her away to a hastily set table. With every bone screaming for release from the agony of three wintry days on the trail and release from the agony of a horribly hurting heart, she wanted to forego the leftovers of what had obviously been a sumptuous supper.

Phoebe set before her a serving of Christmas pudding and poured warmed brandy butter and rum sauce over it. Although it was her favorite dish, Catriona wanted only to curl up in bed and pull the quilts over her head. She nudged it aside. "I canna eat, Phoebe. Me stomach does flip-flops at the thought of food."

The woman eyed her with a happy anticipation. "Ye are carrying a bairn?"

She frowned. "Ye sound like Jacob, ye do. Nae. We havna had . . . I am most certain I am not with child."

"Still, ye must eat. I'll warm ye a bowl o' Cock o' Leekie soup."

After she ate as much of the soup as she could stomach, the tyrannical woman shooed her off to one of the upstairs bedchambers, where she hoped to bury herself in the oblivion of sleep.

But upon opening her trunk to remove her nightrail, she found, atop it, wrapped in red velvet and tied with a white satin ribbon, her gold hairpin.

~ ~ ~ ~ ~ ~ ~ ~

Fergus departed before dawn of the following day, with not even a by your leave. However, the next week between Christmas and Hogmanay passed more quickly than Catriona would have expected. Each day, she received at Anne's rented home friends, who had driven out in their coaches or rode out on their mounts to call upon her.

But mostly she spent time with her family and Anne and Flora – and, quite naturally, Barrett. Sometimes they played backgammon, at which her father beat them all soundly.

It was the afternoon of Hogmanay, New Year's Eve, more important to Scots, most likely, than even Christmas, because during the Protestant Reformation Christmas had been banned in Scotland. For hundreds of years, Christmas had been seen as being Roman Catholic.

Despite the biting air, she and Barrett idly walked along the riverfront, speaking only of pleasantries until, further along, they reached the two-story high falls. Since their childhood days, a wooden railing had been erected alongside the path.

How pitiful was she that her attention was not on the handsome Barrett but on a shadow of a boy, watching from the leafy concealment of alders bordering the falls the girl she had been.

She and Barret paused by tacit agreement at the railing. The fall's spray rimed his eyelashes and congealed her smile. "What will ye do now, Barrett? Emigrate to Nova Scotia or Florida?"

"What? Abandon my friends and contacts here, with my tail tucked between my legs? As long as I do not take up arms, I can return to my office as tobacco agent." He draped one panel of his woolen great cape around her to protect her from the spray. "No, what I shall do will depend greatly upon you."

She ignored the implication in his words and clutched at another topic. "Ye were responsible for having me, and the others with me, taken hostage by the Cherokee, were ye not?"

"Yes – and, no."

Her head canted, and she lifted an inquisitive brow, encouraging him to elaborate.

"Because your husband aligned himself with the Catawba and Creek, Dragging Canoe was already hell-bent on killing and scalping every soul at Kinsfolk Landing. I persuaded him, rather than an outright massacre, to take only you. "

"'Tis unsure I am," she said drily, "whether to thank ye, Barrett Fairfax."

He squeezed her shoulder reassuringly. "Dragging Canoe was calculating that Dare would do anything to get you back. I had not planned on the others being with you that day you were taken captive, but I had planned on easily ransoming you from Dragging Canoe. His cruelty is only surpassed by his greed."

He laid his leather gloved hand over hers, tightened on the railing. "I am prepared to do whatever it takes." He feigned a grimace and added, "Even if that means facing the mighty wrath of your father and asking for your hand, I will do so. I know how he feels about we Sassenachs."

She felt a tightness in her chest, a sighing of her spirit – what others might call the winter blues. It seemed she spent each hour wishing things had been different between her and Jacob. Wanting so badly that it hurt merely to walk with him again along the forested avenue to their cabin. Remembering his mannerisms, like keeping his long rifle ever near or the way he held his sensual mouth when he shaved. Longing for the sound of his purposefully considered words and the feel of his long fingers grazing her shoulder or hip.

"Give me time, Barrett." She squeezed his hand. "I have yet even to file for an annulment."

"Odysseus might have been willing to wait twenty years to be reunited with his fair Penelope, but, as for myself, I would be grateful if you would shorten the suspense of my suffering."

"I . . . I will think upon it seriously."

"Alas," he conceded with a smile, "the slings and arrows of misfortune are my possible fate."

~ ~ ~ ~ ~ ~ ~

That evening, the clans prepared for Hogmanay. Some said it was the Gaelic New Year's celebration of Samhain. Other folk believed it came from the celebration of the 'Yule' by the Vikings, which later contributed to the Twelve Days of Christmas. Regardless, as soon as the clock stroke twelve, bells were rung in every town and village throughout North Carolina's Highlander settlements.

At that point, one of the Hogmanay customs was to stand in a circle, cross over the arms, and, holding hands with people on either side, sing the old folks' song dating back beyond recent memory about auld lang syne.

Another custom, though, dated back even further, through the mist of time – that of the superstitious First Foot, the first foot to step into a house after midnight. To ensure good luck for the household, the first person entering the front door should be male and dark. Blond and redhead first-footers were considered bad luck.

In the most secret spot of her heart, Catriona was hoping, come midnight, for the dark, enigmatic half-breed Jacob Dare to be the first to cross Anne's door step. But Catriona knew, as well, that she and Jacob both had done so much to each other . . . knew that her fervent hope would be unfulfilled.

So, she was not surprised when the golden-haired Barrett, along with the Reverend Hamilton, who had no hair, and old Angus who was gray of head appeared at the door.

"While we may not be the Three Magi," Barrett quipped, "we do come bearing gifts."

Their gifts, the traditional shortbread, black bun, and salt were added to the accumulation brought by other guests' contributions – coal, rum, and, of course, whisky.

Then Barrett surprised her with yet another gift. With a boyishly triumphant smile, he produced from behind his back a dulcimer. "Bought it off a Loyalist family, returning to England. They wanted to sell out quickly. Anne told me of your dulcimer, how it had gotten crushed in the traveling."

Fearful she might tear up again, she hugged him before he could see her weepy expression. "Oh, Barrett, ye so understand me," she mumbled against his embroidered coat. She drew slightly away, the dulcimer in one hand, her other clutching his. "But I have nothing for ye."

"You know what I want from you," he said quietly.

Yes, she knew – and knew he was her perfect match. As Barrett had said, cut from the same cloth, they were.

Once every bite of the Hogmanay Pies was eaten, Catriona's mother suggested a *ceilidh*. Angus took the floor with his story of the bog people, and Anne played on her spinet the quaint old Celtic songs

But this time, Catriona could not bring herself to join in the Hogmanay *ceilidh*. Still too fresh in her memory was of the last *ceilidh*, at the Highlander Games, when Jacob Dare had sat in the shadows, watching her with that same intensity and icy precision that he used to bring his long rifle up and take a bead on the object he meant to bring down.

He had brought her down.

The first quarter of 1777 was dark with winter's wrath – and dark, too, for the fortunes of the Loyalists. With a stroke of genius, Washington had evaded General Cornwallis and his 8,000 Redcoats at Trenton, New Jersey, by leaving his campfires burning and muffling the wheels of his army's departing wagons.

Now, throughout the newly united states, Loyalists knew they most likely either faced exile or humiliating repatriation. That March afternoon, cloudy, cold, and wind-whipped, Anne's chilly parlor had to be lit by both candlelight and firelight. Anne and her mother and Catriona and her parents and brothers occupied the settees and chairs grouped around the hearth's flickering flames.

Catriona's father set a section of oak onto the andirons. Tongues of fire licked hungrily at the wood. "Come spring, we can expect Cornwallis to turn his sights in our direction, if that is any comfort."

"'Tis said his Hessian mercenaries plunder and rape when they take over a town," Flora murmured, without looking up from the sock she was knitting.

Robbie, his red hair catching the fire's light, grumbled, "Even the Black Watch has refused battle honors on their regimental colors. They feel tis not right, this war between kith and kin."

Flora laid aside her needles and looked around at the fire-warmed faces. "I had a letter in the post today. Me husband and Annie's are to be released from the Philadelphia prison. I am no' certain exactly when, but we will definitely sail for Scotland once that happens."

"Flory," Enya exclaimed, "that is wonderful news. For ye. But I dunna know how I shall fare without ye here."

Robbie, the eldest of Catriona's brothers, pivoted from pacing, hands clasped behind his back, to confront them. "I say we also return to Scotland, Da. We have lost everything here."

"But there is no land for us in Scotland," their father reminded them in a chiding tone.

Anne rose to pour more tea, as if by moving she could forestall other worries. "Nor work to be had."

"Well, we have something here still," Catriona's mother said, pausing to take a sip of the watered-down tea. "We have opportunity."

Over the rim of her cup, she peered meaningfully at her husband. Then to Catriona, "Ranald and I have been talking. About uniting our future with the United States' future. Almost every week, ye hear of entire communities, organized by tacksmen, migrating westward, over the Blue Ridge to Kentucky territory. Ye must have learned a lot those months at Kinsfolk Landing about pioneer life that would serve us in guid stead."

Catriona tightened her red plaid around her now gaunt frame, then gently swished the tea in her cup. She had shared little about her captivity with the Indians and nothing about its horror and Barrett's role in it. Although he was known to have worked with the notorious Tory Rangers, her parents were wise enough to wait until she felt ready to volunteer details. "I knew enough to get by – with a lot of help from the settlers."

"If the family," her mother paused to bestow a collective nod on Catriona's father and brothers, "should decide to migrate to Kentucky, would ye be willing to accompany us come spring, when the river runs full?"

She had not expected this. She realized she had been drifting through the darkness of depression these last wintry months. Food was ashes in her mouth. Sleep evaded her. "Barrett has planned on asking you, Da, for me hand."

He studied her closely. "Why has he not?"

"I have put him off until I can file for an annulment."

"And why have ye not yet filed?" he asked, more softly than was usual for his confrontational manner. "What for be ye waiting?"

What was she waiting for? The answer was obvious. Barrett

fitted her way of life so perfectly. As Abigail fitted that of Jacob's. But surely Félicité did not. Did she?

For all Catriona's reasoning and logic, she could not control her feelings. Her feelings were chips of iron brought close to a magnet, swerving abruptly and invariably toward a man whom she sometimes feared, so well did he read those feelings and therefore so easily did he have the upper hand.

Yet there was something to that adage that opposites attracted – and complimented one another. Life was certainly not boring with one's opposite. On the contrary, it was the adventure Jacob had once predicted.

Was she once again stalling for time, waiting for the Highlander Games to reconvene and hoping for Jacob to come to claim her as he had that first time . . . when she knew in her heart of hearts he would not. When would she learn?

What a fool she was, wanting his happiness beyond her own, even knowing that happiness meant another woman in place of her, in his life, in their bed, bearing his child.

"Well?" Andrew asked her. That was so like her brother, always prodding her to venture further up the tree's spindly top, deeper into the creek's swishing water, closer to the tail-bristling skunk.

"In all truth, I feel somewhat stifled here. Surrounded by people and houses and things. Hemmed in."

She missed the solitude of the wilderness – and the independence it afforded. She glanced down at the horsehair wedding band she had yet to remove. It had chaffed the skin of the fingers on either side of it until the flesh there had callused.

"Aye," she conceded softly, while covertly working the ring from her finger. "I'll move with ye to Kentucky."

Jacob would never find her in that wilderness. And she hoped thoughts of him would not either. Beyond the parlor window, the last rays in the whole world were fading.

~ ~ ~ ~ ~ ~ ~

April's Highland Games arrived, with a much lesser turn out of able bodied men. They were away fighting for either the Loyalists or the Patriots – or they had died in battle. And, of course, Jacob Dare made no appearance.

Her own appearance, according to her brother Jamie, left a lot be desired. "Tis knackered, ye look, Sis."

And her father agreed. "Ye've lost too much weight, *mo ulaidh,* and your eyes look like gray coals."

Aye, the fire had gone out of her. She was a nothingness.

The next week, under the dappling shade of spring's leafy oaks and ashes, Barrett joined her and her family on the public square as they made their farewells to the aggregation of friends. "Despite being a rejected suitor, I am here, nevertheless, to send you off. I shall walk you down to the docks."

She laid her hand in the crook of his elbow, and he patted her fingers. "As you have yet to file for an annulment, I do not suppose it is too much to hope that you may soon be widowed?"

"Knowing Jacob Dare, I would say nae."

"Alas, I would have to agree. He will most likely be one of the few plucky souls on the frontier to live to old age."

"But I do have in mind for ye, Barrett, a lovely, high-stepping French lady that I wouldna be surprised if she were shortly widowed – Félicité Newell of New Bern."

"Can she hold my interest, as well as you? You know how easily polite society bores me."

Frivolous Félicité? "She would lead you on a merry chase." The two would strive to outdo one another with never a boring moment between them. She smiled at him. "But then, why dunna ye find out for yourself?"

Yet Félicité could already be ensconced in Jacob's cabin. With that thought, Catriona's heart felt like a mop being wrung dry.

Moored alongside skiffs and schooners was the Kincairn's huge, square barge with its three sheds, one wagon, two canoes, a number of horses, and seven people, not counting the four polers.

With its flat bottom and shallow draft, it could negotiate the small rapids and falls, running fuller than last year, more easily than a periauger. The first day on the river, cold spring rains pelted the passengers, who took refuge in their deck sheds.

Within the shed that Phoebe bond Catriona shared, she lay listlessly on her pallet and, wrapped in a woolen blanket, watched between the slits of boards beside her head the forested shoreline slipping by. When that evening the barge nosed in at a small side stream, the welcoming caucus of squirrels and woodpeckers and frogs surprised her. She had forgotten how the town sounds had drowned out nature. Even with the gently rocking barge, she could not sleep.

"Turnin' and tossin' ain't gonna git ya what ya want," Phoebe cracked from her pallet.

Catriona did not have to ask what the woman was talking about. "He dunna want – or need – me."

"Yewr too prideful, Missy. A mon like Jacob Dare would be the kind to love his woman till the day is long, but also the kind that would 'spect his woman to come to him."

"What if there is someone else?" Unwanted came the memory of Félicité's open ogling of him and Abigail's shy giggling that last night to taunt her own deficiencies.

"Only one way to find out."

No. She simply could not face him again, could not endure that easy assurance he had that bordered on arrogance. It was not his rejection she feared, as much as that impassivity as he watched her flounder with her words, words that should have been her superior defense against his superior strength.

Still, she knew she would be on deck the next day, even if the heavens poured, to watch as the craft breached the falls, then wallowed past the dock of Kinsfolk Landing, and past its higher bluff one mile beyond.

Dawn delivered one of those perfect spring days – mild temperatures and the cloudless sky a clear crystalline blue. By mid-afternoon, the scow rounded the point for which she had been watching. Men, none of whom she recognized, paused from their work to wave greetings.

A mile farther along rose the highest point of Kinsfolk Landing's cliffs. Heart thumping, she put her hand over her eyes to shield them from the sun. Craning her neck, she stared up, up to the bluff's rocky rim. Nothing. Had she foolishly expected that Jacob, given his acute intuition, would be standing there with his ever-present long rifle cradled in the crook of one arm?

After all these months, she could still recall him quite clearly. Recall the long, lean, and muscle-roped body, gloriously naked in the morning . . . recall the strong line of his jaw and the quizzical, forest-dark eyes regarding her as she moved around their cabin. And all too readily recall that smile, slow to come but powerful enough when it did to change her world.

She plopped down on a coil of rope. It was all she could do to keep from crying or cursing. Confusion, pain, longing and guilt – they were her traveling companions. The rest of the day, she simply watched with unseeing eyes, only sensing the shoreline changing, the river narrowing, and the trees canopying the barge.

Instead, images of Jacob continued to besiege her. The way he moved, with an erotic grace, slow and easy and yet as quick to spring as Red Rover. That damned unblinking regard, as if could read her every thought, as if he understood her better than she understood herself.

When the barge once more put in for the night, she forced herself to join the others gathered around the deck's cooking fire, built atop a square of sheet iron propped on bricks. Not that she felt like eating, but because she owed it to family to stop behaving like a disappointed, spoiled child.

She sought a seat next to her mother. Enya wrapped her comforting arm around Catriona's waist. "Passing Kinsfolk Landing . . . I could tell . . . ye are hurting like the saints, are ye not?"

She swallowed and hugged her own arms around her waist, bending forward with the acute pain. "Aye, Mam" she mumbled into her lap. "But how do ye make your heart stop loving someone?"

"This Jacob Dare, he is a mon who loves fearlessly. Like your father does. Ye have confronted life fearlessly. Can ye do no less now?"

That night, curled on her pallet in the shed, Catriona knew she could hurt no more than she already did. Toward dawn, she stealthily rose so as not to disturb Phoebe, softly snoring. She collected her red plaid and the precious item wrapped within it. Slipping on both, she headed toward the murky light thrusting through the slit of the blanketed doorway.

"I'm going with ya," came Phoebe's crackly voice behind her.

She nearly shrieked with surprise. She turned to stare into the darkness and whispered. "I am only going to relieve myself."

"No, yewr not. Besides, ya need me to help ya row the bloody canoe."

"You would leave mam and da – after all these years?"

"Got my sights set on another husband. 'Sides, I'm determined to see ya yet whelp a passel of brats."

She squinted at the woman. "Another husband? That wouldna be Fergus Monroe, would it?"

"Stop yer blathering. We need to shove off."

"I had wanted to break the news to Mam and – "

"I 'spect they already know."

The air was nippy. A rosy light rimmed the tree tops. Birds were beginning to chatter and critters were stirring. The canoe slipped loose from its mooring, and Phoebe, floundering with the oars, muttered, "The canoe's a creation of the Devil hisself."

The fast current sent the canoe and its two paddlers fleetingly downstream, so fast, it made Kinsfolk Landing by midmorning. They caught a wagon on its return trip up the bluff, after having unloaded barrels of pitch dockside. But barrels of pitch no longer manufactured by Jacob's distillery, Catriona thought guiltily.

She climbed down from the wagon and, rubbing her damp palms on her skirt, she marched with Phoebe inside the dimly lit trading post. At the sight of Jacob's old friend, she felt a drumbeat of genuine panic. There was no mind changing now.

Fergus turned from where he was looping a spool of fishing line over a peg. At the sight of her, his hooded eyes flared, and a genuine grin parted his whiskers. Then, his gaze took in Phoebe, and his grin compressed abruptly into a sour scowl. "Well, I'll be a cornholed polecat if'n my gut didn't have a feelin' this was gonna be another one of those bloody mornin's."

"'Tis gonna be yewr lucky mornin' for once, Fergus Monroe," Phoebe said, slapping her bony palm on the counter. "And ya be daft if ya don't recognize it."

From behind them, at the open doorway, a female's voice called out, "Fergus, dost thou 'ave – Mistress Catriona!"

Slowly, she pivoted to face Abigail – an Abigail visibly with child. Sunlight haloed her, the Madonna.

A maelstrom whirled around Catriona, so that she saw nothing, heard nothing but a roaring anguish. Instantly, tears backed up at her throat. Her mouth went dry as bone. Bile churned in her stomach. Her hand groped for the support of the counter's knife-notched edge. God help her, she had wrought both her fondest desire – that higher part that is unselfishness – and her worst nightmare.

Eventually her vision cleared, and Abigail was beaming, her palm placed atop the mound of her stomach. "Guess I surprised thee. It was a surprise for me and Jethro, too. Just hoping the circuit rider makes it to Kinsfolk Landing in time to marry us before another new member is added to its population."

The corners of Catriona's mouth tilted in a broad smile. She crossed the puncheon to cup Abigail's heart-shaped chin and plant a kiss on her forehead. Why, the young woman was perfect for Jethro, Catriona realized. How had she not seen that from the outset? Abigail would take him firmly in hand and guide him. "Ye will make a beautiful bride, Abigail. Ye are already a beautiful mother."

As she hoped she would one day be. But she hoped for so much more. For someone to share the unbearable awe and majesty of a blue heron soaring and skyrockets flaring and, just maybe, later, a wee bairn's gurgling.

There was only one way to find out.

~ ~ ~ ~ ~ ~ ~

Jacob had been gone for five days. He got out his steel and flint and started a small fire with the tinder. Then he peeled off his wet hip-length leather wrappers and moccasins, both of which were cold and clammy. He set them on the stone hearth to dry. Naked, he strode to the cupboard to fill the brass kettle with water and added it atop the coals.

While waiting for the water to boil, he turned his attention to the priming of his rifle, recharging the piece and untying the leather cover from its lock to set it on the table. His gaze alighted on the pewter cup with its six-month-old dried wildflowers. Sturdy lavender and larkspur, most had lost their petals, but some still stubbornly remained. As she did in his thoughts. Cat.

His long fingers reached out in that habitual gesture to crush the flowers. Then, as he always did, he shrugged and returned to examining his long rifle. Crushing the dried flowers would not crush the sweet musky scent of her that he would swear was still present in the cabin. And it would never crush his voracious want of her.

His mind's eye all too easily would catch him off guard and sneak in the sight of her corkscrew hair in pleasing disorder around her bare shoulders in the first light of dawn; her shapely forearms and calves, exposed when she pushed up her sleeves and hiked her skirts to do laundry; the flush of her cheeks when he simply stared, not hiding his desire for her, and the responsive flame in her gray eyes . . . and always her lilting brogue to vanquish the cabin's crushing silence.

One striking image of her claimed his thoughts most often – her standing on the bluff that first day at Kinsfolk Landing, her hat dangling from its ribbons that she held. The breeze played with the curly tendrils of her fire-red hair and seductively hugged her water-ruined wedding gown tightly about her body's curves.

Yet it was her expression as she stared off into the vista that haunted him. In her features, elation and excitement and reverence were all combined. He had known then he had not made a mistake in using all his resources – contriving and wrangling and maneuvering – to make her his wife.

Abruptly, he swung the rifle toward the door. After having been absent, he had scoured the perimeter of the cabin that morning, searching for prints – any disturbance of the sumac vines and other ground cover – to indicate unwarranted visitors. He had found nothing. Some moments elapsed before the shadow appeared, but the rifle was at his shoulder, his finger easing back the trigger.

Then she stepped inside. Cat. His wife. Her left hand, the one wearing his horsehair ring, was fisted upon her breast. The fingertips of her other rested on Red Rover's head. As always, the unexpected sight of Cat stirred in him a throbbing thrill. But this, this feeling far exceeded anything he had ever felt.

His wife's eyes flared at the sight of both his long rifle aimed at her and his blatant nudity. Quickly, her gaze dropped down to Red Rover and her fingers busied themselves, lightly stroking its reddish fur. The cat's tail switched lazily, and its purr rumbled through the room's significant silence.

He strained mightily to keep his words spaced, without inflection. "You are back to stay?"

Her shoulders shot up defensively and her lively face shuddered over. "I dinnae ken if it was me ye wanted or merely a wife, strong of arm and able to bear your children. Ye dunna speak much. So, I came to find out, once and for all."

Half afraid she would bolt for the door, he eased a step nearer it, seemingly for the sole purpose of restoring his rifle to the hooks above. Blocking the doorway, he turned to her. So close to him she was that his very flesh prickled with the sheer intensity of his need for her. He could smell the heat of her, could hear her heart pounding.

Or was it his? He was afraid to say something that would scare her off. He doled out his words carefully. "What made you decide to return here? To find out for sure?"

"Your Christmas gift." She looked him in the eye now with a cool steadiness. "But I was not *sure* that ye still felt as I. That we were meant to be together from the first. We have done so much to hurt one another, ye see."

He felt a lump in his throat. "And you are sure now, Cat?"

The ends of her lips hinted at a tremulous smile. Her gaze dropped purposefully to the new pine floor that had taken him weeks to build. Her foot drew an imaginary circle on its smooth surface. "Ye ken I would come back?"

His grave gaze moved from her vibrant hair, to her throat where her pulse pumped wildly, to her expressive mouth, and back to her watchful eyes. "I knew you would realize that men like Barrett are not for you."

At this, her smile widened. "And ye are?

"Yes. I just did not know how long it would take," he said gravely, "for you to realize this." He knew he was the better man . . . if it could be discounted he was a man who kept others at a distance until he was certain of them. And that he would do what it took to have what he wanted. Even if it took decades to have what the boy in him had wanted. "You realized this sooner than I expected."

She flung herself at him, her arms wrapping around his waist, and looked up at him with gray eyes glistening. "I ween I realized it all along in me heart. From that afternoon, when ye informed me in such a resolute tone – a declaration that took no heed of objections – that I *would* marry ye."

He tunneled his fingers through her hair at her nape to press her cheek against his bare chest. He settled his chin atop her head. He felt her wet fingertips tracing his chest's blue tattooing. But he was not sure if they were wet with her tears or his. This feeling of jubilation was new to him. His joy far more than he could ever have anticipated.

And then he spoke the Cherokee words that had been pierced into his flesh by his mother, so that he would never forget. Never forget that love outlasted everything, even estrangement or death. The words were strangers to his tongue but not his heart, "*Gvgeyu*, my wife."

She grinned up at him through misty gray eyes. "As I said, ye are a mon of few words. And translated into English those three are mighty few. But they be the most important ones."

Her hand slid from his chest down his washboard stomach and

below, and he sprang to life at her tentative touch. "Ye believe that actions speak louder than words," she murmured, almost shyly, "so, I am counting on your actions to make a believer of meself."

Throughout that night, Red Rover's caterwauling outside the cabin occasionally echoed Catriona's ecstatic outcries within. And from within that cabin, their cabin, Jacob Dare heard the words he feared never again to hear from another soul in his lifetime, those same three words translated now into her Gaelic tongue, "*Tha gaol agam ort.*"

§§ AFTERWORD §§

The 90 million acres of primeval forests comprised of vast longleaf pine vanished, and with their passing vanished North Carolina's industries of naval stores and tar and turpentine – the keystones for Kinsfolk Landing's existence. Scrub trees and overgrowth claimed the vanished settlement site.

But Jacob and Catriona Dare did not vanish. The Dares and the Kincairns and their children and their children's children – all untamed and stouthearted pioneers, who recognized no other higher earthly authority – challenged the frontier's hardships and savagery to establish time and again new settlements, ever opening the way Westward.

I'm dancing on sunshine because you have dropped by my little part of Parris's Paradise. We have some things in common ~ that we believe good overcomes evil; that love triumphs over everything, even death; that we love a tension-packed story; and that we feel the best books enhance our lives.

I write for the reckless of heart. Not surprising, I identify with my novels' characters, both the protagonists AND antagonists. I suffer with their angsts and bewilderments and rejoice in their joys and triumphs. And I believe that if we heroically hold fast to our own vision for ourselves in the face of our journey's confrontations, then Life WILL manifest our dreams and goals and visions, as it does for my characters in my novels.

Parris Afton Bonds is the mother of five sons and the author of more than thirty-five published novels. She is the co-founder of and first vice president of Romance Writers of America. Declared by ABC's Nightline as one of three best-selling authors of romantic fiction, the award-winning Parris Afton Bonds has been interviewed by such luminaries as Charlie Rose and featured in major newspapers and magazines as well as published in more than a dozen languages. She donates her time to teaching creative writing to both grade school children and female inmates. The Parris Award was established in her name by the Southwest Writers Workshop to honor a published writer who has given outstandingly of time and talent to other writers.

Prestigious recipients of the Parris Award include Tony Hillerman and the Pulitzer nominee Norman Zollinger.

Subscribe to my mailing list to receive a FREE novel, as well as, notices of new releases and Free E-Book giveaways. Your information will never be shared, sold or given away.

http://parrisaftonbonds.com/subscribe/

www.ingramcontent.com/pod-product-compliance
Lightning Source LLC
Chambersburg PA
CBHW050526190726
48284CB00003B/952